CW01022437

SKINNING THE COYOTE

NICK MCANULTY

WICKED
HOUSE
PUBLISHING

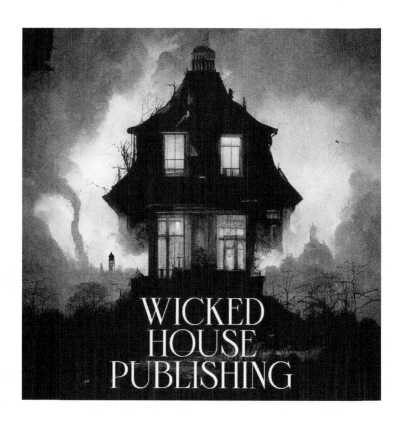

Skinning The Coyote
By Nick McAnulty

Wicked House Publishing

No part of this publication may be reproduced, stored in a retrieval system, or transmitted in any way by any means, electronic, mechanical, photocopy, recording or otherwise without the prior permission of the author except as provided by USA copyright law.

This novel is a work of fiction. Names, descriptions, entities, and incidents included in the story are products of the author's imagination. Any resemblance to actual persons, events, and entities is entirely coincidental.

Cover design by Christian Bentulan
Interior Formatting by Joshua Marsella
All rights reserved. Copyright © 2023 **Nick McAnulty**

CONTENTS

PROLOGUE

THE BENTLEY FARM

i. Isaac

*W*orking the extra hour so he could avoid confronting his father would be the second last mistake Isaac would ever make. If he had put down the axe and gone inside just a few minutes earlier, maybe he wouldn't have seen *her* and things could have been different. Perhaps the Bentley family would have slept through the night without a clue what was dwelling in their barn. Isaac didn't know *it* was lurking in there yet, nor did he know his final mistake wasn't far ahead of him. Right now, his only focus was on the work; the steady, monotonous, yet pleasantly calming work.

He swung his axe rhythmically in a race against the dying daylight, hurrying to chop through what seemed like a never-ending pile of wood to his side. The evening was cooling down quickly, the pleasant warmth from the day's sun slipping away as though it were never there. It was becoming harder for his eyes to focus as the sun dipped behind the horizon, but he refused to let that break his rhythm. He knew the pile would still be there for him to split in the morning, but it wasn't worth the disapproval he'd face from his father. That would sting far worse than the September evening air.

His father had been silent all day, his mood soured after another early morning visit by the pig-nosed man from the bank. Isaac recognized the man from his previous visits, each of which left his father in a fouler mood than the last. A little over a month ago was the first time; the same man had come through with an exciting prospect to buy up their land for a tidy sum. He claimed he would bring the ever-expanding railway through their farmland, *paving way for the future,* as he put it. Isaac's mother thought it was a godsend, but his father was having none of it, politely thanking the man for his time and sending him on his way. But the pig-nosed man was as persistent as a hungry dog begging for table scraps, coming back a few times with several other men in fancy outfits. Each meeting was more tense than the last. It always left his father simmering and ill-tempered, and Isaac knew it was best to steer clear afterwards.

Isaac had been shooed away during today's visit, but he needn't have heard any of the exchange to know the atmosphere had been more hostile this time. His father remained quiet on the issue after the pig-nosed man left, and immediately sent Isaac off to work for the rest of the day. Isaac now shivered as he chopped, figuring there was no harm in putting things off a little longer, especially since he was still getting work done.

He began to lose track of how long he'd been at it. Place the log, swing, split, toss. Place, swing, split, toss. He thought about what a magical thing time was, able to both stand still and creep along when you're lost in a trance. It was tiring work, but peaceful, a feeling he enjoyed because it made him feel grown up.

It was the awful, frightened cry from the horses in the barn that broke him out of his reverie. He'd never heard a horse make a sound like that before; it was closer to a woman's cry than an animal. It scared him in a way he hadn't felt in a long time, not just the awful sound but the disturbing silence afterwards. He waited for a moment, hoping the next sound from the barn would signal everything was okay. But nothing came. Nothing else dared disturb the quiet evening air.

He knew he was going to have to turn around to the barn and face whatever had caused the cry. But he didn't want to. Turning around would make it *real*, into something he couldn't deny. He wanted to ignore it, chalk it up to an imagination running wild after a hard day's work. But he was almost a man now, and that's not what men do. Men didn't imagine silly things, not according to his father. They faced their problems head-on. He thought of his father's face, the scowl he'd get if he knew his son wanted to run and hide rather than face what he'd heard. He took a deep breath and turned, ready to make whatever it was *real*.

Of all the things his mind could have conjured up, nothing came close to the disturbing, surreal vision before him. It was so brief, he almost convinced himself he had imagined it. Standing in the doorway of the barn was an improbably old woman, ancient beyond anyone he'd ever seen in his life. She was completely naked, with frail old skin as grey as the wispy, thin hair on her balding head. Isaac had never seen a naked woman before, even though he wanted to, but he knew that it wasn't supposed to look like this; the sight brought him no pleasure at all. She was covered in wet blisters and sores that looked infected and painful to the touch. She had an oddly calm expression, looking almost pleased to be there.

He wanted to call out to her, but any words he tried to get out were caught in a lump in his throat. Instead, he just watched, watched as she turned and stepped back into the barn where the awful sound had come from. The sight scared him, far worse than the cries of the frightened horses. He wanted to ignore it and go back to chopping. Go on like he hadn't seen any of it, just a horrid thing his mind made up after working too long.

But he didn't.

Instead, he made the final mistake of his life by running back to the house to tell Pa.

ii. Bonnie

Bonnie clumsily stirred the rabbit stew with her free hand while she rocked Baby Anne in the other. Normally she'd scold Bill about taking care of one of them, but after hearing today's tense meeting with the nice man from the bank, she knew juggling both would be far easier than pestering him on the matter. Besides, it was *quiet* now. Baby Anne was content, and Pearl was sitting on the floor reading to herself. Even Bill had seemed to temporarily forget his troubles as he sat in front of the fire, sketching away at one of his charcoal drawings in silence. Apart from the crackling of the fire, the only other sound was the distant, rhythmic thuds of Isaac's axe.

When the chopping turned to silence, she realized Isaac must finally be ready to come in. She knew he was avoiding his father, but it was getting too dark to work and supper was ready. There would always be more wood to chop and there was no reason for him to avoid his father any longer, at least not tonight. Tonight, they could relax, forget their troubles, and enjoy the quiet, peaceful evening together.

The peaceful silence broke when the door slammed open.

"Pa, come quick," Isaac pleaded, out of breath.

He looked exhausted, partially from all the chopping, but there was something else in his eyes. His brow was covered in a cold sweat, his skin a pale tone, but it was the glassy emptiness in his eyes that chilled Bonnie to the bone.

Baby Anne started crying, setting off a chain reaction of

anxiety that shot over to Pearl, who stared at both her parents with dread. Bill wasn't as taken aback by the slam of the door as everyone else, nor by the urgency in his son's voice. He remained calm, gently putting down his charcoal as he turned sternly to the boy. Bill knew panic was contagious, something that spread all too easily if you accepted and shared it. He opted to let his confidence and authority be known before tackling any problem, a tactic that usually put most people at ease.

"What did I tell you about bursting in here like that?" Bill said with the voice of God.

Whatever fear was behind Isaac's eyes calmed slightly, letting in a little room for respect as Bill continued. "You know damn well it upsets your baby sister."

Isaac took a gulp to compose himself, hiding the quiver in his voice as best he could.

"There's someone in the barn," Isaac said as bravely as his voice would allow.

Bonnie nervously resumed stirring the stew to distract her mind. She worried for Isaac but didn't want to get involved, instead opting to watch her husband and eldest son exchange words. Pearl pretended to go back to reading her book, but curiosity had her hanging on every word.

"Someone?" Bill scoffed. "Did you bother to go look to see who it was?"

Bonnie could see the look of shame hit her son's face, a hot redness filling his cheeks. She couldn't help but admire the boy as he forced himself to tackle his embarrassment, looking his father in the eye when he responded. She could see the boy inside swallowing his fear, trying to drum up the man he was becoming. She hoped Bill recognized it as well.

"It's mighty dark out there," Isaac nervously reasoned. "Didn't know if it would be safe to go in and check alone."

She worried this would set Bill off and shot him a look that told him what they both already knew: *Go easy on the boy, he's trying.*

Bill could feel her gaze and gave a slight nod of understanding.

"Alright," Bill said, both warmly and firmly, "let's go see who's there and what they want."

With a huff, Bill grabbed his old Winchester and the oil lamp they kept by the door. Bonnie proudly observed the two getting ready when she caught a glance of something in Isaac's face that unsettled her. He was a good boy, wise beyond his years, yet she hadn't seen him that scared since he was a small child. Bill didn't catch it, handing the oil lamp over to Isaac like it was routine. Isaac let the lamp hang in his father's hands, almost afraid to accept it.

"Something *bad* was going on in the barn," Isaac blurted out, embarrassed but knowing it needed to be said. "Something mighty menacing, I ain't never heard the horses make a sound like that before."

Bill held up his Winchester slightly, suggesting any problems they might have could be solved with the tool in his hands.

"Good thing there's two of us then."

It was reassuring enough for Isaac to take the lamp and head out the door.

Bill gave Bonnie a warm look before following the boy out; the look only parents share when they are in it together. Bonnie could see he was really trying, and it felt like a good end to what had been a bad day.

iii. Bill

It was darker outside than Bill expected. His eyes had to adjust, and he was barely able to see the barn ahead in the cloak of the approaching night. They weren't the ideal conditions for swinging an axe, and that sent a tinge of guilt over him as he thought of his son toiling away in the dark. Sure, the boy had a good work ethic, but Bill knew in his heart that the real reason the boy had stayed out so late was to avoid him after the incident with the parasite from the bank. The idea upset him, making him ponder if he really was that menacing to his own son.

Trying to sense his son's thoughts, Bill wondered what he saw in the barn that sent him running inside. Whatever it was, it must have spooked him real good to make him break the silent treatment they'd been giving each other all day. He was doing his best to keep his composure in front of the boy, but a worry stung in the back of his spine that had him wondering if maybe the prospectors had sent someone over to the barn to spook him a little bit, just to make the idea of selling more attractive. He began fuming, questioning if that was something they would have the balls to do. He fantasized briefly about delivering them a belly full of lead as his answer.

The walk to the barn was quiet and felt much further than the countless times he'd done it before. Part of it was the awkward silence between them, neither one of them addressing the tension that had been lingering between them all day. The other part was the unspoken concern he was hiding from Isaac, wondering who the hell they'd find in the barn and what they wanted. He couldn't put a finger on what was causing it, but his imagination seemed to be running unusually wild tonight. He always liked to face his problems head-on, believing it was the only way that any man of worth should conduct his business, personal or otherwise. The difficulty was trusting banks to adhere to those same standards.

He wanted to say something to Isaac, reassure the boy that none of this had anything to do with him and that everything would be alright. But the words didn't come, staying in his belly as they walked. Bill reassured himself with the thought that maybe checking in on the barn like this together said everything he needed to. Real action instead of soft, empty words. It was better that way.

iv. Isaac

The inside of the barn was supernaturally black. A damp, yellow stench hit Isaac's nose the moment they entered, bringing with it the sour taste of turned milk into the back of his throat. He was thankful it was dark enough that his father couldn't see his face turn at the putrid smell, and he composed himself as best he could before he lit the lamp to get a better view. His stomach was doing somersaults as he braced himself for another run-in with the horrid old woman, still unsure if she had been real or not.

It was quiet. Not hearing an intruder should have brought immediate relief, but the lack of sound from the horses made Isaac think back to the terrified cry they gave just minutes ago.

Whatever anxiety he had about his father earlier was instantly gone, replaced with the comfort of having him there by his side. Isaac hadn't really wanted to ask his father for help, but it was a lot better than coming in here alone. Now all he had to do was use every ounce of bravery he had to not let his father see how afraid he actually was.

Besides the eerie silence, everything seemed fine as they took their first few steps into the barn. No rotting old woman, no horses in distress.

That changed when they saw the blood.

Isaac only noticed a few ruby drops splattered at first, but as the light from the lantern hit the hay, he saw a larger pool of dark red liquid drawn across the ground. The trail led deeper into the barn, and it was clear that something had been dragged across the floor, violently fighting for its life every inch of the way.

Despair grew rapidly in the pit of his stomach, a feeling that made him wish that he had come alone just so he would have had the luxury of leaving and pretending nothing had happened. If he'd come alone, he could have ignored everything in the barn, at least until the morning when he'd have the comfort of daylight. Knowing his stubborn father, there was no way they were going to leave until they got to the bottom of this.

"Jesus," Bill muttered with a hint of fear hidden in the back of his throat.

Isaac admired the way his father kept it together, mimicking his behavior as best he could as the two of them continued to follow the trail. A morbid fascination propelled them along, like a magnetic force pulling them against their will. Each step brought more blood, splashed and spread with increasing violence the deeper they went. Bill clutched his rifle like a totem, ready to fire at whoever, or whatever, they encountered.

He wavered, though, when they came across the horses.

Isaac wanted to retch at what he saw. The horses had been torn apart, effortlessly strewn across the barn into mutilated piles of flesh, their blood and entrails everywhere. The sight of the painted streaks of chunky red and black from the animals insides was enough to make him want to scream, the betrayal of his other senses rushing to him. The smell was disgustingly familiar, like meat that had been left out for weeks. His mind raced as he tried to reconcile the stench of spoiled food with the sight of the beautiful horses he'd tended to for years. Layered on top of it all was a sticky, uncomfortable heat that rose like hot death in the barn.

But the worst was the sound, the drone of flies buzzing around the corpses of the poor animals. They hummed in horrid unison, a thousand times worse than the high-pitched whirring a mosquito makes when it burrows deep in your ear. It was the music of death, an ungodly drone that made him want to poke a knife in his ears if it meant he'd never have to hear it again.

"Good God," his father chimed in, breaking up the nightmare symphony with the sound of a man witnessing unfiltered horror, "who would do something like this?"

The initial shock of the scene had worn off slightly, but the sickening sight and smell provided no comfort. Isaac went to throw up, but a stern look from his father quickly solidified the mess in his stomach.

"Hold it together, son," Bill said with surprising compassion. "Now isn't the time to lose your wits."

He was right. Isaac had heard his father lecture him countless times about how he'd have to be ready to face manhood head-on one day, and he recognized that the moment had rudely arrived today unannounced. He nodded dutifully and held the lamp up for a better view. Sensing his son's strength, Bill clenched his rifle tight and continued forward.

The aftermath of the massacre only got worse when they turned the corner. Isaac's mind morbidly wondered how much intestines could be held in one animal, calculating the mass he was witnessing strewn across the barn. A gut instinct stopped them from pressing on, realizing that any further would mean running into whoever did this. Better to keep their distance, especially if the intruder came charging at them.

"I'm going to give you one chance to come out and explain yourself," Bill hollered into the darkness.

Isaac's mind raced, thinking about the old woman he still wasn't sure he really saw, refusing to believe that she could have done this. He thought of how frail she was, and how she seemed barely able to stand on her own.

"You've got to the count of three," Bill shouted, halting Isaac's thoughts. "After that, I'm going to start shooting for what you did to these poor horses."

They were greeted with silence. If there was someone there, they were calling Bill's bluff.

"One. Two. Three," he counted.

Nothing. They stood in silence, Bill holding his rifle aimed into the darkness. Gooseflesh crept up the back of Isaac's neck as the two tried to hide their fear from one another.

Maybe there really was nobody there, but Isaac knew his father wasn't going to leave until he was absolutely certain. Isaac's hopes of turning around and heading back to the house were shattered when his father took another step into the dark void.

"Pa..." Isaac squeaked with warning, frozen still while his father continued onward.

Bill raised a finger to his mouth, motioning for Isaac to keep silent. Isaac gulped down a hard lump that felt like a rock in his throat and followed his father deeper into the gore-filled barn.

The journey felt endless as they inched forward at a snail's pace. Isaac had been in here countless times before, but the barn had never felt so large. They pushed on in muffled silence, eventually reaching the darkest corner on the far end. The point was black beyond darkness, sucking away any trace of light into its cloak. Isaac wanted to throw the lantern in, thinking the light given off by the fire would be less menacing than the nothingness he saw ahead.

Bill stepped into the void, reaching his hand forward for guidance, only to find nothing. He betrayed himself by letting out a sigh of relief, his heart grateful for the momentary respite. Despite the horrific scene of the slaughter around them, the tension in the barn had been lifted somewhat. They were finally allowed to breathe again.

That changed when the intruder attacked.

Everything happened in front of Isaac's eyes too quickly for his brain to register. The first thing he saw was the flash of a shadow swooping over his father, pulling him into the shadows in an instant. Isaac couldn't make out *what* the shadowy figure was, other than a mass of darkness that lifted Bill into its maw like a leaf in the wind.

The true terror wasn't what he *saw*, but the unforgettable things he *heard*. Bill hadn't begun screaming yet, he had been pulled in too quickly to react, but deep snarling along with hot, heavy breathing filled the air. It almost sounded like a bear, yet the tone of its snarls were deeper and larger. It was only when the first splash of blood splattered across Isaac's face from the darkness that Bill's horrible screaming began.

"Pa!" Isaac shrieked, as his father's blood-curdling cries filled the darkness.

Isaac swung the lamp to try to get a better view of their attacker but could only catch quick glimpses of his father's body flailing around helplessly like a ragdoll.

The squishy crunch of flesh and bone cracked through the barn like thunder. This was followed by a gurgling cry from Bill, and another crimson bath sprayed Isaac like a red baptism. Isaac tried to mutter something back to his father but found his voice paralyzed.

The flailing continued until something flew from the blackness at Isaac, hitting him in the mouth with enough force to knock him over. He lost his grip on the lantern from the blow; his mouth filled with the copper taste of blood as the lamp shattered on the ground. It wasn't until the flames began to spread that he realized he'd been hit by his father's severed arm, still clutching down on the rifle. The grip was so firm it seemed the arm would spring back to life and start shooting.

Another scream snapped Isaac out of his daze, instinctual survival telling him that he needed that rifle at all costs. He grabbed the arm that had been attached to his father only seconds ago, only to have the shadowy thing from the darkness pull the limb away like a vicious dog hoarding a piece of fallen table scraps.

The hay fueled the flames, growing at a dangerous and alarming pace. The darkness gave way to the light from the fire, giving Isaac a clearer view of his father's body just as it was unceremoniously tossed his way seconds later. The boy locked eyes with his dead father, saw the frozen look of terror permanently etched on his face. Then, Isaac forced himself to look up.

It was then, through the glimmering light of the flame, that Isaac saw the pair of deep, poison-filled yellow eyes of the dark figure looking back at him. Despite the myriad horrors he'd just witnessed, the sight of those eyes was the worst thing Isaac had ever seen. The empty pupils tore into the core of his soul, making him feel as if they were going to burn a hole right through the back of his head. Mustering every ounce of will he could find, he tore himself away from the hypnotic glow of the amber eyes and ran out of the barn faster than he had ever run before.

v. Bonnie

Bonnie cherished the few quiet moments she could find in the house, which mostly occurred when Bill was away and the baby was sleeping. But this was different, this was an uncomfortable sort of quiet; it felt menacing. It was almost enough to make her want to shake Baby Anne awake, or yell at poor Pearl just to get a reaction. Anything would be better than this goddamn silence.

That's when she got her wish. She could hear Isaac calling to her faintly from outside. It sounded distant, muffled. There was something off in his voice, something frightened and juvenile that made him sound like a little boy again. Something was wrong, he was scared, and he needed his mama. She put Baby Anne back down in her crib and moved towards the door.

"Ma!" she heard him call.

She knew something wasn't right and found herself suddenly wishing she could go back to the uncomfortable silence from a moment ago.

She opened the door and saw him running, racing like his life depended on it. She couldn't see what he was fleeing from or make out the look on his face, but there was a disturbing manner in the way he moved. She didn't know what had him so spooked, but she could feel that it was something sinister, something evil.

"The rifle!" Isaac screamed. "Ma, get the rifle!"

He was five years old again in her eyes. Bonnie wanted to run out and hug him, tell him that everything was okay, but every ounce of sense in her brain told her to listen to his commands and grab the extra rifle immediately.

But she didn't. Instead, she froze, paralyzed as she caught a glimpse of the shadow chasing her terrified son. She couldn't move. The sight of whatever it was that had her boy looking so frightened caused her to freeze up, standing numbly in the doorway as he ran helplessly to her. She just stopped and watched what happened.

Isaac made it a few more yards before the thing chasing him pounced like a cat, bringing him to the ground in one swift motion. Her boy, now a mouse, disappeared into the shadows. She squinted, straining to see what was happening, barely making out the thrashing struggle being fought between Isaac and the dark figure. Tears welled in her eyes, her skin turning to ice as her eldest child let out an ear-piercing scream that echoed through the valley. She was transfixed, her mind conjuring up horrific images of what she couldn't quite see. It was the voice of innocence that brought her back to reality.

"Mama?" The voice squeaked behind her.

She turned and saw Pearl, frightened but somehow knowing that now was the time to act like a big girl. The thought of her babies snapped Bonnie to attention. She shut the door and ran to Anne, grabbing her tightly, trying to keep from dropping her as her hands trembled.

"Mama, what's going on?" Pearl asked, her voice shaking.

Bonnie wanted to cry and hold her little girl, tell her that everything was going to be okay. But she knew that was a lie, that Mommy had to be brave and lead by example, even if what she really wanted to do was scream until her vocal cords snapped.

"Pearl, baby," Bonnie strained, handing Baby Anne to her big sister, "you take your baby sister, and you hide in your room. You hide and you don't make a peep, no matter what. You hear?"

"But I'm scared, Mama," Pearl confessed, her eyes welling up with tears.

"I said not a peep or your daddy is gonna give you a whippin'," Bonnie lectured with a scowl.

Fearing it was the last face Pearl would ever see her make, Bonnie forced a smile that had a hint of warmth but still meant business, as she ordered her daughter off.

"Now you be a brave girl and go hide for Mama."

Pearl seemed to understand that now wasn't the time to protest. Bonnie felt a contradictory mix of fear and pride as she watched Pearl take her baby sister and head towards the bedroom, her once helpless child now the protector. She knew right then that she'd never get to see her little girl grow up. She wanted to squeeze her and say goodbye, but more than anything, she wanted her safe.

The moment Pearl and Anne were into the bedroom and out

of sight, Bonnie dropped the brave face and ran to grab Bill's extra rifle. She thanked God that the Winchester was loaded, then made her way to the door.

She clenched her eyes shut, quietly mumbling a quick prayer as she prepared for whatever was out there. She raised the Winchester and braced it tight against her shoulder. It felt much heavier in her arms than she remembered, but her aim was steady as the terrible rumbling sound drew near. With her senses so heightened, she almost forgot to breathe as she waited for the intruder to make its move. Each passing second felt like hours, and it seemed every natural sound had been sucked from the room. The only things that existed now were Bonnie and whatever was approaching on the opposite side of the door.

A few hour-long seconds passed. Silence. She kept the rifle held up with bated breath as a few more seconds crawled by. Nothing still. She waited, never blinking, her breath still, until the horrid crashing on the door began.

BANG

The door loudly shook, the hinges buckling from the impact on the other side. She steadied her aim, suddenly feeling calm and ready for whatever was to come.

BANG

BANG

A heavy bead of sweat inched down her forehead. It itched like the devil, begging to be wiped away. The pounding continued, the pauses between becoming shorter and shorter as the rhythm intensified, the door ready to burst open at any moment. Bonnie remained calm with her rifle drawn. The only comfort she had left was the thought that nothing was going to come for her family without going through her first.

vi. Pearl

Pearl hid in the dark sanctuary under her parents' bed, lying as still as she could. She'd sometimes practice to see how long she could hold her breath, and her daddy would yell *you're going to make yourself pass out* when he'd catch her. She swelled with pride now, having the opportunity to use this seemingly useless skill, confident that she had become good enough at it to remain completely silent. Unfortunately, she wasn't the only one she had to worry about.

She cooed at Baby Anne, who was resting calmly, cradled in her arms in the cramped space under the bed. She mentally willed her little sister to stay quiet, amazed that the trick somehow worked. She felt they were in their own safe bubble, one that protected them from the chaos that was erupting out in the front room.

She heard a loud crash, then the sound of the front door being smashed off its hinges, followed by the ear ringing *bangs* of two gunshots fired in rapid succession. The sounds were followed by the horrified screams of her mother, cut abruptly short moments later. Pearl kept calm as she blocked out the images of her mother's life coming to a sudden and violent end just a few short feet away. Miraculously, Baby Anne remained quiet through all of it, sleeping as if nothing was going on. They remained quiet when the loud thud of their mother's body hit the floor, reverberating throughout the house, followed by the worst sound of all. Silence.

The world stood still for Pearl. The only thing she could hear were the tiny breaths of Baby Anne, who she was worried would start wailing at any moment, alerting whatever was out there to their hiding space. Yet, her baby sister remained quiet, which only served to amplify the horrid creaking of the floorboards as heavy footsteps sauntered towards the bedroom.

The steps grew louder, closer, finally stopping right outside the entrance to the bedroom. The door creaked open; the squeaky hinges never sounded louder.

Pearl could barely make anything out in the dark, straining her eyes as she struggled to see what was there. Buried under the shadow of black, she saw what appeared to be two massive, multi-pronged hooves. They looked like they belonged to a giant, deformed elk, effortlessly standing on its hind legs, politely waiting at the entrance.

The *thing* loitered at the doorway for far too long, seeming to debate if it wanted to enter the room or not. Pearl could hear it smelling the air, its flaring nostrils snorting loudly. The mysterious *thing* reached into the frame of the door with its front claws and pulled, ripping a large chunk away to make room for its massive body to enter. Pearl could feel the air in the room being sucked away as the door splinters hit the ground, her ears perking up to the sound of the creature sniffing like a wild dog hunting its prey. Instinctually her young mind started to worry that no matter how quiet she was, no amount of silence could hide her scent.

The snorts grew louder, the creature's breathing became labored. Pearl could feel her heart pounding rapidly, thumping like it was trying to smash through her ribcage to escape her body.

Thump. Thump. Thump.

It pumped like a drum, the loudest noise she'd ever heard.

Please, just go, she thought, *leave us alone and never come back.*

After what seemed like an eternity, the creature stopped and turned to leave. It appeared to have given up, satisfied that there was no more damage for it to do here. Her silent prayers had been answered. Frustrated, it made its way to the door. They were safe.

That's when baby Anne started crying.

A deafening, angry snarl spouted from the intruder. It

turned from the doorway, pouncing violently towards the bed. Pearl instinctively covered her hand over Baby Anne's mouth.

But it was too late.

The bed went flying, easily tossed across the room like it was nothing more than an apple core.

Exposed and vulnerable, Pearl found herself hypnotized, her eyes trying to make sense of the *thing* standing above them in the darkness. Her brain tried to process what she was looking at, but the only thing she could make out were the awful, yellow eyes. They gave off a hypnotizing glow, two burning amber orbs. They would be the last thing she ever saw. She let out a scream, clutching her baby sister in her arms.

CHAPTER ONE
PLAYING THE OLD PART

i. Weston

*I*t was cool, even for late September. Maybe it was the early hour, but the sharp pain of the morning chill on Weston's cheeks made him think winter was threatening to arrive sooner than anticipated this year. Then again, the air was always cold first thing in the morning before most of the world woke up. Despite the cool weather, the calm at the edge of the woods was always nice, especially at this hour. It was as if time stood still here, or didn't exist at all.

He broke out of his own head when he heard a wicked screech, the sound of a wild predator reduced to prey with an effortless snap. It wailed in pain like an infant, giving a howl that shook Weston to the bone. He gripped his rifle and ran toward the cries, pushing through the branches as quickly and safely as he could.

When he got close enough that he knew he wouldn't miss, he stopped and raised the rifle. Lining the wounded coyote up in his sights, he could see it had caught its hind leg in one of his traps. His father had taught him how to make the trap, but he was never confident they were as good as his, until seeing it now in horrible action. It worked, and judging by the pain on the coyote's face as it gnawed on its own leg, it worked well.

He was aiming for a kill shot when the coyote suddenly looked up at him, stopping the biting and screeching in one frozen movement. A deadly calm descended over the coyote's features as it locked eyes with him. Its eyes showed recognition, not quite pleading, but rather as if it wanted to tell Weston that it knew that he was the one that did this. Weston continued lining up his shot to finish the job, but his finger gave a slight tremble as he went to pull the trigger. The coyote's hypnotic gaze was nearly powerful enough to stop him from following through. All he could do was stare back.

He heard the loud *crack* of the bullet before he saw the impact whiz through its heart, killing the trapped animal instantly. The thunderous sound echoed through the trees, sending off every bird in sight. The coyote's corpse jolted a few inches from the impact, falling lifelessly to the ground. Weston turned to see his father pointing his rifle at his target, smoke still rising from the barrel.

As the echo of the bullet evaporated in the sky, Weston waited for the certain lecture he was about to get as his father's footsteps crunched towards him. He tried to ready a rebuttal but was unable to squeak one out before his father laid into him.

"Why didn't you shoot?" he asked coldly.

The past couple years had been hard on his father. Though only in his forties, he looked like a worn version of himself, frozen in time like petrified wood. Mounting hardships, combined with his hard drinking days, had visibly aged him. He was like an old statue, a decaying version of the face Weston remembered growing up. The worn leather look of his skin made Weston more uneasy around his father now than he was when he was a small child, even though the fists didn't fly as easily or as often as they did in those years before he sobered up.

He had to look away from his father's piercing stare as he stammered his words, cursing himself for not finding the right response. Shame got the better part of him before he could get out an answer, and his father snapped back at him with even less patience.

"You should have put it down," he commanded coldly, making Weston feel four years old again.

That inner youth regression immediately betrayed Weston, his tone switching to a defensive rebuttal.

"It looked innocent," Weston pushed back with as much authority as he could muster. "I thought maybe I could help it."

"It *was* innocent," his father responded. "When it hunts, it steals from the farm. It's only doing what's in its nature."

Weston knew the lecture before he heard it, but looking the poor coyote in the eyes made him feel differently.

"Seems cruel to shoot it just for that," Weston countered, trying not to sound too defensive.

His father gave his brow a slight scratch, the pause hitting Weston in the pit of his stomach. Sure, the scratch could have been a genuine itch, but it felt more like a dismissal.

"If I didn't shoot it, it would have gnawed its leg off to get free of the trap," his father explained. "It'd be cruel *not* to put it down."

Cruelty was a recurring theme in their family. What happened to his mama was cruel, as was his father hitting the bottle afterwards, in turn causing the incident that forever put him out of work as a lawman. Weston was raised to accept cruelty as a fact of life, so why was the fate of the coyote any different?

"Mama used to say that human nature was cruel," Weston told his father plainly.

He rarely brought up his mother, knowing the pain it brought them both, but he also refused to put any of her lessons aside for the sake of politeness.

"Maybe," his father responded, with a slightly kinder tone in his eyes that suggested he agreed. "She also wanted you to be better than someone who just gave in to their selfish instincts."

His father's response was both kind and cruel. Weston suddenly felt a sting of shame for suggesting they be like everyone else.

The moment passed quickly, interrupted by the sound of a rider approaching the property. His father was the first to notice, squinting to see who it was before his face relaxed with recognition. Weston could tell that their conversation was over, trumped in favor of more pressing matters the rider was sure to bring.

"Un-trap the carcass and bring it to the house," his father ordered. "The fur's still salvageable."

Weston didn't hesitate, nodding dutifully as he went to free the animal from the trap.

ii. Shane

An early morning gunshot echoed across the sky as Shane pulled up to the farmhouse. He didn't realize just how tired he was until he stopped. The aches, hunger, and thirst rushed to him immediately as he pulled his horse up to his old friend's place. His news felt like it couldn't wait when he first rode off, but now it crept to the back of his mind as the thought of getting inside where it was warm selfishly dominated his headspace. It was cold riding this early in the morning and the thought of riding back out with Eli so soon after arriving wasn't appealing, but the opportunity he had was too good to wait on.

He spotted Eli and Weston off in the distance, the boy

lagging behind carrying the carcass of a healthy-sized animal. They looked good, all things considered. Shane had witnessed Eli struggle through his fair share of ups and downs over the years and thought he looked on the upside today. While he always wanted the best for his friend, he hoped catching him in a better mood would sweeten his proposal.

"Mornin Shane," Eli greeted, friendly with a hint of suspicion.

"Mornin Eli," Shane politely replied. "Heard a gunshot." He noted Weston off in the distance carrying the carcass. "Catch something?"

"Coyote," Eli muttered. "They've been getting extra aggressive. Sons-a-bitches got another one of our pigs the other night." Eli nodded over to Weston, his face shifting from annoyed to proud. "The boy caught it in one of his traps."

"Weston set it up?" Shane whistled with admiration.

It looked like a clean kill, one that put Shane's trap setting to shame.

"He's getting good at it." Eli beamed before his face soured a bit, "He didn't want to put the thing down, though."

Shane could sense the distaste in Eli's voice but didn't want to join in on insulting the boy further.

"Can't blame him," Shane scoffed, jumping to the boy's defense. "I'd have let the fuckin thing rot in the trap. Let the bastard starve out there."

"Not if you were tryin to raise a boy right on your own you wouldn't." Eli winced, clearly disagreeing.

Even at his age, Shane could easily be embarrassed, especially by Eli. He stammered for a moment, trying to think of a good retort before he opted it was safer to just apologize for the crude comment. After all, they had a lot to discuss, and this wasn't the right foot to start off on.

"Sorry, Eli," Shane stated humbly. "I didn't mean anything by it."

"It's nothing." Eli brushed it off. An uncomfortable silence followed.

A gust of wind filled the void, amplifying the morning chill. Suddenly feeling the temperature, Shane used every bit of discipline he had not to shiver. He was grateful when Eli killed the silence by changing the subject.

"So, what's going on, Shane?" Eli bluntly asked. "Bit early for a visit. Unless of course there's some baggage involved."

Shane was racking his tired brain for a way to broach the subject when Weston finally caught up to them, allowing the topic to shift as their attention turned to the dead coyote.

"Mornin'." The boy politely nodded.

Shane noted Weston was getting bigger, his face starting to resemble his father more and more every day.

"Weston." Shane greeted him with a smile, both genuinely happy to see the boy and relieved he could put off business for another few moments. "Your pa tells me it was *you* that caught that bastard."

"Yeah, but I learned how to make the trap from Pa," the boy said modestly, his eyes drifting to his feet, "so technically it's *his* trap."

"Own your accomplishments, son," Eli lectured. Shane sensed Eli would be prouder if the boy stood up for himself over the actual achievement itself.

"Looks like whoever put it together did a good job," Shane said. The catch was impressive, and he thought the boy should feel proud of what he had achieved.

"Thank you, sir," the boy said before going silent again.

"So, what's going on Shane?" Eli asked, cutting back to the point.

Shane never had the strongest poker face, and his old friend could always read him a mile away. There was business to discuss, but Shane kept deflecting, knowing it was nothing the boy should hear.

"Weston, if you wouldn't mind," Shane said with as much authority as he felt comfortable displaying. "I would like to have a private word with your Pa."

"Go take the carcass to the barn," Eli commanded, "You can get to skinnin it while it's still fresh."

The boy dutifully nodded, taking his kill to the barn without another word.

The two men were now alone; the questions lingering in the air finally had room to bubble to the surface.

"Come on inside," Eli said. "You look like you could use a warm drink."

iii. Eli

Eli observed Shane's hands fidgeting as he handed him the warm cup of coffee. Shane was always easy to read, but today more so than usual, with an obvious mix of nerves and adrenaline getting the best of him. Eli took a sip of his own coffee, relying on the burning sensation on his tongue to help him put on a neutral mask while he thought about the far-fetched plan that had colorfully poured out of his old friend.

He knew he should have shut down the proposal immediately, considering how dangerous and arrogant it was. If they were caught, it wouldn't just be humiliating but possibly suicidal. On the other hand, there was something in Shane's giddy voice that kept him invested in talking it through. There was a glow coming from the old man as he played everything out, beaming with a contagious energy that captured Eli's full attention.

There was no denying that the money played a strong factor

in Eli's consideration, but there was something more to it that was just as appealing. Something about the romantic idea of stepping back into his old life. He liked the fantasy of the two of them getting back on the right side of justice again, even if they were just playing make-believe.

He took another sip of the bitter coffee as he digested the pitch. It was a lot to consider without the luxury of time to think it over. A sudden craving for something stronger than coffee crept up on him, the desire for a drink to help focus and calm those nerves itching at his throat. Nothing overboard, just a splash to bring sanity back into the equation. But no, that couldn't happen. Not anymore. Coffee would have to do.

"Dead isn't an option?" Eli asked.

He knew it wasn't really something that was on the table but felt it was at least worth asking. No harm in exploring any wiggle room they might have that would make the whole idea feel slightly less crazy.

"Dead won't do," Shane answered, shaking his old hound dog face. "Miles wants the kid alive. There are too many questions that need to be answered."

No shit. Eli had questions too. *Everybody* had questions about what happened that day. Even off-duty all these years, Eli still heard the stories about Kit 'The Gentleman' Boone. The rumors only became more interesting, and far-fetched, when 'The Gentleman' nickname was swiftly dropped after the Silverton stories began to circulate. From his years of experience, Eli knew better than to fall for old legends that romanticized outlaws, but there was something about the massacre in the Silverton story that kept him intrigued. There was a tangled mystery around what really happened, along with enough gory details that it brought out his worst morbid curiosity. It was a hell of a mess, landing a massive price on the kid's head that was now dictating their conversation.

But as intriguing as the story was, the whole thing never added up to Eli. Why kill all those innocent people for no reason? Why did the kid suddenly become a cold-blooded killer when his reputation was so clean before that? It didn't fit the pattern of the dozens of stickups 'The Gentleman' had committed before, building on his reputation while contradicting it at the same time. It was that mystery and lingering questions around the incident that mandated the *alive* stipulation to the bounty.

"It's risky as hell," Eli mumbled as these questions gnawed at him.

There were a lot of factors they'd have to consider, almost none of them in their favor. First, the plan was ballsy and arrogant. A lot of things would have to go right for them to waltz into Blackcreek like they belonged, before snatching the kid out of there alive. Even if he cooperated, it would only work if every asshole they encountered believed their lie.

Then there was the issue of getting their prisoner to his destination, which was unfortunately *very* specific. Eli's name wasn't worth spit in most law circles anymore, making trust an issue when it came to who they'd hand their bounty over to. Blackcreek was out of the question and neither of them trusted anyone local anymore. Their best and only bet was old Miles Kelly, the sheriff in Arkell. The ride to Arkell wasn't a slouch of a journey, essentially doubled after the ride to Blackcreek, but Miles was probably the last man with a badge that Eli trusted after the *incident*.

"Everything will be fine if we stick to the plan," Shane reassured him. Despite all the risks, the youthful gleam in his eyes didn't waver. "All we have to do is slip on the old hat and stars to play the part."

Play the part. It hurt to hear it put into words out loud like that. It diminished everything he once was into a silly game of make-believe, like something those traveling actors he saw a few summers ago would do. It had never been just a part to him, it had been his goddamn life. But that didn't work out so well, did it? Maybe he *should* have treated it like a part. Maybe then he would have taken it more seriously and wouldn't have let things slip the way they did.

"It's not my hat to put on anymore," Eli conceded with shame.

It wasn't that he didn't want to do it; he really did. It was because of Ada's voice, creeping into his ear the way it sometimes did to lecture him about doing the sensible thing now that it was just him and the boy.

"I don't know if I can just play the part when we used to do it for real, with purpose. We used to do it to deliver justice."

"This *is* justice," Shane countered defensively. "You'd be able to make good with the banks while doing the right thing at the same time. Justice is served and you and Weston don't have to worry about those vultures bothering you anymore."

Make good with the banks. That's what all this was really about. They could argue all day about justice and right and wrong, but the dirty truth was that Eli needed the goddamn money and he needed it badly. Calling it justice was just a lie they could agree on to feel good about the whole affair. There wasn't really anything to debate, only the charade of pretending there was a debate to begin with.

"You're *sure* it's him?" Eli stressed, lying to himself that there was more to his decision than the financial implications.

"I wouldn't be coming to you if I weren't," Shane answered.

His friend's eyes looked older than usual, the crow's feet tightening. But they also looked *sure*. Looking at the confidence in those old eyes, another thought began chewing away at Eli. He thought about the reputation the kid had built after the Silverton incident and how far that infamy must have spread.

Whether it was the reward money, justice, or good old-fashioned revenge, he knew they couldn't be the only party interested in tracking the kid down.

"If he's hiding out in Blackcreek," Eli pressed, "how come nobody there has done anything about it?"

"Everybody in Blackcreek has their own sins to worry about," Shane reasoned. "They all have enough shit to worry about without giving a damn about every gun, hick, and stranger that rolls through their pathetic little shit-hole town. Besides, if they knew who he was and cared, he'd be dead already."

It was true. Grim, but true.

"Is he riding with a posse?" Eli asked. "Even just four men doubles the two of us."

"Nah," Shane dismissed. "He's running scared. Scared men hide alone, it's the only way to stop yappin tongues from getting them caught."

Shit, the old man had an answer for everything. He looked cocky, the confidence shedding years off him. It was enough to make Eli think that maybe they really could do this. His throat ached again for a swig from the bottle to help level out the nerves.

"If he really is there and he's alone," Eli warned, "he won't be sticking around for long."

"That's why I came straight to you," Shane answered with confidence.

There were a dozen reasons not to go along with the crazy plan and just one reason why he should do it. But the one was stronger than the dozen combined.

"It's your call boss," Shane concluded.

Boss. Eli liked how it sounded and wondered if that's why Shane threw it in.

"If you think it's too risky, just say the word."

Eli soaked in the scenario, letting it marinate into his bones to wash away the doubts that would tell him not to do it. Out the window, he saw Weston laboring away trying to get the damn sows in line. He was hard on the boy, yet the kid always took it in stride. Weston had been through far too much over the last couple years, and things would only be worse for him if the banks ended up taking the place away from them. None of it was the boy's fault, but he'd still be the one who would have to pay for it. There was only one choice.

"We better get going then," Eli answered calmly.

Shane didn't know how to respond to the sudden decision and sat there gawking like a dumb mule as Eli got up.

"Right now?" he asked.

Eli liked catching the old man off guard. Made him feel like the old times, the good times before he went and fucked everything up.

"If he's still there," Eli started, with a one-track mind that no longer had second thoughts, "he can't be staying for more than a night or two. We go now, we can make it by dark to get the jump on him."

Shane didn't have to hear another word.

iv. Weston

Weston could feel the blisters starting to form on his hands as he tightened the rope, securing the gear on his father's horse snugly. He didn't dare question the hasty job his father did securing his blanket and rifle. Instead, he quietly stepped in to make sure everything was secure. His father always stressed to him the importance of doing a job properly, even if he didn't always adhere to his own rules. Weston may not have been happy about his father taking off so suddenly like this, but he couldn't keep himself from at least making sure the old man's things were packed correctly.

"I'll be back in a week at most," his father told him, his voice infused with an oddly giddy confidence.

Weston had been banished outside while his father and Shane discussed the matter at hand in hushed tones. He knew the subject must be serious after being evicted, but didn't expect them to be in such a hurry to get out of there so shortly after. It wasn't like his pa to rush like this, no matter what the issue. If he really had to go, Weston would have at least appreciated his father letting him know where he was going. If he was old enough to watch the farm, then surely he was old enough to know whatever secret business had them rushing out of there.

"Tend to the animals and keep a close eye. Especially the pigs at nightfall," his father commanded. "And watch for anyone who don't belong creeping around. You're in charge of keeping things in order while I'm gone."

You're in charge. The words should have carried more weight, but they came off dismissively, like he couldn't wait to ride off with Shane and be done with it.

His father never went into detail about what they wanted, but Weston had seen the sharp-dressed men from the bank come around a few times and was able to put the pieces together. He knew the strain it was causing his father, and his assumption that he was riding off to find a way to get a little bit of money to keep the bank off their back for one more season wasn't unrealistic.

At least that's what Weston hoped he was doing.

Deep down, he feared that his father was finally cutting his losses, riding off and never coming back. He'd be gone forever, leaving Weston alone with nothing but debt and a couple goddamn pigs. He wanted to confront his father, ask him where the hell he was going and how he could just abandon his only son for God-knows-how-long. Or better yet, he wished he had the courage to give the old man the beat down he deserved, finally hitting back and showing him he wasn't a little kid anymore.

"I will Pa," he squeaked. He had a million things he wanted to tell his father before he left, instead letting out the weakest words that came to him out of habit. "Be careful."

He hated himself for cowering. He had readied himself to find the courage to say what he wanted, only to let the moment pass. He just watched as his father gave him a nod goodbye before riding off into the brisk September morning.

CHAPTER TWO

A DISTRIBUTION OF LUCK

i. Silas

"*P*air of tens," Charlie boasted, drunkenly slapping down his shitty hand with that rotten, awful grin of his.

If he didn't know better, Silas would have thought Charlie was holding a royal flush and Maggie's heart judging by the stupid smile on his face. But Charlie was a piss-poor player and a fucking idiot, more than happy to lose his money as long as he got to drink, tell his jokes, and leer at Miss Maggie all night.

It had been a good night for Silas. Hell, he couldn't remember ever having a streak like this before in his life. They'd been playing for hours now, cleaning out a few drunks from the table for what little they were worth. Now there were just four of them left, drinking and playing as Silas' stack of chips steadily grew. Charlie was a lost cause at this point in the game, shamelessly playing dogshit hands repeatedly like they were sweet sugar. John was just as hopeless, more interested in getting pissed up than playing, as his small pile of chips slowly dimin-

ished. Seth was a different story, though. He was there to play a
serious game, but the right cards just weren't coming to him.

Silas could feel the seething anger coming from Seth, especially during the few hands Seth looked cocky about only to
have Silas wisely fold on. Part of him felt bad for Seth, who was
growing visibly irritated as his chips slowly evaporated over the
course of the night. On the other hand, fuck Seth. Why should
he care? Tonight was Silas' night and he wasn't going to let this
sour bastard soil it for him.

He knew better than to boast about his winnings, believing a
gracious winner always outshines a braggart. He did his best to
be a gentleman as he took in each pot, hoping maybe Maggie
would notice and see what a winner he was. A winner and a
gentleman, who maybe had enough chips to convince her that
he could take her out somewhere real nice. Take her the hell
away out of Blackcreek.

The run-down saloon was mostly empty, save for a few
pathetic degenerates. There were the players at the table joining
him, a lone asshole sitting at the bar drinking, the saloon's propri-
etor and bartender Arlo, and his beautiful daughter, Miss Maggie,
who made the place shine as she served up drinks. Arlo was very
protective of Maggie, never letting her tend to the place alone or
get too cozy with any of the patrons. It made it difficult for Silas to
chat intimately with her outside of a few pleasantries and stolen
smiles. He could hardly blame Arlo for his overprotective nature,
with all the shitheels that came in and out of Blackcreek, a good
number of them sure to stop in his establishment. Even tonight,
the small but rowdy group of fellow players and the silent
scumbag sitting alone at the bar, were more than reason enough
for Arlo to be on edge, with an extra close eye on his daughter.

Silas knew he was different then all these assholes. He had
hopes and dreams outside of the drink in his glass and the four

musty walls of this tavern. He deserved a chance to talk to Maggie without having a bar full of drunks giving him shit any time he showed a slight bit of polite interest. But during a rowdy game like this in a hellhole in the middle of a hellhole, the only chance you had to talk with Miss Maggie was limited to strictly business.

"Hey Maggie," he hollered, trying to keep the charm as he eyeballed the stranger at the bar she was serving, "Bring 'nother round, wouldya, sweetheart?"

She smiled in that way that melted his heart like fresh butter. It gave him the confidence to pull a couple coins from his growing stack and hold them out.

"And keep 'em comin'."

Sweet Maggie finished serving the lone creep at the bar and gave Silas a shy nod. God, he didn't like the way that guy looked. *Never trust loners*, he thought, *especially when there's a pretty gal in sight.*

"Looks like that lucky streak of yours is coming to an end," Seth growled, yanking Silas out of his fantasy. "Full house," he exclaimed, laying down his cards, prouder than an old dog taking down a young fox.

Full house. A damn fine hand.

Silas had been watching Seth grow angrier throughout the night and from the stories he had heard, he knew Seth was the type that could snap if the losses kept coming. It was tough because Silas knew he was actually the one holding the hand of the night and that Seth was going to be crushed when his win was robbed from him. He felt a slight touch of guilt as he watched Seth grin obliviously, knowing he was moments away from disappointing him yet again. Still, Silas let the moment linger for his own satisfaction. After all, a good hand doesn't mean shit unless the reveal lives up to it.

John seemed to perk back alive at the reveal, giving an impressed whistle to the hand.

"Shit!" Charlie muttered, tossing down his miserable cards.

Seth was visibly itching to take that stack of chips, growing a little more antsy with each moment Silas took to reveal his hand.

"Not bad," Silas grinned. "Not bad."

God, he wished Maggie was watching. Slow bleeding a bunch of drunks wasn't that impressive, but when you had a hand that could take down a full house and knock a player out of the game? If she saw that, she'd see what a real winner he was.

"You going to show us what ya got or what?" Seth demanded impatiently. There was a cockiness in his voice, but Silas could hear it poisoned with insecurity deep down. "Nobody will judge you for folding whatever shameful shit hand you're holding to yourself."

Silas did everything he could to force the smile stuck on his face away. It was the type of grin his mother warned him would never go away if he didn't stop it.

"I suppose you can't win 'em all," Silas said, showing off his bluffing skills.

"No, you can't," Seth boasted.

"But you can have a lucky streak," Silas countered, his smile creeping back. "And my streak ain't over yet."

He lay down his flush, knowing without looking that Maggie was watching, along with her old man. Hell, even the mute bastard at the bar had to have been curious how the game was going at this point.

"Sorry, Seth," Silas said with the vaguest hint of sympathy. "That's a sore loss, partner."

Charlie and John immediately lost it, hollering like a couple donkeys in a burst of gleeful, drunken laughter.

"A fuckin flush," Charlie giggled. "God damn it Silas, it really *is* your lucky night." He slapped poor Seth, who was staring coldly at the cards that cost him everything, on the back. "You pull out a full-house and *still* lose! Sorry, Seth, that's just bad fuckin luck pal."

Silas's smile was stretched wide enough it was starting to hurt. He couldn't help it, the grin refusing to leave his face as he leaned in to collect the pot. It felt good to win big and he decided he was going to enjoy the moment while it was his. The moment only lasted a heartbeat, though, because that was when the mood of the night curdled.

As Silas collected, Seth snapped his arm in and grabbed him by the wrist. His clammy hand gripped tightly; the cold lizard-like feel of the palm around his wrist made Silas freeze up.

"You wouldn't be fucking with me," Seth snarled. "Would you, Silas?"

Silas knew that letting Seth handle him like this would make him look weak, negating the entire win in everyone's eyes. He tried to shake free from the grip but found it far tighter than anticipated. It *hurt*, Seth proving to be much stronger than Silas would have guessed from his lanky build. His wrist burned from the rub of the grip; panic started to kick in as he tried to keep a straight face. Feeling like he wasn't going to be able to worm out through force, he put on a slick smile to try to bring the fun tone of the room back to where it was just moments ago.

"C'mon Seth," Silas reasoned. "We're having fun and I'm just having a lucky night."

"Nobody's that lucky," Seth said coldly, not in the mood for any of it.

The rational approach wasn't working, but Silas had nothing to hide either. He snapped his hand free from Seth's grip, gaining the confidence to stand his ground and stare him down.

"Sometimes people have a lucky night," Silas said. "Tonight's my turn."

Something he said must have gotten through Seth's thick skull, because he finally dropped the attitude and let out a friendly chuckle. Silas didn't want to let on how relieved he was, but the deflated tension at the table allowed the grin to grow back on his face.

The rest of the table took note, letting out a nervous laughter that seemed to be coming from a place of relief. He thought laughter was always better than a fight, especially when you're the one on the other side of the person who thinks they've been done wrong.

"You're right," Seth conceded, his tone dignified, gentlemanly. "Luck changes hands all the time. Tonight's your lucky night, which I suppose would make it my unlucky one."

A whiff of the tension still lingered until Miss Maggie came over with their drinks, bringing a ray of much needed light with her.

"Here you boys are," Maggie offered, in that way of hers that was sweeter than honey. Silas was going to offer to buy Seth his drink before recognizing at this point it was already assumed.

"Thank you, sweetheart." Silas smiled, offering a crumpled bill from his winnings. It was more than enough for everyone's drinks, but not enough to showboat. She smiled kindly at the gesture, projecting her fondness in a way that even the dimmest of those at the table would pick up on.

"I think ol Silas is sweet on you, Maggie," Charlie interrupted without an ounce of charm before bursting into a fit of giggles.

Goddamn it, Charlie, Silas thought. Couldn't the old fucking drunk keep his mouth shut for one goddamn minute in his miserable life? Silas wanted to play it cool, but he felt his face burning red while Charlie and John had their laugh at his expense.

"Leave her alone," Silas muttered back pathetically.

Fucking hell, he instantly felt all the goodwill from a whole night of winning lost in a snap.

"They're just joshing you Silas," Maggie cooed back in a way that made him feel both embarrassed and prideful as hell. "I think it's because they're jealous," she added with a wink.

The pair of goddamned donkeys lost it again, braying like a couple of asses in heat. They were hooting and hollering at Silas's expense while Maggie drank it up, knowing that the teasing was getting his goat. Silas calmed himself down by reminding himself that a little teasing never hurt anyone. After all, ain't that the way schoolgirls let little boys know they like 'em? At least it meant she was paying *some* sort of attention to him.

Still, he didn't enjoy being the center of all that hollering and teasing, even if it was all in good fun. Even less, he didn't like how that asshole at the bar sat there silently, drinking as if none of this had been going on while the drunken laughter erupted just a few feet away.

That was the last of the laughter for the night and the last time some of them ever laughed again. It was at that point that the night went real bad, when Silas's luck changed.

Maggie had just placed the last of the drinks down when Seth reached forward and grabbed her by the wrist. It was quick, like a rattlesnake striking its prey, the look in his eyes filled with just as much venom.

"I've been having an unlucky day today, Maggie," Seth spat, looking at her with bulging eyes.

She tried to pull away, but his clammy grip was too tight.

"I...I'm sorry to hear that Seth," she said. Silas could hear the fear in her voice, though she tried not to let it show. He was worried for her, afraid of that look in Seth's eyes that said he was in a mean place.

"Tell me, Maggie," Seth asked, "is today a lucky day for you?"

That was enough for Arlo. He lumbered away from the bar with enough authority to make most men step right the fuck down.

"That's enough, Seth," Arlo commanded. He tolerated a lot of shit in his bar, but very little when it involved Maggie. "She's got nothin to do with your beef, she's just serving drinks."

"Stay out of it, old man," Seth hissed.

Something in his eyes was dangerous enough to make Arlo stop in his tracks, leaving poor Maggie locked in Seth's clutches. She watched with mortified betrayal as her dad cowered.

"Quit playing now, Seth," Maggie said, fighting back tears with forced playfulness. "Fun is fun, but it's starting to hurt now."

Silas's heart ached watching Seth ignore her pleas as he tightened his greasy grip.

"Funny thing about luck," Seth lectured, "is that the bad kind is a *lot* more common than the good kind." He eyeballed Silas with a stone-cold stare that promised nobody else was going to have the last word. "That's why we only have one winner at a table full of players. The rest of us are stuck with bad luck, just there to lose."

Just there to lose. Silas couldn't think of any other day in his life where he wasn't the one losing. Why couldn't today have been different?

"So, if today's your lucky day Silas, what do the odds say about what kind of luck Miss Maggie here would be having?"

God, he hated hearing Seth say her name like that. His lips felt like they hadn't tasted water in a week, dry as vulture bones looking for words. He calculated how to respond without putting Maggie in further danger. *Fuck the money* he thought; he just wanted her to be ok.

"C'mon Seth," he finally answered, figuring reason was the only way out of this. "It's just a game of cards."

The reaction was as if those were the worst combination of words Seth had ever heard in his life. Silas was ready for any angry retort Seth might respond with, but not for things to go the way they did.

It all happened in a blink. In one motion, Seth was up from the table with his revolver drawn. He pulled Maggie closer into a tight grasp, pressing the metal of his gun barrel to her temple. She was caught in his clutches before her brain had time to process what was happening, her face frozen in disbelief. She locked her doe eyes with Silas, silently begging for help. She braced herself for that final *bang* while everyone else at the table froze like a painting.

"God damn it, Seth!" Arlo hollered, sounding like half a man for the first time that night. "Let her go!"

Seth shot his piercing eyes at Arlo, making the old bartender back down once again.

"One more peep out of you, old man," Seth warned, "and you're going to have to hire a new girl to come in and clean up the mess I made out of this one."

With all sense of heroics gone, Arlo shriveled back from man to worm, helplessly watching things unfold.

The lone man sitting at the bar remained unmoved by the situation.

"C'mon Seth," Silas pleaded, realizing the only weapon he had to save poor Maggie was humility. "It's only a stupid game."

"I had a lot of money riding on that stupid game," Seth hissed.

"You can keep the money," Silas promised, feeling none of his words were getting through. "Just let Maggie go."

Seth spat a green mucus that gave an audible splat as it hit the ground.

"I don't want you to *give* me the money," Seth barked with offense. "I want you to tell me *how* you won it." There was hatred in his eyes. Not hatred from losing, but at the thought of being swindled. "You've been cheating, admit it."

Silas wished he'd been cheating just so he *could* admit it and put an end to this. Seth might have put a bullet in him out of anger if that were the case, but at least he could take the blame and Miss Maggie would be okay. But that was the damn problem: there was nothing to admit to. He played nothing but an honest game. Cheating hadn't even crossed his mind: he just had a good goddamned night. He could have lied about it and *said* he cheated, but he wasn't that good of a bluffer. The reasonable part of his brain was hoping that Seth could see that, and they could chalk the whole thing up as a good old misunderstanding, something they could laugh about later over a drink. Instead, the hate in Seth's eyes told Silas that they were beyond the point of reasoning tonight.

"I told you." Silas gulped down a huge lump of humility. "I didn't cheat, I just had a lucky night."

For some reason, this was funny to Seth. That crooked smile of his started to grow, every single one of his rotten teeth showing as he cocked the hammer of his pistol.

"Lucky?" Seth spat through a grin you could smell. "Too bad you've been hogging all that luck and not sharing any of it with poor Miss Maggie here."

Seth pressed the cold barrel harder against Maggie's temple. She squeezed her eyes shut, tears pouring down as she did her best to prepare herself for the end.

Nobody was going to save her. Not Silas, not Arlo. Nobody. Sweet Maggie was going to die, here in this awful place, by a lousy drunk just because he lost a few bucks playing cards. Silas wished he could do more for her. Instead, he used those last seconds to dream about the life they could have had together while he waited for the inevitable.

That's when the stranger at the bar drew his pistol and fired.

ii. Kit

Kit had been nursing each drink at a pace slow enough to keep his wits, yet respectful enough that he wouldn't raise any eyebrows as he tried to blend in with the barstools. *Keep em' comin'* was his motto of the night, sitting there thinking about what his next move would be. The place was the perfect kind of dump to lay low in without suffering from complete isolation.

The tradeoff was contending with the local grime. The poor girl working the bar looked eighteen, tops, too young and too pretty for the type of people a shithole like this attracted. Kit felt bad for her, watching her serve the group of lousy drunks playing a game of poker where only two of the players appeared to have any skin in the game. It wasn't fair for a girl like her to be stuck in a place like this. But the world wasn't a fair place and there was nothing special enough about her to make him risk putting his neck on the line to whisk her away out of here. Even if he wanted to, how would he? He was still trying to figure out how to get *himself* out of the mess that had him hiding out in this hellhole in the first place.

Blackcreek was a rough town, but rough was a good thing for Kit's situation. Rough meant heroes didn't usually come sniffing around, allowing you to blend in with your fellow lowlife in peace. You only had a problem in a place like this if you were weak, the smell potent to the local wolves looking to take advantage of lambs. But weakness had never been a problem for Kit despite his youth and pretty face. Sure, he'd had his share of run-ins where the odd tough tried to put him in his place, but usually a glare that said *don't fuck with me* had them leave him alone and move on to weaker prey. And for those that didn't move on, there were a few stories out there someone was surely telling about the poor bastards that had made that mistake.

But there would be no mistakes tonight. Tonight was about

biding his time and plotting his next move. Maybe he'd even enjoy his drink if he let himself. Problem was, he rarely ever let his guard down long enough to relax and enjoy anything. Even now, as much as he wished he could turn his mind off, enjoy the whiskey, and let the bartender's daughter distract his mind, the group of goddamned players harassing the girl was stopping him and getting on his nerves.

He could sense things growing tense over at the card table. The one player flirting with the poor girl all night was too stupid to cool down on the gloating about the streak he had found himself on. It was the type of attitude that would get you killed one day, something Kit had seen many times before and was damned worried he'd be seeing again tonight if the man didn't lay off. The thought of the mood turning sour made his finger twitch, instinctively readying itself to draw if he had to.

Not tonight though. The plan for tonight was to lay low, blend in and mind his own business. No matter how much trouble some poor son of a bitch was looking at getting himself into, it would be nothing compared to what Kit would be facing if anyone here figured out who he was. So, he'd ignore them. He'd remain an unremarkable face, blending in with the barstools as another rummy that nobody remembered.

That was the plan. But his plans often had a way of going wrong lately, and tonight was no exception.

The table inevitably started arguing when the sore loser of the group was humiliated during a tense hand. It was one of those common situations that happens during games that either fizzles out quickly or ends up with one of the players picking up their teeth. Or, in a place like Blackcreek, ends with a bullet in the gut of the slowest draw. Kit had hoped to avoid being around a situation like that, but if it happened, he'd let it play out and things would be fine. Tragic but fine. Someone else getting themselves killed over a card game was a damn shame, but it was someone else's shame and something Kit could ignore and let go.

What he couldn't ignore is when they had to go and get the poor girl involved.

It started innocently enough. Well, as innocent as an angry drunk grabbing at a poor bar girl can be. Kit could tell by the sound in her voice that the drunk was grabbing her wrist too hard, her voice scared under her tough demeanor. He also knew it was all in the name of boasting, meant to put a little fear in the winner to make him look weak. It didn't matter how many chips you were holding, if you looked weak in front of the girl you fancy, you suddenly became the one who was the loser. Kit knew how it went; words would be exchanged and eventually they'd take it outside to settle. He'd seen it before and wasn't going to ruin his cover by stepping in before it happened again. He just had to let it go.

Just. Let. It. Go.

His reaction time must have been slipping, because the conflict rapidly barreled forward beyond the point of no return before he could make a move. He knew the blowup was inevitable but didn't expect the loser to escalate so much of his anger towards the girl. Around the point that usually ends with the demand to *take things outside and settle this like men*, the loser was up in a blink with the barrel of his iron pressed against the poor girl's temple. Clearly, he knew the other player was sweet on her, striking at his weak point to show how dangerous he was. Never show your rival your weaknesses. Never show your cards.

Instinctively, Kit wanted to jump in to help her. But he forced himself to play it cool. He knew there were three other men at the table against one, plus her daddy, the bartender, who wouldn't stand for this. The bar was full of other people who could play the hero. All Kit had to do was blend in and get the hell out of there if things went south.

The bartender sheepishly stepped forward, but Kit could see his yellow colors the second he opened his mouth. After a few heated words exchanged, the man quickly shriveled up like a slug on a hot rock. Disgusted, Kit wanted to put a bullet in him just for being so pathetic.

The two losing drunks gawking at the table didn't do a goddamn thing either. They just watched the exchange with slack-jawed stupidity while the loser held his pistol to the poor gal.

The only chance she had was from the guy that cleaned the loser out. He was sensibly using the only weapon he could in the situation: his words. Unfortunately, those words were falling on deaf ears.

It's not my problem, Kit kept trying to tell himself, recognizing that very soon that wouldn't be the case.

"Too bad you've been hogging all that luck and not sharing any of it with poor Maggie here," he heard the loser say to his opponent.

Kit wanted to believe that he was bluffing, and that the girl would be fine, but there was something in the man's eyes, an unhinged craziness that he'd seen far too many times, which always ended with bloodshed. Tears were starting to pour down the poor girl's cheeks, her fear contagious. Her face said what Kit knew; the crazy asshole really was going to shoot her.

You could slip out of here right after he shoots her and everyone scrambles over the commotion, Kit thought, *you'd be invisible walking away from her dead body.*

You've done it before...

The guilt forming in his throat from the thought made him want to be sick. He heard their whimpers again, coming from beyond the grave and landing here in this shithole of a bar to haunt him. But the whimpers didn't belong to *them*. They were too vivid, too real. They were here. They were hers. And she was still alive.

But she wouldn't be if he waited any longer. He couldn't stop himself. He drew.

BANG

The first gunshot cracked through the bar like lightning shattering a tree.

BANG

A second followed that shook the tavern still.

Kit didn't intend to shoot the man, but that beautiful combination of instinct and muscle memory did the job for him. Before he realized what he'd done, his smoking pistol was facing the now-dead drunk, who never knew what hit him. The poor woman stood there in dumb shock, her blood-covered face fooled into thinking she was the one who was dead.

The sulfur smell of gunpowder gave the air a threatening aura. The group at the table turned their attention to Kit, peering through the cloud from his pistol, wondering what happened. He stepped through the smoke, giving himself a better shot at anybody who might have any fatal ideas.

"He was right," Kit said calmly, breaking the stunned silence of the tavern. "It wasn't his lucky day."

It should have ended right there. But it never does, which is why he didn't want to get involved in the first place.

Letting bravery overtake logic, the two rowdy drunks now appeared stone sober as they clumsily reached for their pistols.

Neither of them were fast enough.

A double *BANG* cracked through the bar like an angry bullwhip. The two shots punctured the lungs of the first drunk, sending him crashing through the table. A third *BANG* from Kit's revolver was mercifully aimed at the second drunk's trigger hand, blowing two of his fingers clean off and sending his iron to the floor. It took the poor bastard a second to realize his fingers were gone before he let out a shrieking scream of pain, adrenaline, and confusion. He'd never play the piano again, but at least he'd live to see another day. There was no screaming from the first drunk, who wheezed his way through his last moments on the ground.

The winner at the table, who started the whole debacle, was now going for his sidearm, but his eyes told Kit that he didn't feel confident in his choice. This was a man who tried to use his words to defuse a situation moments ago, so Kit reasoned that maybe he could give him an out using just those. Kit locked his sights on the miserable fucker and cocked his hammer.

"You have a split second to decide how you want this to play out," Kit threatened. He could tell the man didn't really want to draw, but that he might be dumb enough that he'd still have to be talked out of it. "You've had a pretty lucky night so far. If I were you, I'd make the right decision to keep that lucky streak of yours going."

Kit never let his eyes waver, the other man's eyes doing nothing but betraying him. Kit may have used the man's preference for words to solve this exchange, but the man had no words left to respond with. The scared son-of-a-bitch moved his hand away from his revolver, letting the will to live outweigh his pride.

"Good boy," Kit responded with a hint of admiration.

Maybe the man's appreciation for sparing him and saving his lady friend would buy Kit enough goodwill to let him quietly get his shit together and get the hell out of Blackcreek before he drew any more attention. He could just give a friendly nod and make his way out of here, becoming nothing more than a story of another stranger that came and went through town.

It would have been nice if things went like that.

THUMP

Things went dark instead.

iii. Silas

"Holy shit," Silas stuttered in disbelief. "It's him."

Charlie was screaming like a banshee while John bled out like a stuck pig, but all Silas could focus on was the man knocked out in front of him. Was it really him? Did he just survive a shootout with the Silverton Butcher himself? He couldn't believe it, feeling both grateful to be alive and like a fool at a loss for anything meaningful to say.

He owed his life to Arlo, who had managed to sneak up on the stranger, cracking him in the back of the head with the butt of his shotgun and knocking him out cold. Silas didn't really think the stranger was going to kill him at that moment, not after he had saved Miss Maggie like that, but that was before he realized who the man was.

A dozen contradictory thoughts ran through Silas's mind as he stared at the unconscious man. The stranger had shot the place up with deadly accuracy, leaving Seth and John dead and poor Charlie two fingers shorter than he was a minute ago, but he had also saved Maggie, something Silas was eternally grateful for. He felt conflicted but didn't rule out the thought that maybe the bastard had stepped in because he had some other nefarious plans for Miss Maggie. The thought made Silas click his jaw in anger, logically concluding that butchers like this never do a good deed without an ulterior motive. If that was the case, he'd be more than happy to string the fucker up.

"Maggie," Arlo barked, his shotgun confidently aimed at the stranger, ready to shoot if he had to. "Get the rope."

CHAPTER THREE
THE LAW COMES TO BLACKCREEK

i. Eli

*T*he hours it took to get to Blackcreek passed quickly for Eli, his mind occupied with pleasant distractions the whole time. Part of it was that they never stopped riding once they left the ranch, and that it was good quality time spent riding with his old friend. The other part was that beautiful feeling that he hadn't felt for a long time. The feeling of fear.

True, his life as of late hadn't been completely absent of fear; the fear that the banks would take the farm. The fear that his boy might take off one day and never return. The fear that the years he wasted on the bottle would catch up to him and force the last of his good memories to fade away the same way they had for his daddy once he got up in age. But those were all the bad kinds of fear, the mundane fear of everyday life. They weren't like *this* fear. This fear was the fear you get from going into the wolves den, the fear of being a gunshot away from being nothing more than a memory.

The good fear.

He still couldn't decide if their plan was exceptionally stupid or brilliant. Shane did a great job of selling it as a breeze, but even with the blur of the bottle fogging up his memories of his years with the law, Eli had seen enough to know that it didn't take much to cause shit to go sideways real quick in a bad situation.

He'd faced down his share of trouble in his former life, but a lot of the things they'd done in the past weren't easy; the bottle had just made those difficult tasks easier to go down. He didn't have that luxury today. Today his head was clear as a clean brook, that clarity front and center as he rode with glee into the mess he knew awaited them. Clarity was a double-edged sword, helping you think straight while also causing you to think too much. Thinking too much about what could go wrong.

If they could get to the Boone kid before anyone in Black-creek recognized him, it would be stupid of them to assume he would leave with them without putting up a fight. Eli played out a dozen scenarios in his head of how things might go, and there wasn't one of them that didn't end with bloodshed of some kind. The kid was supposedly a crack shot, which didn't help their situation, and even if they *did* get the jump on him, they couldn't shoot him since he wasn't worth shit to them dead. Dragging a dead man to Arkell would only make Sheriff Kelly think Eli was back on the bottle, a stunt that might make him decide to hang Eli instead. Nope, dead wasn't an option. They needed him alive, and that wasn't going to be easy.

But fuck easy. That thrill he was feeling in his belly came from knowing deep down that this whole crazier-than-a-rat-in-a-shithouse plan was going to be the goddamned furthest thing from easy.

"Woah," Shane called out, pulling his horse to a stop.

Eli was so lost in his self-satisfied thoughts that he didn't notice they'd already made the outskirts of Blackcreek, and from the look of it back here, things in town seemed to be buzzing.

"Looks like Blackcreek ain't so sleepy tonight," Shane mused.

Even from this distance it was clear that some sort of commotion was going on in the middle of town. Everyone was crowding around about something, and for something to stir up that much interest in Blackcreek, Eli got the bad feeling that maybe everyone had figured out who their latest resident was.

Yep, it wasn't going to be easy.

ii. Silas

Silas felt like a coward as he slunk behind Arlo, who was leading the stranger out of the bar with his shotgun. Even with the man's hands tied behind his back, Silas wanted to keep a safe distance after seeing what a quick and precise shot he was. The shotgun should have made him feel a little safer, but the lack of worry on the stranger's face was a gentle *Don't fuck with me* reminder that he *did* just shoot up half of Arlo's tavern mere minutes ago.

Silas felt guilty about how everything went down. He'd known Seth well enough from playing a few card games with him that he figured with enough time, he'd probably convince himself that Seth was just messing around and that there was no way he would have *actually* hurt Miss Maggie. At least those would be the lies he'd tell himself to sleep better at night, a way to justify putting his head down while the stranger who saved Maggie's life was taken out to the slaughter. Silently, he knew the truth was that during those moments in the bar, Seth *was* going to pull the trigger and kill her. He saw it in Seth's eyes and had never been more afraid of anyone or anything before in his life.

There was no denying the stranger saved Maggie, maybe Silas too. Watching Maggie cry as Seth held his pistol to her beautiful face made Silas sick. He would have done anything to save her at that moment, and this stranger did just that. The lump in Silas's throat was begging him to plead to save this man, but reality has a funny way of coming back and making a liar out of the promises you made to God after a desperate moment passes. The man he should have given anything in the world to save was being marched off to his death, and all Silas did was watch.

Life would eventually move on for Silas and he would find a way to justify the hanging. Later, when the stranger would be dead and buried, everyone would be drinking to celebrate getting rid of one of God's worst and he'd find a way to bury his doubt by focusing on the tall and horrid stories about the man that saved Maggie's life. Eventually, after enough booze and time, there'd be zero guilt or questions lingering as he moved on with his life, blaming the man's death on his own rotten crimes that put him on the wrong end of the noose.

As for now, Silas would have to find a way to get rid of the heavy doubt he carried about the man who saved the only good thing in his miserable life, as he watched him being marched off to the jackals. He might have seemed like a savior to Silas in the bar, but knowing he was involved in the Silverton tragedy was a nice way to help put that gratitude aside. After all, you start giving gratitude to the devil, you ain't far away from starting to make a deal or two with him.

Things were even murkier since they were serving justice to the stranger when justice didn't belong to them. Justice didn't really belong to *anybody* in Blackcreek, yet most of the townsfolk hypocritically lapped it up like a greedy cat with a saucer of milk when they were given the chance. The general understanding was that anybody staying in Blackcreek was there for one reason — to have people stay the fuck out of their business. If you were there to lay low, you respected other people's wishes to do the same. Generally, that meant you kept to yourself, but the boredom of isolation had its way of riling everyone up in the makeshift little town every once in a while, if they had a reason. And having a piece of shit like the Silverton Butcher shooting up Arlo's bar was more than reason enough.

Now justice, at least Blackcreek's farcical version of it, was an issue you'd take to Dante if a situation requiring it came up. Silas felt like nobody in Arlo's bar was equipped to deal with this dilemma, so that's exactly who the stranger was going to have to answer to. Charlie had run ahead to let Dante know who they'd discovered while Arlo was tying the stranger up, and it didn't take Dante long to get the whole town red-hot and ready to serve some of their own home-cooked justice. If there really was a window of time for Silas to have a change of heart about the whole thing, it was gone the moment Dante became involved.

Dante's towering presence made Seth look like a tame kitten in comparison. Nobody had listened to Seth during his short and miserable life, doomed to be a loser who only came at you when he was scared and humiliated. People listened to Dante though. Dante carried authority by simply *being*, commanding your respect with just a look. Most people had to raise their voice to intimidate you, but Dante only had to say a couple haunting words while flashing you a seemingly friendly smile to have you shitting in your boots.

That smile was the first thing Silas noticed now as they marched their prized prisoner toward him and his rag-tag posse. The moonlight reflected off his perfect teeth, his grin growing with each step as they approached.

"I'll be damned," Dante purred with his velvet voice. "When I first heard about the slaughter on the Silverton train, I said that I'd do *anything* to string up the bastard who did it myself." Dante kept his eyes locked on the stranger as he marveled at the opportunity. "I thought it was just wishful thinking, one of those cute thoughts you have to yourself to push the ugliness of a terrible story away. I didn't realize that I'd actually have the pleasure of making it happen one day."

Dante's words struck a chord with Doc, a giant bear of a man that was never far from his side. Doc stepped his huge frame forward, clearly wanting a piece of the judgment that was being thrown around.

"Ira Baker was on that train," Doc shared solemnly. "So was his boy, not much older than ten."

He wasn't loud or boisterous about the claim, but every word landed with the growing group. As a man of few words, Doc's input said a lot.

The theatrics were starting to draw a crowd. Everyone knew the story of Silverton, and each of the new lurkers wanted their own taste of the ready-to-spill blood. The murmurs of the rattled group were starting to grow, feeding an energy to Dante that he reveled in.

One old-timer stepped forward, finding the courage to add his two cents. His face looked like he'd seen a ghost.

"Did you hear about the poor souls at the Bentley farm?" the old man squeaked, his voice shaking with fear. "Someone slaughtered the entire family. Baby and all."

The mention of the dead baby was enough to mutate the crowd's whispers into an angrier buzz, like a hive of pissed-off bees. The anger gave the old man enough confidence to direct his ire toward the stranger, nodding at him with vengeance.

"This cowardly cocksucker was probably the one that did it."

His accusation was trial enough for the crowd.

"I don't know anything about that," the stranger said, shameless with the matter-of-fact tone of his denial. "I carry my share of sins, but I had nothing to do with that."

The old man's story about the farm had transformed the stranger's expression from a stone-cold neutral stare into genuine offense. He hadn't tried to deny anything that had been thrown at him up until that point, only chiming in now to defend himself against these gruesome accusations about the Bentley farm. Something about that response made Silas almost believe him, though the energy from the crowd suggested he was probably the only one.

"Save it for the reaper," Dante responded. "You'll have plenty of time to cry to him about what you did and didn't do soon enough."

Dante shot Arlo a commanding nod, beckoning him to bring the stranger forward. Any last-ditch effort to object to this farce of a trial remained silently on Silas's tongue.

The moment the stranger was within Dante's reach, Doc grabbed him with his meaty paws and marched him toward the town's crudely prepared gallows. The stranger squirmed and struggled to break free from his grasp, but struggling against Doc was like trying to break free from the grip of a python. Doc flung the dirty noose around the stranger's neck, leading him up onto the rickety barrel beneath it. Doc gave the noose a good tug, enjoying every ounce of pain he knew the rope burn would give the murdering bastard.

The crowd fed into every hostile moment, building up to what would be a collective cathartic experience that would allow this group of bad men to briefly feel good about themselves for bringing a far worse man to justice. Dante let the approval of the crowd wash over him, playing up his self-appointed role as a ringmaster to the world's most fucked up circus.

"Any last words?" Dante crooned with false sympathy, glaring at the stranger as if he were a disobedient dog.

"Shouldn't there be some sort of trial?" the stranger asked with complete sincerity. "I don't see one lawman here amongst the lot of you."

The tense air broke, the crowd bursting into laughter at the inquiry. It was a completely legitimate question, while also being the stupidest fucking thing Silas had ever heard in his life. Yes, a trial conducted by officers of the law was how things were normally supposed to go, but *normal* had no fucking place in Blackcreek — especially when it came to the law.

"A lawman in Blackcreek?" Charlie brayed in his signature donkey laugh, suddenly wanting to have his moment with the crowd. "That's cute. We could have a nice trial, get you to tell everyone your side of the story."

Everyone laughed even harder. Everyone but Dante.

"We'll leave the trial for the devil," Dante said with a cold smile. There was no joke behind his words, stated as pure facts.

"I'll be seeing you in hell then," the stranger replied, a cool grin on his face.

Maybe he was trying to intimidate the crowd, or maybe he just didn't care anymore, but nothing about him looked scared to Silas.

"I'm banking on it, child slayer," Dante retorted. Any guilt Silas felt about the situation evaporated as he let himself become absorbed in the theatrics of the back and forth.

Dante used the momentum of the crowd's energy to move forward with the main event, strutting towards the rickety barrel his prisoner was teetering on. He gave the grin of a mischievous child, signaling to the crowd that it was time to send the stranger to his maker. Blackcreek wasn't known for being full of people doing the right thing, but there was something almost poetic about the way Dante got the crowd riled up in support of his form of makeshift justice.

Silas knew the stranger's death would be greeted by cheers and that things would build from there into an all-night party, like an out-of-control wildfire. They'd forget about the blood-shed that started the night and celebrate with drinks like it never happened. Hell, maybe it would give him a chance to turn the charm back on with Miss Maggie as the drinks flowed. They could reminisce about what a crazy night they had, maybe even share a dance if some music started up.

There Silas went, getting lost in his thoughts again, wandering so far into his own mind that he almost missed the hanging.

Except the hanging never happened.

The roaring energy of the crowd was stopped by the all-too-familiar sound of a gunshot cracking through the sky from the edge of town. The thunderous *bang* echoed throughout the square, bringing everyone to a silent halt.

Damn gunfire ruined his chance with Maggie for the second time that night.

iii. Shane

"Shit," Eli muttered, recognizing what the commotion in town must be about.

Shane could see the panic in his old friend's face, worried that they were too late. The crowd had figured out who they had on their hands and decided they were going to string the poor bastard up themselves.

"Ain't the law gonna step in?" Shane asked hopelessly. He felt stupid as soon as he said it. He knew the answer before the words left Eli's lips.

"There ain't no law in Blackcreek."

The crowd was too large for the two of them to even think of taking on, even with the element of surprise. Add in that everyone was pissed off and likely liquored up, it would be nothing short of suicide to go in to try to stop them. The only options they had were to hopelessly watch their payday hang or turn around and get the hell out of there.

Anything but going forward to face the crowd.

"We're going in," Eli said confidently.

Shane knew his friend was desperate for money but didn't think it was bad enough that he had gone fucking mad. He hoped Eli was just posturing, putting up a bluff so that Shane would have to be the one to shut the idea down to save face. Shane wasn't too proud to back down from a failed plan, but before he could get another word out, Eli fired his rifle into the air and started riding into town like a man with nothing to lose.

His gut told Shane to turn the other way and leave.

He didn't listen. He galloped after his friend, straight into the hornet's nest.

iv. Kit

No matter how many close brushes with death Kit had over the years, he never once got used to the idea of dying. He had the unique gift of being able to give the impression he didn't care whether he lived or died, but he was scared shitless every single time it almost happened.

He had far too many of these *too close* situations to count, every one of them ending with him laughing things off over a few drinks. But the drinks were really just as much of an excuse to calm the nerves as they were to celebrate. Yes, there was a bit of a thrill in the aftermath that made him thankful to be alive, but he never truly enjoyed that moment of *almost* like he pretended to. It was easy to look back and enjoy the close-call stories because the present gave you the luxury of being in the position of knowing that everything turned out fine at the end. But at the time of every single one of those stories, he felt sure that it really was the end.

Like this time. This time definitely felt like the end. You could only gamble with the reaper so many times before you lost to him. And when you did lose, as you inevitably would, it was a bet that he damn well would collect.

But just like every other time, even if he was frightened like a small child deep down in the pit of his stomach, he still played it cool. He played it cool with his speech after he shot up the tavern. He played it cool when they blindsided him, knocking him out and dragging him into the streets while ranting about some deranged sort of justice. And he was playing it cool now in these last moments, a noose tightened around his neck while this blowhard of an asshole gave a boastful speech to drag on the show. But this time really did feel like the last time. There was no posse coming, no escape plan, and no words he could say that would charm him free. That snuggly fit noose was doing all the talking for him. He was scared, and like all those other times, it felt like the last time.

And like all those other times, somehow it wasn't.

It was the familiar *bang* of gunfire that saved him once again. It was a sound that usually brought him dread, but tonight it was an invitation to freedom, a sound that he'd never been more relieved to hear as it echoed through the air. The first shot was followed quickly by a second, accompanied by the incoming sound of galloping horses. It didn't sound like a big group approaching, but they sure as hell sounded confident.

"Let that man go," he heard one of the approaching riders shout to the group.

It was a voice he recognized as that of authority instead of fellow scumbag. It was a voice that said the law had somehow made its way to Blackcreek.

The crowd's tension from the gunfire released when they saw the pathetic size of the party riding in. Expecting a full posse, they were instead greeted by two lone men riding without backup. Kit could see the collective expressions on several of the townsfolk's faces, thinking it was some sort of joke, but he couldn't help but admire the confidence of the two men who rode in with the courage of a dozen.

"Two? Where's the rest of 'em?" he heard Dante question, projecting that same bit of smug theatrics he had been displaying all night. "I see the cavalry really sprang for you, boy."

He snorted obnoxiously, giving Kit a smack on the shoulder hard enough to make him nearly lose his footing.

A few of the yokels in the crowd giggled at this lazy attempt at a joke. But the two outsiders didn't waver, staring down the crowd without the slightest bit of fear in their eyes. One of the riders fired his rifle in the air again, to show that they were indeed serious, silencing everyone.

"Marshal Eli Cooke," the man with the rifle announced.

There was an unspoken understanding that kept the law out of most of Blackcreek's affairs, making even the hardest of lawmen think twice before waltzing in. But this marshal had the icy stare of someone who could care less about what he was *supposed* to do, his own safety being the furthest thing from his mind.

"As the only law enforcement presence here," the marshal continued, "I demand you surrender this prisoner into our custody immediately."

The demand should have brought more laughter from the drunks who had been wound up for blood, but instead they responded with respectful silence. The marshal's demeanor had cut through the crowd, stealing their attention from Dante's showman antics. Kit could feel Dante seething behind him at the suggestion of handing over his prize pig to a couple lawmen so easily.

"Marshal," Dante barked, the word oozing with frustration, "as much as I'd *love* to hand this man over to you, he is wanted in connection to the Silverton massacre."

The mere mention of the word *Silverton* got some of the men in the crowd nodding in agreement, a sentiment Dante quickly built on.

"Some of the people here knew men on that train and would like to see this coward pay for his crimes," he crooned, adding a punctuation mark by grabbing Kit by the back of the neck as he spoke his next words with oily salesmanship. "This piece of shit deserves to be strung up."

The crowd was a powder keg just waiting for a match to light it, yet the lawmen didn't waver. They remained calm, confident, like veterans of the job.

But something about the lawmen struck Kit the wrong way. He admired how bravely they stood up to an angry mob, but he wondered why he wasn't familiar with their faces. He would have made a point to be aware of any officer this brave, the stone-cold type of lawmen he made a careful point of avoiding at all costs. Yet he couldn't recall coming across anyone like them in recent memory. The composure they carried, it was mesmerizing and not something he'd easily forget.

"What you're saying may be true," the marshal responded with an understanding tone, "but it is also my job to make sure that justice is properly and legally carried out, and that this man is brought in to receive a fair trial. Just like any man here deserves and would be granted for whatever sins he had committed."

There was another murmur in the crowd that took this as an attempt at humor. Blackcreek was the place you went to if you were trying to stay as far the hell away from anything fair — especially a trial.

"Fair trial?" Dante asked with disgust, the theatrics toned down as genuine offense began to creep in. "Do you think there was anything *fair* about what he did to those kids at the Bentley farm?"

"I told you I had nothing to do with that," Kit snapped back after hearing the accusation brought up again.

He didn't like getting defensive, he thought it made him sound weak. But he also didn't like being accused of things he didn't do. Hanging or no hanging, he wasn't going to stand there and let them sully his reputation by accusing him of killing some innocent kids. He had done a lot of terrible shit in his life, but he wasn't one of those animals that boasted about claiming more bodies to the pile than he was responsible for. Of course, his protests didn't matter as various people in the crowd hissed for him to *shut the fuck up*, but he knew he couldn't go to the grave peacefully if he didn't at least try to defend his name.

The marshal raised his hand in a way that somehow calmed the crowd again, like a pastor to his congregation. It was goddamn impressive how cool he was about the whole thing, using balls of steel to stand his ground.

"This isn't about being fair," the marshal said, sounding like he could justify hanging Kit there on the spot if it were up to him. "It's about the law."

This exchange set the big bastard Doc off; he started reaching for his pistol in retaliation. Kit should have spotted it but was too engrossed watching the unfolding of what was either going to be his rescue or his doom. Who *did* catch it was the older and quieter of the two lawmen, who aimed his rifle at his would-be attacker before he had a chance to draw.

"You draw that pistol and I'd have the legal right to put you down," the older deputy warned, matter-of-fact. "You wanna talk about fair? I don't think it would be fair that while this man gets a trial for his crimes, you'd be the one that was put down like a dog for drawing on an officer. It wouldn't be *fair*, but it is what'll happen if you don't get your hands off that iron."

The old deputy looked his would-be shooter down like a disobedient dog. His unblinking stare went on long enough that

Kit thought it had to be an optical illusion, like he was looking at a statue. Ice ran through Kit's veins, reaffirming his view that these were clearly veterans of the job.

"Not fair at all," Doc finally bellowed back, wisely moving his hand away from his revolver.

Who were these guys? Kit didn't know if he should be relieved or scared shitless that he might be leaving Blackcreek with them.

"We appreciate everyone's enthusiasm for justice here," the marshal announced as if he were conducting routine business, "but this is in the capable hands of the law now. We'll be on our way and will gladly turn a blind eye to any questionable activity anyone here might be up to, for your cooperation."

The crowd was dead silent, captivated in pure disbelief. It wouldn't have taken much to push just one of them to build up the courage to draw a firearm, setting off a chain reaction that would end with two dead lawmen. Killing a marshal was a hangable offense, but it's damn hard to hang a man if every single person there denied it happened. But no rogue shot came, everyone collectively buying what the lawmen were selling. They came here to take the outlaw away and even if there were only two of them, it looked like they were going to do just that.

Yet there was still the feeling of needing *permission* to let them go lingering in the air. All eyes turned to their de facto leader for confirmation on how to proceed.

Dante finally submitted and gave a slight nod of approval, prompting a couple lackeys to cut Kit free. Kit took a delicious gulp of air as his neck was freed from the grip of the noose; a small pleasure cut short by the angry shove behind him that pushed him toward the marshal to face the next chapter of his fate.

"You won't get away with this," Doc mumbled to the lawmen. Anyone in their right mind would have buckled hearing a threat coming from such a mountain of a man, but the marshal and his deputy seemed disinterested as they collected their prisoner.

"Not tryin to *get away* with anything," the marshal calmly answered." We're just doing our job."

The burn of the noose marks was now starting to set in, but Kit hardly minded thanks to that unbeatable sensation of cheating death yet again. He knew as he was pushed away from one death towards the lawmen, that they were surely just planning to take him to a different, more civilized death, but he still considered a delay from death to be cheating enough. After all, every passing second of every day was made up of finding ways of delaying our trip to the inevitable end place.

The marshal dutifully helped Kit onto the front of the elder deputy's horse, securing his hands behind his back to make sure he didn't try any *funny business,* as he'd been warned about in a dozen or so similar situations before.

They were ready to ride off when confidence came back to Dante, reintroducing the bravado in his tone.

"You gentlemen could still save yourself the hassle of making the journey," Dante hollered. "Not to mention, avoid any undesirable folks on your way who might want to see your passenger dead."

The threat was thinly veiled, but it felt weak to Kit. After all, there were *much* worse people out there looking for him than anyone in Blackcreek; ballsy marshals included.

"That's not who I'd be worried about," Kit couldn't help but call back.

"You got something to say, boy?" the big bastard Doc injected, clearly irked by the comment.

"I'd be a lot more worried about anyone out there who wants me *alive*," Kit clarified with his winning grin.

Underneath that smile he truly *was* scared of who was

waiting for him out in the world. If *they* ended up finding him, his fate would end far worse than being strung up by a bunch of assholes in some dipshit shanty town.

He forced himself not to worry about *them* at this moment. Instead, he savored the feeling of freedom by flashing a smile that said *Sorry to leave you, friends, wish I could stay* to a whole goddamn town that wanted him dead.

"You got him secure?" the marshal asked his partner.

They were strictly business, exchanging logistics as if they didn't have to worry about being shot in the back when leaving, before ending the exchange.

"Then let's go."

The horses started pacing, steadily picking up momentum as they rode out of Blackcreek for the next stop with Kit's delayed date with death. He expected everyone in town to come after them and start shooting, but there wasn't much more than the sarcastic holler of a "we'll see you around *real* soon, marshal," behind them as they rode off.

So long death, sorry you missed me yet again tonight, Kit thought as they rode along. *Maybe we'll meet up again tomorrow.*

CHAPTER FOUR

BIT BY THE SNAKE

i. Eli

*T*he drop in temperature hit almost instantly when the sun went down, skipping the gradual stage that helped you acclimate to the cold. It felt even cooler to Eli because he was sweating under his clothes, thanks to the tense escape they had miraculously pulled off earlier.

The events of riding into Blackcreek under the guise of his old life had been racing through his mind ever since they left, pushing other important details, like his body temperature, out of his head. They'd pulled it off so convincingly that he'd actually believed he was wearing his star again in the moment, feeling like a hero as they barked orders to the scum of Blackcreek. The old hat felt right, making him feel more like a marshal now than when he actually was one.

Now that the thrill started to wear off, the question *what happens now?* started creeping in to occupy its place. Shane's plan of getting their prisoner over to Sheriff Kelly in Arkell seemed simple enough, but there were still too many variables to consider now that they were in the thick of it. Most immediately, if anyone from Blackcreek held a grudge for the stunt they pulled and came after them. They were riding through an isolated open stretch, a terrible place to be if you were outnumbered in an ambush. Even if they weren't bothered by anyone from Blackcreek, the comment the kid made earlier about *anyone else who might want him alive* struck Eli the wrong way. There were too many uncertainties, the doubt making Eli feel like Arkell couldn't arrive soon enough.

"Nights are getting colder," Shane commented, filling the quiet with the start of comforting small talk. "Winter's creeping up on us."

"It's earlier than usual," Eli observed, his mind drifting to the thought of Weston at the farm alone.

Leaving home for a job like this ran the risk of you not making it back. It *was* getting colder, and he worried about how much harder it would be for the boy if he had to tackle the impending winter alone if the worst happened.

"You prepared?" Eli asked, shifting his thoughts to Shane instead of his own responsibilities.

"Prepared as an old fool like me can be," Shane laughed.

Shane wasn't shy of self-deprecating humor, but he was always good at keeping on top of things. Without him, a batshit plan like this would never have got rolling, leaving Eli stuck scrounging like a rat for other ways to pay the banks off.

"What about you?"

What about you? Eli thought, the question twisting the dagger of the image of his boy stranded alone. If they did manage to get Kit to Arkell, the bounty sure would make the winter a hell of a lot easier. But if something happened to them on the way? The winter, the banks: it would all be a damned burden for Weston to carry on his own. Eli started to feel nauseated, the guilt for taking off bubbling in his chest. He'd have to push those feelings aside if they wanted to make it through this.

"Not as much as I'd like to be," Eli finally answered.

He never liked thinking about the winter, but the crisp night air was a threatening reminder that it would arrive before they knew it, whether he was ready for it or not.

"Been finding as much extra work as I can to keep the banks off our backs," Eli mused, trying to lay out facts instead of feeling sorry for himself. "The boy's growing though, so he can do a lot more than he could before, which is a blessin'."

"That is a blessin'," Shane agreed.

The look on his friend's face made Eli beam with pride as he thought about the boy. He was a good kid, strong and hardworking. Eli was proud of his son and truly did love him, though he rarely showed it. Too much praise could make a boy soft.

"Eats more though," Eli added half joking, half feeling sorry for his pockets.

It was true, the boy could do his share of work, but what they say about growing boys' appetites was no joke.

"Sometimes feels like there's more than just two mouths to feed," he chuckled, "especially considering his mother ate like a sparrow."

The comment stumbled Shane into silence. Eli hated when people acted like they had to tiptoe around Ada being gone. It may have been a sensitivity, but it was also a fact.

The flu had taken her a few winters ago, a tragedy that pushed his drinking over the edge to the point that led to the *incident*. At first, he did nothing but feel sorry for himself, drinking the days away and letting everything slip. But something about seeing his boy watch his only parent left submit to the drink forced him to crawl out of the darkness. He threw away the bottle, found odd jobs where he could, and moved on. If he could move on, why the hell couldn't everybody else?

Shane was better than most about not letting Ada's name suck the oxygen out of every conversation, but even he stumbled for a moment at the mention of her. Eli silently appreciated when he was able to pick the conversation back up as if nothing was said.

"He's just growing," Shane said, as if the topic of dead wives had never been broached. "He's a good kid, turning into a fine young man."

The comment felt sincere, Eli feeling that pride from it again.

"I hope so," Eli said truthfully, without any of that forced modesty bullshit that people try to fall on when they can't just accept a compliment. "The world has enough bad men in it. Don't need another one."

The comment drew a smirk on Kit's face, turning from the front of Shane's horse to let his amusement be known. For a bit there, Eli was so engrossed in catching up with his old friend that he straight up forgot their prisoner was with them. In his marshal days, he probably would have ignored the smirk's invitation to talk, but it was a long ride to Arkell, and the kid hadn't been a pain in their ass thus far, so he decided he'd bite.

"So, you are with us," Eli commented, indulging the kid." Been so quiet up there I thought you might have nodded off."

It was a gentle rib, friendly enough that Eli didn't consider it hostile. The kid must have felt differently, facing forward and going mute again. It appeared any chance of sharing some friendly chatter with their prisoner to kill time was a fool's errand. That or perhaps Eli wasn't using the right approach. Some people just didn't like to be ribbed, friendly or not.

While he at least had Shane to talk to, he had heard all of Shane's stories a dozen times before and knew where all the small talk led to. He loved the old guy, but stories of the glory days and fishing accomplishments didn't compare to what must be going on in the mind of the man accused of the Silverton slaughter.

To hell with letting it rest, Eli thought. This kid had a story to tell and the more he resisted, the more Eli wanted to hear it.

"Not the talkative type, are you?" Eli asked, trying a new approach.

He was greeted by more silence, amplifying the sound of horse hooves clopping away. The stubborn bastard really didn't want to talk. Or at least that's what Eli thought, until a few minutes later when the kid opened his mouth, proving that even an outlaw can only stand so much boredom.

"What should a man in my situation say?" Kit asked play-fully. "We ain't sitting around playing a friendly game of cards and you're not exactly taking me somewhere to get my pecker sucked either."

Eli almost let himself laugh at the crude comment, holding it in as he opted to hide his crasser side and keep things a little more formal.

"It's a long ride to Arkell," Eli countered. "I just thought some friendly conversation might help us pass the time."

"*Time* is all I got," the kid squawked with a little laugh that sounded like he was genuinely amused, "and there ain't *nothing* friendly about taking a man to hang."

The kid had a point. Hard to call a conversation *friendly* when both parties knew how things ended once their journey concluded. Eli truly *did* mean for the conversation to be friendly. Despite where they were headed, none of it was personal.

"There's nothing malicious about it either," Eli responded, hoping he didn't come off like he was trying to defend himself too much. "We're just taking you in to be dealt a fair judgment, rather than let the mob deal out justice."

The words felt true as he said them. Yes, a hanging was never pleasant but at least it would be handled with more dignity than what the cheering, drunken crowd in Blackcreek had planned.

"You ever stop to think that maybe the mob *deserved* their

justice?" Kit asked.

He didn't sound like he was trying to be cute or going for irony. He sounded like he genuinely meant the question, as if part of him felt bad for the angry people of Blackcreek being deprived of their hanging of the stranger they so quickly and passionately despised.

"Better a group decides what's fair over one man with a badge," Kit mused. "Wouldn't you agree Marshal..." he trailed off.

"Marshal What-was-it-again?"

Eli didn't like the kid's tone. It suggested a little too much, coming off with a hint of a threatening edge. He would have much rather been given a crude *I forgot your fucking name* over this suggestive bullshit.

Or perhaps it was just the long journey getting to him. Eli carefully thought about his response before giving the kid an answer, not wanting to overplay his hand, while also recognizing that the question, without the layers of tone and context, could honestly be an innocent one.

"Marshal Eli Cooke," Eli answered with as much pride as he could make himself pretend to believe.

Saying it out loud after hearing the tone in Kit's voice made him question if he still believed it himself. He hated that bit of doubt. He didn't owe the kid shit, let alone an explanation.

"Marrrrshal Eeeelli Coooke..." Kit repeated, dragging the name out with a drawl like tobacco was stuck in his gums.

It was too playful for Eli's liking, the smile teasing that there was more probing to come.

"Tell me Marshal," Kit started in a way that felt like the beginning of a bad story, "why is your word on justice more valid than an entire town full of men?"

Eli had heard different variations of that same question countless times during his law days. Like now, it always happened when he was hauling someone away for breaking the law and doing something they generally shouldn't have been doing. And like now, they were always dead serious when they asked it. The answer was simple and true, even if the truth was a little muddier in this particular case.

"Because it's the law," Eli answered plainly, believing the answer as truth instead of placating bullshit. "The law dictates that every man deserves fair passage to his judgment no matter who he is or what he's done. Those men back there had no respect for the law, nor your fair judgment."

It was a good answer. Better than that, it was a no-bullshit answer. Eli believed it as every man should with any question he answers. But no matter how good an answer it was, he could see Kit wasn't going to just accept it and let the matter go. It wasn't necessarily that the kid didn't *believe* him, but that his mind was pulling apart every possible variation of this moral code while contorting it with his own perverted views on the matter.

"Let's say that the man in Blackcreek who wanted to hang me drew his pistol on you," Kit inquired. "You would have shot him dead, correct?"

"Indeed, I would," Eli said, not sugarcoating the answer.

"Now, if you did that," Kit mused, "the only thing he would have done wrong was trying to stop you from preventing him from bringing a bad man to justice."

The kid had a point, even if it was a cliched one that Eli had heard time and time again. For Eli, that point stopped mattering the moment you drew on an officer of the law. He'd always taken that stance but wondered how it applied now. Without the badge, he was nothing but another scumbag pretending to be something he wasn't. He quickly pushed those thoughts aside, rationalizing his duties as he gave another truthful answer.

"If he drew on me and I put him down, it would be because of the choice he made," Eli affirmed.

His daddy always warned him about his choices when he was a kid, the advice being the only good thing he ever gave him. Eli had always tried to pass these half-remembered thoughts on to Weston, now sharing them with this poor bastard as something to think about before he met God at the end of a rope.

"Doesn't make someone a bad man if they get on the wrong side of things," Eli lectured. "Just one bad decision."

The solemn note brought silence back among the men. Eli meant for it to be a bit of friendly banter, chit-chat to get the kid to open up and maybe give them some info about what the hell happened on that train. But no, he let his lecturing views get in the way with his goddamn biblical stance on right and wrong.

It was damn quiet, and Eli wasn't quite sure how to spark the conversation back up again. Thankfully, Shane broke the silence and tried another approach.

"You referred to yourself as a bad man," Shane said with almost academic curiosity. "Is that how you see yourself?"

A smirk that seemed to hide a bit of pain hit Kit's face, an expression hiding shame with the cover of bravado.

"I don't know if I'm a bad man. I was just trying to speak on your level," Kit answered humbly. "I was only presenting myself the way you see me. Call it trying to relate."

"I never said you were a bad man," Shane answered.

"No," Kit agreed, "but you *thought* it."

Shane's calm demeanor wavered. Like most men, he didn't like being told what he did and didn't think.

"You don't know what I think of you," Shane scoffed.

"No?" the kid began. He really wasn't letting things go. Eli couldn't help but admire how slowly Kit was gaining the upper hand, reeling Shane in like a trout that didn't know it was hooked. "Please, enlighten me and let me know what you *do* think of me?"

Shane took a moment to really think about his answer, a

quality that Eli always appreciated. Where most men would snap when they realized they were being wound up and react with colorful responses like *asshole* or *cocksucker*, Shane made sure his insults were well thought out and rang true.

"I think you're sneaky," Shane finally answered calmly.

All he did was tell the truth, a simple trick that made the best insults sting the hardest. Nothing makes a man fret more than holding up a mirror, reflecting what he already knows about himself but hopes nobody else can see.

Kit let out a good chuckle at the takedown of his character. It was one of those great, full-bellied laughs that only happen when you get the perfect cocktail of sincere and hostile smashed together.

"Sneaky?" Kit asked, his laugh suggesting Shane picked the wrong word and giving him a chance to try again.

"Yeah," Shane said, standing his ground. "I think you're sneaky."

"Sneaky implies I'm up to something unexpected," Kit countered, easily pushing the laughter away to make his point. "It's like saying a rattlesnake is sneaky because it bit you when you picked it up. Sure, you can be pissed at the snake, but it was your own damn fault for picking it up in the first place."

"So, you're saying you're a snake?" Shane questioned.

He sounded like he didn't buy the argument, yet it was a good enough hook to draw him in to want to hear more.

"No," Kit warned, "but like the snake, you should have known exactly what you were going to get when you picked me up."

That's when the snake bit him.

Distracted by the lecture, Shane's nose exploded into a ruby geyser when Kit violently jerked his head back in one quick motion. Shane's vision was lost in a dark, red splash from the sucker head-butt, toppling him off his horse into the dirt.

Even with his hands tied behind his back, Kit didn't miss his opportunity to escape. He thrust his heels into the horse's side, barreling ahead while Shane ate dirt. Eli could barely register what had happened before the kid had a good hundred-yard lead on them.

"Shit!" Eli growled, instinctively drawing his pistol.

Old habits had him ready to fire on the escaped convict, stopped only when Shane gave a desperate tug at his leg from his pathetic spot below.

"He's no good to us dead," Shane warned, ignoring the blood covering half of his face.

The only thing that mattered at that moment was their prize, and it was getting away.

"Goddamn it," Eli grumbled, holstering his pistol.

He galloped after the kid, the stupid warning about being bit by a snake replaying in his head. The snake warned them, and it was right. They should have known *exactly* what it was going to do when they picked it up.

ii. Kit

Kit couldn't believe it worked. He'd always hated his daddy but was loving his useless old fables on *the nature of snakes* that distracted the minds of these simpletons long enough for him to make the move that set him on his way to freedom.

Later, he'd have time to reflect on how stupid and reckless his escape attempt was. How he should have spent some time building up their trust, or at least waited for them to fall asleep before trying to get away. Impatience is a bastard like that though, causing instinct to snap on and snatch that opportunity as soon as it presents itself. Instinct will do whatever it takes to break free.

Of course, now that he was free, the odds were stacked heavily against him. Most pressing was trying to steer the damn horse with his hands tied behind his back, a skill that was difficult, but not completely impossible. He cockily thought of the two times he'd done it before in his life: once, recklessly to impress a plump farm girl who later showed him *how* impressed she was by the foolish act, and the second in a situation not dissimilar to this one where his life depended on it. But just because you got away with poking the bear once or twice before didn't mean you should keep doing it. Alas, here he was, after poking that damn bear again, finding himself fleeing hands-free as it chased after him just as it had countless times before.

Then another uneasy thought started gnawing at his mind. *What's to stop them from just shooting me in the back?* They may have preached about fair trials and justice, but Kit had been at odds with enough lawmen to know they'd *always* bring you in dead over letting you escape. So why *hadn't* they shot him yet?

BANG

The answer cracked behind him, his mind jumping to the conclusion that this indeed might be the end. But as the *BANG* echoed through the canyons and his brains remained safe firmly inside his skull, he started to recognize the shot for what it was; A warning shot.

With the law, there were no warning shots. The only *warning* shots he'd ever experienced were the shots that missed, and the one that just whizzed by missed by too wide a margin to be a mistake. The law generally not only had good aim, but they *loved* to shoot to kill. Give them any excuse to put a bandit down and they'd prove time and time again that murder was the true desire that lived in their black hearts. Lawmen always shoot to kill.

The lack of direct gunfire from his pursuers added another point in favor of his growing suspicion that questioned how reputable these lawmen truly were. He wouldn't have made it this far from a real marshal. He'd be dead.

"Stop!" he heard muffled under the galloping hooves trailing behind him. "Don't make me kill you."

BANG

Another warning shot. That was two too many. It gave Kit the go-ahead to gallop faster to his freedom. These men weren't after him for justice, this was a bounty hunt.

"No reward for a dead man!" Kit called out, antagonizing his pursuer.

The taunt felt good, complimenting the wonderful feeling of air blowing through his auburn hair as he chased that brief, fleeting feeling of freedom.

iii. Shane

Dark ruby clumped in the dirt beneath Shane, the heavy stream from his nose refusing to stop flowing. He spat a huge wad of the coppery liquid out of his mouth, bitterly realizing that his nose was likely broken. Letting his vanity get the better of him, he rolled his tongue along his front teeth to double check that they were all still there, thanking God for the small miracle that he still had a full smile.

His nose hurt like a bastard, the familiar pain of a hangover ringing through his skull. He cursed the kid who already had a good lead on them, riding off with his horse and their dreams of a payday. If Eli couldn't catch up to the kid, Shane hoped he'd at least shoot the bastard to pay him back for the nose.

That and to get his fucking horse back.

iv. Eli

Eli hoped his warning shot would make Kit think twice and stop, but the fucker just kept riding. The kid *was* fearless, Eli had to give him that.

"Stop!" Eli hollered, firing another shot in the air. "Don't make me kill you."

"No reward for a dead man!" Kit laughed back.

He was right, which only made Eli want to shoot him more.

"If I'm leaving empty handed," Eli screamed, his pistol drawn and ready to kill, "I might as well get the satisfaction of putting a bullet in you for what you did to Shane's nose."

It was a reasonable argument rooted in truth. While Eli didn't really *want* to kill the kid out of spite, he would still do it if that's what it took to get Shane's horse back.

"Then fire away, *lawman*," Kit taunted, calling Eli on his bluff.

Eli hated the way the kid had said *lawman*. It was like he was telling Eli he knew it wasn't true while still playing along with the lie just to taunt him. It was condescending, causing that urge to shoot him to come roaring back. Thinking of the pay, Eli resisted the urge, holstering the pistol and channeling his pissed-off energy into riding.

Weston. The farm. The money to get the vultures off his back. All fleeing right before his eyes, leaving him with nothing but Shane and his busted nose. It wasn't happening, not today. He gave his steed a sharp heel, hard enough that he'd normally feel guilty about, but efficient in getting the horse to pick up speed. A few more kicks pushed the horse as fast as it could go, putting Eli within arm's reach of his should-be prisoner. He was impressed that the kid managed to keep such momentum and speed with his hands tied behind his back, figuring the lack of control should have intimidated him from pushing the horse so hard. Then again, countless others had made the fatal mistake of underestimating men who had nothing to lose.

He stretched his arm forward, pulling back empty-handed. He reached for the kid again, stretching his fingers beyond their limits. Their horses ran parallel at the same blinding speed, Eli at least having the advantage of being able to navigate with both hands while not having to worry about being shot in the process.

He reached again, filled with that stupid optimism where you know it just *has* to happen for you this time. That ignorant way of thinking that if you visualize what you want bad enough, it will make it happen, somehow worked for him. He managed to grasp a snag of the rope binding Kit's hands, clenching down and forcing the kid to halt in place as his horse continued onward without him. Kit was violently thrown to the ground, along with enough momentum to pull Eli off his own horse.

The two of them hit the dirt with enough speed to give a little bounce before skidding to a stop. Eli was thankful that the kid broke most of his fall, but that didn't make the tumble any more enjoyable as he scraped up his arm into a fine mess of dirt, blood and pebbles. It took Eli a minute to get a hold of himself, groaning as he caught his breath. He could feel every fiber of his body in the worst way possible, signaling nostalgic waves of pain from old injuries he hadn't felt in a very long time. He felt sure that the kid wasn't going anywhere, curious how bad he must be doing after taking the worst of the fall.

He was aching all over, but any resentment he had towards the kid minutes ago was now gone. Yes, he was dirtier, bloodier, and in more pain than he had been in years, but he felt good. It felt good to have won. The kid was probably half his age and had a head start, yet Eli still managed to take him down. Pain or no pain, a feeling like that was worth a tumble. He used that satisfaction to pick himself up, hiding the pain as best he could as he hobbled over to the dirty, bloody mess of a prisoner. Any cocky grin Kit had when he was fleeing was gone now.

"That's probably enough excitement for one evening," Eli gloated. "What do you say we call it a night?"

CHAPTER FIVE

SOMETIMES THE MONSTER IS REAL

i. Shane

*T*he seemingly never-ending stream from Shane's nose had finally stopped bleeding, thanks to the necessary recipe of applied pressure and time. What wouldn't end was the steady level of pain, paired with a ringing headache that made him feel like his skull was going to explode.

Christ, the kid could hit hard, he thought, musing how his nose hadn't bled like that since a bar fight he was involved in some twenty-odd years ago.

At least his sense of smell wasn't gone, and he could still enjoy the aroma of the rabbit roasting. Eli had managed to shoot a couple after they stopped, more than enough to make a meal for the two of them and possibly stretch out to a third if they felt like generously sharing with their *guest*. The pain in Shane's nose crawling up to his brain made him feel less charitable towards the kid, making the idea of sharing the grub a pretty big *if*.

Their experience in the bush during the old days made them resourceful at pulling together meals like this on the fly. They'd cooked their share of rabbits in those days, and from the smell coming off of the one Eli had rigged up now, Shane was confident that his old friend hadn't lost his touch. He took a deep whiff of the roasting vermin, an act which had the unfortunate side effect of reminding him of how badly his nose hurt. He touched it out of instinct, wincing from the pain immediately.

"Looks broken," Kit remarked, the first words out of his mouth since the tumble.

They had securely bound him in a way that Shane should have found satisfying, but the kid's words still grated at him. Shane knew the comment was bait, refusing to give the satisfaction of a response. Instead, the three men sat in silence, quietly listening to crackling embers as the rabbit finished cooking.

Satisfied with his gourmet creation, Eli expertly pulled the roasted meat from the fire and ripped it into two generous chunks, handing one to Shane before greedily gorging on his half. It was damn good, almost good enough to make the pain in Shane's nose disappear. The smell of it lit up the kid's eyes, then a sad realization dawned behind them that he probably wouldn't be eating tonight.

"You gonna give me any of that?" he asked as if he had a right to claim a share.

"Fuck you," Shane scoffed with smug satisfaction.

Eli subtly shot Shane a look of disapproval. The remark was crass, but it felt good. *That's right asshole,* he thought, *This is MY dinner.*

"That's a funny way of saying grace," Kit joked.

Hunger had broken his silent streak, getting the kid nice and chatty as he revved up for the negotiation phase which would eventually decay into full-on begging.

"You ain't gettin shit after breakin my fuckin nose," Shane scolded.

He didn't want to show the kid that he was still pissed off, but sometimes letting the anger out felt better than the smug satisfaction of holding it in.

"It wasn't personal," Kit replied.

He didn't sound like he was insincere, or that he was just saying it to mooch some of their meal. It felt honest, like he was sharing a fact as true as water being wet. This pissed Shane off even more, wishing the kid would beg for scraps like a dog, rather than try to share his point of view.

"Well, *this* is," Shane replied with petty glee as he took a big gluttonous bite of the rabbit.

He barely registered the taste as the hot meat burnt his tongue, but he pushed the pain aside with a shit-eating grin to let Kit know it was the best thing he'd ever tasted.

"De-fucking-licious," he gloated with an audible smack from his lips, chewing with his mouth open.

The moment of satisfaction was short-lived when Kit turned his attention to Eli, looking for sympathy where he was more likely to get it.

"Whaddya say, marshal?" The kid spoke with a little bit too much shuckster desperation. "Spare anything for your guest? Looks like there's plenty to go around."

Shane was impressed by the chilly, silent response Eli gave. His friend wasn't normally the type to let a man go hungry, but their trek was long enough without broken noses and chases thrown into the mix, that it felt warranted.

"C'mon," The kid whined, getting pouty now. His hunger was starting to cause him to lose a bit of that cool exterior. "It's a long way to Arkell."

Eli's generous spirit got the better of him, ripping off a hunk of his supper to share with their prisoner. While Shane disapproved, the generosity was also part of what he liked about Eli. When most men in the world are cold, why judge the rare ones that show a little warmth? Eli kindly held a piece out for Kit to eat, a gesture that made the kid's face look a little insulted.

"You're going to hand-feed me like a baby?" Kit asked sarcastically.

"I really don't see any other option," Eli answered.

"Well," Kit began, the charm instantly starting back up, "you could untie my hands and let me feed myself with a bit of dignity." He added a smile to punctuate his last point. "You can trust me."

"I wish I was able to do that," Eli said, smiling right back with just as much charm, but with that added glee of knowing he was holding all the cards. "But I've learned my lesson for the day about handling rattlesnakes."

"What if I promise to be a *good* rattlesnake?" Kit asked with a devilish grin.

The response made Shane feel icky. It was a little too cutesy coming from someone so vicious.

"I only see two options," Eli said, enjoying a bite from his dinner. "One, I can feed you like a baby and you can be thankful for what you get."

"Or?" Kit asked, as if option one wasn't going to be the best offer on the table.

"Or Shane and I dine alone." Eli punctuated his answer with another generous bite.

"Which is how I'd vote," Shane interrupted. "You sneaky son-of-a-bitch."

Not afraid to trade hunger for a little humility, Kit playfully opened his mouth to show that food with compromise is better than no food at all. Without dragging things out any further, as lesser men might do, Eli ripped a chunk of rabbit from the bone and plopped it in Kit's mouth.

"Thank you, marshal," Kit said humbly. "I appreciate it."

Eli ripped off another hunk of meat and fed it to Kit, who

took it gratefully. For a few moments, the three men ate in silence that felt damn near civil. Between the warm fire and the stars above them, one could almost confuse the situation for a comforting gathering of friends. The only giveaway was a few bound limbs and broken noses thrown into the equation.

The comfort of the makeshift meal seemed to put Eli in a friendlier mood, lowering his guard around their prisoner. And with that comfort came the need for conversation.

"You're not the way I imagined," Eli observed freely.

"How so?" Kit asked. His tone was genuinely intrigued, like an old friend sincere about discussing big ideas.

"When you're not breaking people's noses, you're very polite." Eli observed this with a touch of admiration. "Not in that snaky way used by those assholes you see riding into town trying to sell you miracle tonic, either. It's genuine."

"Mama taught me that it never costs anything to be polite," Kit said proudly.

"Smart woman," Eli agreed, "I just find it a little surprising, considering the stories."

Shane hadn't really thought about the Silverton incident since they stopped for the night. Part of this was due to the adrenaline from the kidnapping and getting out of Blackcreek alive. The other part was that the kid's personality was actually pretty fucking likeable, minus an escape attempt or two. But the biggest reason, the reason Shane didn't want to admit to himself, was that the stories of the Silverton robbery were just too goddamn grim to think about. Even if the tales were exaggerated, the darkness at the heart of them was something you didn't want on your mind when traveling with the man responsible.

"Tell me, marshal," Kit asked with curiosity, "what do the stories say?"

The question caught Eli's tongue, making him think long and hard before answering to make sure he chose his response carefully. The subject matter was heavy, so he wanted to make sure the words he used would cover the cost.

"The stories call you a butcher," Eli stated calmly, not letting emotions get in the way of facts. "They say that you went from the gentleman robber to full-blown killer that day."

Shane studied Kit closely as he awaited his answer. The kid was doing an admirable job of holding back every bit of shame, regret, and anger that came from hearing Eli's judgment, but he spotted a small twitch in the corner of his eye that showed the cracks beneath the cool demeanor.

"You keep bad company, and a bad reputation will find a way to start following you," Kit replied, a solemn look on his face.

He looked afraid, justifiably so, when the next question came out of his mouth.

"Have you ever heard of the Walker Brothers?" he asked, his voice sounding like he could use a stiff drink.

The mere mention of the Walkers sent a chill through the air that brought the three men to silence. Of course, Shane and Eli knew who they were, damn near any man with law ties did. Gideon and Bronco Walker, more commonly known as the Bloody Walker Brothers, were a pair of ghosts. Nobody ever seemed to have encountered them in person, but every man on both sides of the law knew the horrible tales. They were the monsters from a children's story that broke into the real world, their atrocities exaggerated to various horrific degrees that only got more twisted, depending on who was telling the story.

"Stories of monsters like that have a way of traveling," Eli managed to reply. He looked like a scared father trying to hide his fear in front of his children, burying his feelings as he reassured, "but they're just stories."

"Stories gotta come from somewhere," Kit said, dead serious, his face hiding regret layered on top of fear.

"The Silverton train..." the words fell out of Shane's lips as he made the connection.

"Most stories you hear exaggerate what really happened," Kit said. "They always embellish to make things bigger. To make the bad guy badder. More money, more bodies, more danger. All that bullshit."

He looked shaken, forcing himself to continue his story while he still had the momentum to use as courage.

"But once in a while, the story is true. Sometimes the monsters *are* real."

ii. Kit

Kit wasn't sure why he decided to tell them what happened in Silverton. Maybe it was his stomach being thankful for getting a morsel of their meal. Or maybe it was because he was grateful that they didn't put a bullet in him over the escape stunt he tried to pull earlier. But the real reason was probably closer to him just being tired. Tired of keeping it all in. Tired of not having an outlet to get it off his chest. Tired of carrying the burden, the blame, and the guilt.

The unspoken rule among criminals, at least the good ones, was to never admit to any of the misdeeds you committed. In Kit's mind, anyone that bragged about their feats was either a liar or a fool, or a terrible combination of both. When somebody did brag about something, they were usually simple robberies or a murder that they didn't attach a name to, filled with foggy details. Not things to be proud of, but things you could learn to live with after enough time, distractions, and dates with the bottle.

Silverton was different from all that, the memory bottled up in a way that wanted to break free like a mad bull. He'd never uttered a peep about it to another soul, even though he thought about it non-stop. It was a weight that had become too much to carry and one he'd been carrying alone for far too long. If he was going to hang for it anyway, why not get his side of the story out to someone while he had their ear? Better to tell it in front of the warmth of a fire with the illusion of being a free man, instead of in a cell to some sheriff who was just listening to it as a formality.

Despite the drinking, the distractions, and the running, he had dreamt about that day every single night since it happened. At this point, he wasn't quite sure which of the details were completely true and which ones had been embellished and changed by the combination of memory, liquor, and dreams merging together. The only factor that he was certain was true was the perfect clarity of the screaming faces of the people on that train, a haunting detail burned into his brain that he couldn't forget.

Before Silverton, Kit always found robberies to be fun. Every day was an adventure that made a man eternally youthful, defying the decay that crawled over most men as they went about their mundane lives. That feeling in your stomach of being an eight-year-old kid doing something wrong every time you danced with danger was worth it alone, while the monetary reward made it possible to make a living without breaking your back if you knew how to do it right. And good lord, Kit knew how to do it right.

Pick a shit-hole tavern in any no-name town and you're guaranteed to find someone that considers themselves a bandit. The credentials to wear the title were zero to none, drawing in a share of men with little morals and low ambition that proudly wore the name like a badge. There were a lot of degenerate assholes and bullies who liked the power dynamic and excuse to hurt people that give the profession a bad name, but Kit felt that you didn't have to be a violent asshole to be a good bandit. He found that you could be a bit of a gentleman, being polite while you robbed someone instead of using violence. Most people were responsive to the approach since you usually weren't even taking their money when it came to banks and wagons anyway. And if it *was* their money you were taking, you were probably robbing a bigger crook than you, so there was no harm to any of the good people of the world. It was fun and if you were good at it, it was easy.

That was how it was before Silverton happened.

He'd first heard about the train in a card game with Lee Pickford, a weasel-faced nobody who was in over his head with nothing left to bet but information. Kit rarely would have let Lee play when he was tapped out like that, but he'd been on a good streak that night and was feeling generous. Stupid, but generous. Curious about how valuable Lee's information really was, Kit laid down real money against what were likely to be empty words, because that's what cocky young men with fat wallets do. When cash is coming in and out, you don't mind throwing it around on something useless when you're having fun.

Except it turned out ol' weasel-faced Lee's information was far from useless.

The story Lee fed required a specific type of individual that Kit just happened to be. They needed someone quick on both the draw and on making decisions that could keep a crowd in check, with a calm demeanor in case things got out of hand. If Lee met a person fitting those requirements, he could connect them with the right people that could make that individual a lot of money. Of course, Lee would require a finder's fee for making the connection, but that bargaining chip was off the table after he played and lost it during their card game.

His story claimed that an unassuming pedestrian train leaving Silverton was set to discreetly ship out two dozen bags of gold coins, all hidden under the guise of bags of coal in the engine room. The strategy of using a civilian train and a decoy product was put in place to hide the valuables in plain sight without raising suspicion, a detail that suggested that they were likely meant for a bribe that nobody wanted on record. It was a smart idea that should have kept bandits clear from the train, if greed and resentment hadn't allowed loose lips to get that information out to the wrong people.

The pedestrian shuttle strategy had its share of advantages for a robbery. The need for discretion would mean lower security than a standard gold shuttle, and robbing supplies from the engine room over individual passengers meant you were far less likely to run into anyone trying to be a hero. *Don't worry, ladies and gentlemen, we're just here to take a few bags of coal and we'll be on our way.* It was the type of robbery you could pull off without having to fire a single bullet if you did it right. The perfect job for a gentleman.

On the surface it was flawless. Kit's daddy had taught him that if something seemed too good to be true, it probably was. On the other hand, Kit learned hard and fast from his stickup career that most advice really only applied to people that were too afraid to take what they wanted in this world. If you want something in life, you had to have the balls to take it, and this sounded like an opportunity just begging to be taken.

Talking things through with Lee, Kit learned that most of the planning had already been taken care of. Most bandits and stickup artists had huge egos that didn't like to go into a pre-formulated plan, but Kit knew a good thing when it was presented to him. He figured there was nothing to complain about if all you had to do was show up, do your job, and make a hell of a lot of money. All the plan needed was a few extra hired guns, which Kit was more than happy to accommodate.

He accepted the job and recommended recruiting his old sometimes-partner, sometimes-rival Jim Tulley to join him as backup. Jim was reliable and had a good enough head on his shoulders, so Kit figured pulling in a familiar face would help things run smoothly. In the end, the job would end up costing Jim his life, but at the time, Kit thought he was doing a favor for the closest thing he had to a friend.

There were plenty of chances for Kit to say no to the job. He could have said no when Lee tried to gamble something in the pot that wasn't money. He could have said no when he thought about how ridiculous it was to put this much faith into a story being told to him by a scumbag like Lee Pickford, who couldn't even cover his bets. He could have said no at every stage up until he met *them*. What he couldn't do was say no the moment he finally met the Walker Brothers.

Things with the brothers didn't start out half bad. He immediately liked Gideon Walker when he met him. It might have been different if he had known the stories at the time, but Kit found the man charming enough that he probably wouldn't have believed them if he did. Gideon was well-spoken, charismatic and meticulous. He looked you directly in the eye with every word he spoke, along with a smile that let you know that you had his full attention. Knowing what he knew now, these traits would be remembered as off-putting details that would go on to haunt Kit. But then and there, Kit found these qualities charming, blindly dreaming of all the money they were going to make together.

He felt differently about Bronco. The younger Walker brother barely said a word, his stone face never changing its cold expression or showing emotion of any kind. Gideon assured Kit that his brother was just a little slow and that he didn't speak much to anyone, but that he was trustworthy and that you could count on him to do the job at hand. Kit would later recall this cold silence when he witnessed Bronco shoot a six-year-old girl dead in front of her mother.

The plan for the robbery was deceptively simple, effective and efficient without the flair you saw from amateurs who were trying to make their mark. Gideon had devised a way of getting them on board, half of them as passengers and the other half as workers in the most efficient areas on the train. Once the train pulled out of Silverton, Gideon and Bronco were to run crowd control if their cover was blown while Kit and Jim offloaded the bags hidden in the engine room.

Despite his skepticism, the far-fetched story he had been told about gold hiding in plain sight on a pedestrian train miraculously turned out to be true. The finer details of what happened from there and how they unfolded, though were a blurred mess in Kit's memory. He was unsure of which parts he was remembering correctly and which had been perverted by the alcohol-fueled nightmares since. He clearly recalled things starting off smoothly, how they managed to blend in with the crowd and get on the train without issue. He remembered pulling his mask on and the simple stickup of the two featherweight guards that brought them into the engine room without a fuss. And he remembered opening up those big ol bags of *coal* and seeing more gold than he'd ever seen in his entire life. Hell, he even remembered the crude joke Jim proudly told him earlier while they were waiting for the train.

You ever hear this one? What do a whore and a saloon have in common? Liquor in the front, poker in the back.

He'd think of that joke every time he pictured the burned-in image of Jim's skull splattering all over his shirt.

Get it, Kit? Poker in the back!

It's when the shooting started that the details became fuzzy, Kit's brain protecting him from the worst of the horrors that day.

He was gathering the last of the cargo with Jim when they heard the commotion coming from one of the pedestrian cars. He assumed their cover had been blown, not panicking since they had accounted for it to happen and were prepared if it did. He heard the unmistakable pops of gunfire, followed by terrified screams. There was no reason for any shots to go off; something was wrong. He should have stayed in the engine room, but instinct sent him to go check it out.

He pulled Jim along to check out the commotion, and they made their way back to the passenger car. The screaming and begging grew more frantic the closer they got, sounding more desperate than the routine cries that traditionally came with a stick-up. The biggest tipoff that something was wrong was the pattern of the gunfire. It didn't sound like the standard exchange between opposing forces, but rather a repeated *BANG BANG BANG,* rhythmically going off from one side.

Jim took the lead opening the door to the passenger car, the screams now reaching an unbearable pitch. They were greeted by the sight of Gideon, a twisted grin on his face, firing on the unarmed men, women, and children in the passenger car without discrimination. Kit's foggy memory clearly remembered Gideon laughing as he slaughtered the passengers, while Bronco partook in the rampage with that same cold, expressionless stare he shared with Kit upon their first meeting. Some of the poor souls were screaming, others pleaded for their lives, but most were too paralyzed with fear and disbelief to make any noise at all.

Their entrance pulled Gideon's attention away from his victims. He quickly aimed his pistol their way and fired. The first shot skimmed Jim in the throat, followed by a second that burrowed into his skull. Poor ol' Jim Tulley's brains splattered all over Kit, the brick-red splash buried underneath a shower of screams and gunfire. Jim's dead body knocked Kit to the ground with him, the horror on the train attacking all of his senses as he fell.

Liquor in the front, poker in the back.

Kit lay under Jim's corpse, the blood from his old rival's brain oozing over his face like a baptism from hell. Across the aisle, he locked eyes with a small girl lying cradled under her dead mother's arms. The girl was quivering, her brown doe eyes refusing to blink as she looked at him for help. Maybe he should have played dead, let the blood wash over him as the Walker Brothers finished their misdeeds, but the little girl's eyes wouldn't let him. They were praying for mercy in a place where it didn't exist. Not knowing why he did it, Kit pulled his mask down and gave her a little nod as if to tell her she was going to be ok. Miraculously, the little girl didn't cry or scream, responding with a delicate nod that let him know that she trusted him.

The rest of the incident started to blur together for Kit, still unsure how he managed to get out of the passenger car alive. Amid the chaos, he remembered getting up and drawing on the Walkers as he scooped up the little girl under his arm. He fired his pistol blindly through the smoke of the nightmare, grazing one of the brothers across the cheek with one of his shots before escaping back towards the engine room. The growing pile of bodies, along with the screaming, clinging hands between him and the Walkers, gave him just enough of a lead to get ahead of them alive.

He found himself between cars, clutching the poor child like she was his own. The girl was crying for dear life, weeping for a mother she'd never see again. He whispered to her that everything would be ok, telling her his name and asking what hers was to put her fragile mind at ease. It was the perfect opportunity to jump off the train, a horrific option but far safer than staying on this ride to hell. The sooner they leapt, the bigger lead they'd have against the bloodthirsty predators.

But that awful gluttony in his belly made him double back. His primal instinct refused to let him leave without collecting his prize. He burst into the engine room with the girl in tow, greedily hauling out the sacks of gold to their haven between the cars.

He desperately flung the bags from the moving train before clutching the terrified child and making the leap himself. He used his body weight to take as much of the fall as possible, leaning into his shoulder to soften the blow. Despite all the bad he'd done in life, he was blessed enough to walk away nearly unscathed from the jump. All of the scars he'd suffer from that day would be on the inside.

The girl didn't fare as well. He heard the audible *snap* of her leg breaking as they landed, a shard of bone visibly protruding out of her ankle. She howled in pain like a fox caught in a snare, the horrible pitch threatening to shatter Kit's eardrums. He did what he could to ignore the wails, dusting himself off and forcing himself up. The train continued to barrel along, the Walkers thankfully still aboard. He still had time to get a good lead on them.

He should have left the girl there. She'd only slow him down, closing the gap between him and the brothers. But he'd seen what they did to those people on the train, and she wasn't going anywhere on that leg. They'd catch her. Torture her to find out which direction Kit went and then torture her some more just for the hell of it. They'd skin her alive like a fish before caving her head in like poor Jim Tulley, whose fresh brains still soaked Kit's shirt. He wasn't going to let that happen.

He slung her over his back and picked up as many of the bags as he could carry, mustering the strength of a mule to power forward. He wasn't going anywhere fast carrying this weight, a walking dead man begging to be caught.

Stumbling along, he eventually came across an elder gentleman on horseback who clearly saw that they were in trouble. Hearing the wails of the little girl, the stranger stopped, dismounted, and kindly offered to help, like any decent person would do.

Being decent was his mistake.

Kit wasted no time drawing on the stranger, demanding the man's horse if he wanted to live. Kit should have shot them both dead on the spot, a bullet being a better end for the girl than if he had left her for the Walkers. No witnesses meant that anyone that could tie his face to the robbery would die then and there.

Instead, he mounted his gold on the horse and rode off, leaving the little girl with the old man. There had been enough bloodshed that day and he didn't think he needed to add two more innocent bodies to the pile. He prayed that if there was a God, he'd have enough mercy to send help for the two lost souls before the Walkers caught up to them.

He'd ride away with his booty, leaving the girl and elder gentleman to later identify him as the lone gunman in the robbery. A new legacy would be born: *Kit Boone, the Silverton train butcher*. He may have been rich now, but how the hell do you spend your fortune when your name is as good as mud?

And then there were the Walker Brothers.

He wasn't sure what happened to them, but he never heard any other names beyond his own being tied to the Silverton massacre. He hadn't gone a waking moment since that day without thinking about what they'd do to him if they ever caught him. If they'd slaughter a bunch of civilians just for fun, what would they do to someone who had ripped them off? They were out there somewhere; God help him if they ever found him.

As for the gold, it was safe. Stashed away, waiting for him.

But there was no reason to tell his listeners about the where-abouts of the gold tonight. No good player shows their hand too early, especially when they need every last chip they have in their increasingly shrinking pile.

The whereabouts of the gold could wait.

iii. Eli

Silence sucked up the air for a long while after the kid finished his story. The crackling embers of the fire took over the conversation, everyone at a loss for words.

When the rabbit first came off the fire, the fresh meat tasted exquisite. But after such an ugly tale of senseless violence, the meat now tasted like ashes in Eli's mouth. He'd seen greed turn situations violent countless times before in his past life, but never with such meaningless brutality. These were families butchered for no reason outside of the glee of a couple of animals.

Hanging in the air was the kid's involvement in the massacre. Kit came out of the story far better than he was going in, but no matter how convincing his story was, it still ended with him playing a part in the bloodbath. It didn't matter how small of a part a man plays in a tale like that, he still left with innocent blood on his hands.

"Nobody on that train deserved to die," Shane said with disgust, taking the words right out of Eli's mouth. "It don't matter who pulled the trigger. You ride with animals like that, you deserve the end of the rope that you're gonna get."

"You ain't wrong," Kit agreed solemnly.

He didn't look like he wanted sympathy, just to clear the burden of carrying such a heavy story to himself.

If the story were true, it put Eli in a rough moral dilemma. The boy would hang, there was no doubt about it, but Eli thought maybe there was some good to glean from it. Maybe there was a way to get true justice after all.

"Being able to help track down a couple wanted men like the Walkers," Eli began, thinking out loud with a little too much put-on optimism, "it could give you some leverage with the sheriff."

He knew deep down that Miles wouldn't want to go easy on anyone involved with the Silverton massacre, but he thought any information the kid had that could help track down the Walker Brothers might prove to be a special exception.

"Perhaps you'd be able to make some sort of deal if you helped find them."

"My date with the hangman sounds a *hell* of a lot more appealing than ever seeing those vicious bastards again," Kit scoffed. The shaking in his voice told Eli that this would be the last he spoke on the subject.

The men went silent again, turning their attention away from each other and back to the fire. A campfire story of slaughtering innocent civilians had a way of killing conversation like that.

Filling the uneasy silence, Eli ripped off another hunk of the rabbit, taking a bite before feeding the rest to Kit, who took it gratefully. As the kid chewed, he sized Eli up and down like he was looking to buy a new horse.

"You know, marshal," Kit said, "*you* ain't the way I imagined either. You're *different*."

Eli found the statement confusing, the tone making it sound like bait. He didn't want to entertain it, but engaging and changing the subject was damn better than silently thinking about the horrors on that train.

"Why would you imagine *anything* about me?" Eli asked, genuinely curious.

"I know you've heard about me, and I know you've heard about the Walker Brothers. Being a lawman, you've probably heard stories about dozens of other outlaws, bandits, bad seeds, and shitkickers," Kit mused. He wasn't wrong, but also clearly wasn't finished. "But people like us, the people you tell stories about? We also tell our *own* stories, stories about the *other* side of the law."

Eli didn't like the presumptuous tone of where this was headed. He wanted to clock Kit right there, but held back by telling himself that the kid was probably just spinning bullshit.

Bullshit or not, Eli still took the bait.

"And what do these stories on your side say?" he asked, trying not to sound too interested.

A smile grew on the kid's face as soon as the words left Eli's lips, telling him he played the wrong hand.

"I consider myself an educated professional. I may not be the best that there is, but I do try my damnedest to educate myself so I one day can be," Kit began.

Fuck, they all loved to build themselves up like that.

"That means that I like to know who out there is chasing me," he continued, keeping his eyes locked with Eli to let him know he took this part of his line of work very seriously. "I try to know the names and faces of every lawman within a fifty-mile radius of wherever I am if I can."

The kid stopped, achieving exactly the dramatic effect that he wanted. Any playfulness left in his voice was long gone when he uttered his next thoughts on the matter.

"Yet, through all of this, I can't recall hearing about a Marshal *Eli Cooke*."

Eli's body went cold, his bones ready to leap free from his skin. He felt his bowels spin and stir, wanting to fail him while a simultaneous urge to vomit crept into his throat. He shot a quick glance to Shane who also looked visibly uncomfortable with the direction of the conversation. He did everything he could to keep his expression frozen in stone, burying the dread he felt inside like a corpse in the desert.

"You just know everyone then, dontcha?" Eli responded, forcefully dismissive.

"When it comes to those that want to see me locked up or at the end of a noose, you're goddamn right I do," Kit said, his confidence pushing into cocky territory. "Which makes me think one of two things. One, you are a long way from home." He paused for what seemed like a full minute, Eli's stomach feeling like it was about to liquify as he awaited the second option. "Or two, you're no lawman at all."

Whether it was in the past or not, the disrespect to accuse him of not being a lawman made Eli want to blow the kid's brains out. He could have drawn his pistol and shot him dead right then and there. He and Shane could have ridden off, leaving the kid's worthless carcass behind and never speaking about this incident again. But that would only prove him right, making him some sort of twisted martyr instead of the monster he really was. So, Eli calmly buried the urge to put him down and responded with the one truth he knew.

"You're wrong, son," Eli said, hiding the offense, "I am a goddamn lawman."

He believed every word as it came out of his mouth.

"At heart, yes you are," the kid responded, not knowing how close he was to eating a bullet just to spin some bullshit that wasn't entertaining anyone. "See, I was racking my brain to see where I knew you from and I just kept drawing a blank." He gave a nod toward Shane, who looked mortified to suddenly be spun into this tale. "Until I started focusing on your old friend here."

The blood drained out of Shane's face, leaving his complexion a deathly gray.

"His mug reminded me of this story I heard years ago about a disgraced marshal that hit the bottle too hard," Kit mused.

The urge to draw his pistol came right back to Eli, realizing he might not be able to suppress it this time if the kid didn't shut his trap soon. But the kid kept on yapping.

"One day, he was so pissed up on a whiskey bender that he drunkenly misfired during an altercation. Missed his target altogether and hit a bystander instead."

"You son-of-a-bitch," Shane snapped, unaware that his interruption probably saved the kid from having Eli shoot him on the spot.

"The drunken marshal was given the choice to quietly step down to avoid going behind bars. They shamed him into quittin the following day when he finally sobered up." Kit turned his focus to Shane, who was seething at every word. "When he did, his old, loyal lapdog of a deputy quit in solidarity. Blind loyalty is a bitch that way."

"You have no idea what happened," Shane spat.

Eli felt embarrassed having his friend stick up for him, but was too paralyzed with shame to speak for himself.

"Don't be insulted. You turned things around and used them to find fortune. I'm impressed," Kit responded, his tone filled with condescension and false admiration. "It takes a special type of man to recognize opportunity when it presents itself. You were smart enough to dig out the ol badge and fool a bunch of yokels, who were too stupid to know better, for the bounty of a lifetime. How do I not admire that?"

Eli didn't like the praise, nor how it brought him down to Kit's despicable level. He thought they covered their tracks, only to have their plan embarrassingly spelled out for them like this. Not only did he have to relive the shameful memory of his past, but be humiliated for being a fraud at the same time. They weren't bad men; they were just labeled that way from one bad decision years ago that they had more than paid for. Who the fuck was this murdering coward to judge them?

Eli took one last bite of the rabbit before throwing the rest of the carcass on the fire out of spite. The act pulled the kid out of his bullshit story, reality crashing back to him as soon as he saw his last chance of getting any more scraps of dinner disappear into the flames.

"Hey, there was still meat on that!" he whined.

The decision to discard the rest of the meat was petty, but Eli felt good about the power trip, like he was ripping the leg off of an ant by sending the kid to sleep on an empty stomach.

"Storytime is over," Eli said, keeping his emotions neutral. He turned to Shane as if the kid was no longer there. "We'll sleep in shifts in case this son-of-a-bitch gets any ideas."

Shane looked more than happy to see they were done with stories of the past and back in the present.

"I'll stay up first," Shane offered. "I don't mind."

His expression told Eli that he really didn't.

Eli nodded appreciatively. Normally he'd insist that Shane get his rest first, but he *was* damn tired and felt grateful for the opportunity to get a little shuteye.

"If he makes a move," Eli warned, "shoot him."

Shane nodded, giving Eli the go-ahead to close the chapter on this never-ending day. He just hoped tonight the dreams would stay at bay.

iv. Shane

Shane was glad to see Eli fall asleep almost immediately after lying down. They shared a few unspoken lies agreed upon by them that allowed them to ignore and never speak about certain aspects of their lives and history. One, without question, was Ada. He knew how hard it was raising Weston without a mother and never brought Ada up by name unless Eli did first. The second was the fateful day that had them turn in their stars after the accident. It was a terrible tragedy and there was no question that Eli had to step down afterwards, but when Shane quit out of solidarity, they both understood that there'd be no more mention of it if they were to continue any sort of friendship. Eli put down the bottle and Shane paid him the respect of silence on the matter.

So, who the fuck did this kid think he was, spinning this tale up now?

They may have told a couple white lies about their standing with the law to bring the kid in, but those details didn't change the end result. The kid was a wanted man and he had to be brought to justice, no matter who it was that brought him there. Badge or no badge, the reward would be the same when they delivered their prize to Sheriff Kelly. They just needed to play the role to scoop the bounty up in the first place, so why did the finer details matter?

"What about you, old timer?" Kit asked, breaking the silence. "Do *you* have any stories for me?"

Shane's first thought was to break the kid's nose. Pay him back for earlier along with penance for getting Eli riled up like that. Of course, Eli wouldn't approve, but he was sound asleep and in no place to object. He might be disappointed to wake up and find the kid with a busted nose, but it wouldn't last any longer than a quick look of disapproval that would never be brought up again. Because that's what friends did, they didn't dwell on each other's mistakes. They let sleeping dogs lie.

But friends *also* didn't do things to disappoint each other on purpose, even with small self-indulgences. Shane knew that his fantasy of fucking this bastard's face up was just that — a fantasy. Going through with it would only show the kid that he had the ability to rile Shane up, something he'd no doubt love.

Nope, he wasn't going to give him the satisfaction. He ignored Kit's invitation to continue the conversation, choosing instead to quietly focus on the fire as if it were his only company. The silence said everything he had to say.

"Looks like it's going to be a long night ahead of us," Kit said with a hint of amusement.

Shane didn't disagree.

CHAPTER SIX

THERE'S SOMETHING YOU SHOULD KNOW

i. Dante

*S*unrise was only a couple short hours away, yet Dante still hadn't slept a wink. While most of his men preferred to stay up into the wee hours boozing and whoring before passing out and nursing a hell of a hangover the next day, Dante insisted on proper rest. Watching a drunk beg for sex he was going to eventually end up paying for was pathetic and grew tiring to watch. Same with pissing away the late hours playing cards with a bunch of assholes that barely respected the game. A man needed his seven hours if he wanted to stay sharp, and Dante *always* wanted to be sharp. He had a carefully crafted persona, carrying himself in a way that made people listen. While part of that came from natural charisma, he believed proper rest was a contributing factor as well. You had to work on your image and keep yourself alert, something a tired man can't do properly.

But rest hadn't come easy thanks to a visit from the law, who suddenly decided that tonight was the night of all nights to make a stop in Blackcreek. He couldn't get over how they rode in on their high horse to a place that was conveniently invisible to them every other fucking day of the year.

Dante never bothered trying to convince himself he was the most honest or lawful man around, but he felt noble about the decision to string up that son-of-a-bitch murderer, only to have that opportunity snatched away from him. This bastard thought he could blend in among his people, drink in his town as if they were the same. Fuck that, his people weren't child killers. If this murderer wanted to bring his trouble to Blackcreek, he damn well should have paid the justice of Blackcreek.

But trying to bring him to justice didn't feel good, because *trying* to do the right thing wasn't the same as *doing* the right thing. The right thing would have been to kick that stool and let him hang while the mystery marshal watched. Some men might argue that handing him over to the hands of the law proper was the right thing to do, but it felt cowardly to Dante and the thought of sleep right now made him feel sick.

He was hanging out alone with his thoughts at Arlo's, fully aware that this was where the whole nest of shit began. He sipped his drink in solitude, dismissing every drunken cock-sucker who awkwardly approached him that night to make sure everything was alright with him after what happened. God, he hated that. Why couldn't a man just sit alone to lick his wounds without interruption?

Thankfully, most everyone had settled down by this hour, either gone, passed out, or lying with purchased comfort in the whorehouse. There was no reason for the place to still be open, and if it was anyone else loitering about, Arlo would have kicked them out long ago. There was a small amount of pathetic comfort in that bit of power he held. *Just try to kick me out, mother-erfucker, and see what happens,* he thought, smiling to himself as he milked a sip from his piss-warm beer at the thought of the imaginary confrontation.

His eyes hurt. They wanted rest. But the face of that murdering coward haunted him, along with the faces of the two mystery lawmen whose presence stunk up his mind the more he thought about them. If you were going to send the law into Blackcreek, why the hell would you only send *two* badges? You'd have to be crazier than big Doc to do something that reckless.

The sound of someone frantically entering Arlo's broke him out of his disturbed thoughts. It was Doc, followed by Tommy McGill, who had stopped at the entrance as if waiting for permission to proceed further. Tommy was a weasel-faced cunt who rubbed Dante the wrong way, a speck of a man who fancied himself a bounty hunter when the prospect was small enough for him to handle. He was dumb as a demented dog, but smart enough to know not to dare chase any bounty that made their way into Blackcreek. His arrival turned Dante's mood even fouler.

Doc looked like something serious was on his mind, a rare occurrence saved for times that actually warranted it. Towering close to seven feet tall, Doc wasn't a man who wasted words when a glare would do the job, so him coming in here looking like speaking was his top priority both intrigued and put a touch of worry into Dante.

"Still can't sleep?" Doc asked with as much concern as a giant like him could muster.

Dante didn't usually appreciate anyone prying into what was going on inside his head, but Doc was quiet enough that his speaking actually meant something. It also didn't hurt that he'd seen Doc break enough men's limbs just for looking at him funny, a fact that made him comfortable giving him a little leeway.

"Any man that can sleep easily after letting a child killer go has something wrong going on in his head," Dante responded respectfully. "I know as soon as my head hits the pillow, my mind will go wandering. I can't stop thinking about how we let that cocksucker go free."

Doc gave a grunt that said he didn't have to go any further on the subject. Dante's focus shifted to Tommy, who was fidgeting like a snot-nosed kid damn near ready to piss himself.

"What's he doing here?" Dante asked, not even trying to hide his disgust.

Doc gave a sympathetic shrug before nodding to Tommy, signaling permission for him to join them. Nobody particularly liked Tommy, so Dante took small pleasures in letting his disdain for him be known.

"Uh, hello..." Tommy started, muttering, already too cunty for Dante to bear.

Doc interrupted him by ripping the hat off Tommy's pecker-looking head, shoving it into his hands to hold out of respect. It shut Tommy up real quick, making the pathetic show of him standing there even sadder. Dante looked at the weasel with his hat in hand, appreciating the way Doc made the little details perfect. Tommy gripped the ugly hat tightly, fidgeting with the rim to try to hide his nervousness.

"Well?" Dante said. "Cat got your cunt tongue? Out with it."

"Hello, sir," Tommy cawed like a chicken being fucked. "I'm sorry to uh, to be uh, bothering you, sir."

Each word he mumbled was more painful to hear than the last.

"Spit it out already," Dante growled, his patience long gone.

He may have still been awake, but Dante thought about how he *should* be sleeping right now, which made him play out a scenario in his head where his slumber had been interrupted by this shit-heel. The irrational thought pissed him off to no end and he was not making any effort to hide how he felt, especially to Tommy-fuckup-McGill. Doc could sense Dante's patience thinning, so he shot Tommy a look that said *Speak now or I'll rip that tongue out of your mouth so you can forever hold your fucking peace.* The look on Tommy's face told him the message was loud and fucking clear, prompting him to stand up straight and get to his point.

"Sorry to be bothering you so late sir," Tommy tried again. "It's about that marshal who took away the boy you were set to hang. There's something you should know."

At this ungodly hour, Tommy McGill, of all fucking people, suddenly had Dante's full attention.

CHAPTER SEVEN

A NEW DAWN

i. Eli

*I*t's no secret that years and memories can be a bit of a haze for any man who spends a chunk of his life living in the bottle. What is less well known is how the lost years spent drinking will fuck with your dreams, making the haze from the whiskey and the haze of sleep blend together into one incoherent cloud. If it gets bad enough, it can be damn near impossible to discern where the foggy memories end and the imagination of dreams begin.

There were a lot of reasons Eli didn't like dwelling on the day his career as a lawman died. It wasn't the guilt, as he already had his share of awful deeds outside of the terrible events of that day to atone for. No, it was that thinking about it too much ran the risk of having it seep into his dreams like poison into a well. Once that poison was in the water of your dreams, there's no telling what damage it might do in polluting the mind. The more he dreamt about it, the more he doubted which version of the events were true and which were part of the dreams. The waking confusion over which reality you actually experienced felt worse than any nightmare.

He remembered it was blistering hot that day. That was true, because feeling the poison of the bottle is a hell of a lot more potent when the heat sweats the worst stink out of you. He also remembered that he wasn't supposed to do anything that day, just relax and enjoy himself. Yes, he let the drink grab a hold of him pretty hard some days, but he still had enough control to not go too hard when he had to work. This wasn't supposed to be a day of him holding up the law though, it was supposed to be *his* day. His day to have a few drinks, relax and enjoy the sun. That hot, blistering sun.

Then he remembered the people coming to him for help.

He remembered hazy visions of a fight.

He remembered the Cries. *Marshal, marshal, stop him.*

He remembered the crowd.

And then the other things he remembered started to blur together. Blurring into intertwined dreams and memories soaked in whiskey.

In the blurs there was some arguing.

There was a commotion.

There was a draw.

There was a gunshot.

There were screams.

There was a dead woman who had no right to die that day.

The noises faded together. As did the faces. As did handing in his badge, and the next couple days preceding the event. Fractions of drunken memories that changed his life. Unpleasant dreams on a bad night. All one, all the same.

But he clearly remembered it was hot.

It was damn hot, and it was *bright*. It was bright *now*. The memory, the dream, it was *now*.

The sun poured through his closed eyelids as he heard his name called.

Eli. Eli. Eli.

It wasn't a dream. He was here, he felt the light of the morning sun. He clearly heard Shane's words telling him, "Eli, wake up."

He did. The dream was over.

ii. Eli

The sunrise cast a beautiful orange glow over the ashy remains of last night's fire, greeting Eli as he was shaken awake. He sprung to life, horrified at the realization that he must've nodded off during his watch. The look on Shane's face was filled with worry, telling him right away that the kid must have escaped in the middle of the night. He looked to his right to see Kit was still there, lying on the ground, out cold. The relief he felt was short-lived, realizing that whatever was worrying his friend must be bad if he looked this upset with their payday still in tow.

Without a word, Shane helped Eli to his feet and handed him his old telescope. Eli could feel a lump of dread forming in his stomach from the implication as he followed Shane a few hundred yards to the edge of the plateau. They had wisely camped in a spot that had given them an uphill advantage to avoid being open prey, but small advantages are still just that — small. Reaching the peak, Shane motioned for them to hunch down and lay on their bellies near the cliffside. He wordlessly scanned the land for any threats, carefully pointing his finger off to the east when he spotted something. The old bastard still had his tracking sense, thank God for small miracles. Eli raised his telescope for a better view.

"Shit," he muttered, speaking for both of them.

Even with the dirty scratches and thin crack on the lens, he could see they had a problem. Their guests were far enough away to be barely visible, but the fact that they were visible at all meant they were too close. The base had maybe a dozen or so men, camped out, most having a bite to eat or catching a quick rest from their ride. The only comfort Eli had was that they hadn't been spotted yet, something he knew because they were still alive. But that wouldn't last long; they were bound to be discovered soon. They had to move and they had to move now.

iii. Kit

A swift kick from the marshal woke Kit to the sight of the old man packing up their things in a hurry. He'd seen men move like this enough times to know exactly what it meant. It was time to run.

"Time to move," Eli demanded sternly.

Kit never loved being bossed around, but it was always worse when it happened first thing in the morning. The lawmen might want to get a move on, but he wasn't exactly in a rush to get to his hanging.

Bug me again in five minutes, and bring coffee, wouldya? would have been his next words if Eli hadn't followed up his order by barking, "Now!"

"Did our friends in Blackcreek finally realize you sold them ten pounds of bullshit in a five-pound bag with that *not-so-official* badge of yours, marshal?" Kit suggested with a chuckle.

"Enough yammering, we gotta go," Eli growled, grabbing Kit by the arm.

"I'm dead either way," Kit reasoned with amusement, letting his weight start to hang dead. "Letting you guys fight it out might actually give me a snowball's chance in hell at escaping."

If the look on the marshal's face didn't say he was serious, his next actions sure as shit did. He drew his pistol and aimed it right at Kit's testicles.

"You're coming with us no matter what," Eli spat, surprisingly calm. "But it's up to you if you want to make the trip to Arkell with or without your balls."

Eli cocked the hammer, a vein pulsing in his forehead, looking ready to pop. Kit really didn't have much bargaining power to lean on. While he wasn't enthusiastic about being sent to hang, he sure as hell would rather sway at the gallows than go on living with his cock and balls gone. He stood up straight to let the marshal know he wouldn't be a problem, hoping to keep his pecker intact *thank-you-very-much*.

"I suppose we should get moving then," Kit said with no hard feeling.

Nobody protested the suggestion.

iv. Shane

Shane could sense how tired his poor horse was, its breathing labored as it galloped. It was subtle and easy to miss if you didn't know what you were looking for, but he was very in tune with the creature, and he'd seen enough poor animals pushed beyond their limits to know that this one would be finished if they didn't stop soon.

He'd witnessed a man break his horse once before, an ugly ordeal that stuck with Shane ever since. The man had been pushing it hard, aggressively riding through the desert until the horse reached its limit and just gave up and stopped. It was sudden and undramatic, as if any spirit the horse retained had suddenly dried up from its body. Pain and thirst had gotten the best of the beast, causing it to set its own terms on how it would exit from this world. The man pleaded with it, yelled at it, even whipped it, but the horse wasn't some merchant that could be bargained with. It just lay down, submitting to a death that was cruelly taking its time. Realizing it would be nothing but a meal for the buzzards soon enough, the man finally showed an ounce of kindness by shooting the horse dead. After that, the poor bastard had to resort to continuing his journey on foot, his old companion left behind to rot under the hot sun. The image haunted Shane, and he swore to himself that he'd never allow it to happen under his guidance. He was ashamed, as the image crept into his mind now, of how he only had concern for his own well-being over the poor animal's. Outside of Eli, his horse was the last friend he had in the world, yet he was more than ready to throw its life away for his own safety.

They had been careful not to overload the horses for their journey, accounting for distance and weight, with appropriate stops to go easy on them. But with Shane carrying the extra rider, they had to take a bit more of a leisurely pace to compensate, which wasn't a luxury they had anymore since discovering they were being tailed. He wasn't positive if they had been spotted or not, but they agreed that distance was the most important factor right now, just to be safe. He initially felt confident about their lead, but hearing the off-rhythm breathing of his steed forced the reality front and center that they couldn't afford to keep riding like this for much longer.

"C'mon," Shane quietly negotiated with his horse, the beautiful creature speeding along as quick as it could carry them.

Sweat poured from his brow in the damned heat, a realization that immediately transferred his sympathies back to the horse. *If you think you're hot, you should try lugging two assholes on your back.*

If the horse gave up and stopped here, out in the open, they'd be easy pickings. *You're doing great*, he wanted to say, encouraging his horse with pride. *I know you can do this.*

Instead, he kept riding, silently praying that they'd make it.

v. Dante

Stubbornness and pride fueled Dante's futile trek, knowing damn well that there was little to no chance of them intercepting the lying marshal. He didn't even know *where* they were bringing their captor for sure, he was taking a leap of faith by banking that Arkell was the most logical choice, based on the story Tommy McGill sold him.

There was a high probability that Dante would arrive in Arkell, discover they were too late, and that the bastard that killed Ira Baker, his wife and kids, and the rest of the people on that train had already been sent to his grave. Arriving there in time was a losing bet, but one he had to take because it was the right one. As long as he had tried to do what he thought was right, he could live with himself and be able to sleep again. Because it wasn't greed that made Dante tick like the rest of the hicks that rode with him — it was his goddamn pride. And right now, his pride hurt.

He stewed on these simmering thoughts during the frantic ride, thinking over and over again about what happened to him in Blackcreek. He wanted to know what this disgraced marshal and his old lackey actually wanted with their prize. Like almost every other piece of shit he knew, his first thought was that they were motivated by greed. They were just looking for that reward money Tommy told him about, for turning the bastard in to face bureaucratic justice, instead of the punishment he deserved.

That's *if* it was the reward the marshal cared about. Dante had also considered that perhaps being shamed from one side of the law was enough to push the marshal to the other. Maybe they showed up in Blackcreek to rescue the murdering bastard and ride off together to retrieve the blood money from the Silverton robbery. It still came down to greed, just a nastier version of it. The problem he had with that scenario was that it was just the two men that came to rescue the prisoner instead of a whole posse. Bold plan or not, those numbers were just plain stupid in Dante's mind.

Which made him think that these men still believed they were noble, justifying to themselves that taking the murderer in for the bounty was somehow honorable. Dante had met his share of bounty hunters, and almost all of them lied to themselves instead of accepting that they were driven by greed. If they weren't true outlaws and really were trying to bring the man to justice, that complicated how Dante would deal with the situation if he caught up with them. He had to pit logic against his fucking pride, two vicious lions tugging at his ideals.

Logic told him that the consequences for killing a lawman, even an ex-lawman, would see him hang. Even if it wasn't in an official capacity, and the law viewed the ex-marshal as an outcast, men of the law had a weird code that put aside any differences they had to band together against anyone that wronged one of them. If he rode down two former stars and shot them like dogs in the street, he'd pay the ultimate price. All the law would have to do was squeeze one of the assholes he was traveling with and they would squeal his name like a piggy to keep their neck out of the noose. Logic knew that killing them was a bad idea.

But his *pride* told him to kill the cocksuckers anyway. And his pride was one nasty fucking lion.

Then, of course, there was the beautiful spot known as *the middle ground*, the logical place that allowed him to put all of these complicated cards on the table and do what he thought was right and just. Logically, he wasn't going to shoot these men for taking his prisoner away. No, he had another plan. He was going to do the right thing and politely ask the marshal to give his prisoner back to him. Nothing wrong with that, it was an approach that everyone should be happy with. The marshal would be grateful he wasn't harmed, and Dante would be happy that he could dish out his own appropriate justice, or claim the reward that was rightfully his.

If the marshal cooperated. And this was where his pride was satisfied with his logic.

His logic *also* told him that any two men riding into Blackcreek alone with a plan like theirs must be desperate. A play like that was gambling with their lives, which was the sign of someone who didn't have much to lose. Men like that were dangerous and not likely to easily give up what they desperately stole. Desperation led to stupid mistakes.

Stupid mistakes, like drawing on a group of men, even when you're outgunned. He'd ask politely for the former lawmen to give up their prisoner and shoot them down when they foolishly drew on him.

As for anybody with the law looking to avenge the marshal's death? There wouldn't be any vengeance if there was no body. Bury the lawmen in the desert and forget about them, like the rest of the world had. After all, nobody gives a shit about a drunk when he's alive, only when he's a dead martyr. No bodies, no trouble.

That is, if they made it to Arkell in time.

So, he kept on riding, playing the scenario over and over again in his head. While his men yammered on to each other about bullshit, Dante smiled to himself as he enjoyed how well logic and pride were getting along today.

CHAPTER EIGHT

THE DEN OF ROT

i. Eli

"Whaddya stopping for?" Eli demanded as Shane pulled his horse up to the old, dilapidated barn.

"The horses are done, they need a break," Shane reasoned, calmly playing down how dire their situation was. "We're pushing them too hard. Mine's not gonna make it if we keep going."

Eli took one look at Shane's horse, recognizing the harsh reality of the state it was in. They *had* been pushing them too hard, and Shane's horse had the weight of the kid to contend with. Mix that with the heat from the lack of any cover and he could see how the rotting, abandoned barn looked like a sanctuary to Shane.

"What if they saw us? We'll be dead if we stop," Eli countered. "We need as much distance between us and them as we can get."

"If we keep riding the horses this hard, we're gonna break 'em."

Eli hated when he was told what he already knew, even if he had to hear it out loud to make it sink in.

"You break the horses out here in the open, we're sittin ducks." Shane pointed to the old barn. "We stop and hide, we can at least let them pass if they come this way."

It wasn't a great option, but it was a hell of a lot better than if the horses stopped in the middle of open land. They were caught between picking two losers, the old barn looking like the better of their options.

There was something about the barn that didn't sit well with Eli. He didn't like how this abandoned place stood alone in the middle of nowhere, as if tempting all passers to stop. It disturbed him how empty it looked, like it hadn't held any love or purpose in a long time. Being in its presence sent a chill through his bones, making him shiver despite the punishing sun. There was no question that they'd be dead if they waited for their pursuers to catch up to them, but the barn had an aura sinister enough that entering felt like it should be a last resort.

"What if they don't pass?" Eli asked, sharing out loud the worry that everyone was feeling. "What if they stop and decide to check the barn out?"

He could see by the look on Shane's face that he had the same concern. More worrisome, the look on Kit's face shared the same dread about the place.

"They'll smell the chicken-shit," Kit stated as fact. "Chicken-shit *stinks*. You can *always* smell a coward hiding if you're lookin'."

Like any man, Eli didn't appreciate being called a coward. Yet he *felt* like one from the childlike fear growing inside him at the thought of entering the barn. Bullshit statement or not, putting out the idea that their pursuers could smell fear made it feel true.

"We have to stop here, we don't have any other choice,"

Shane concluded, "but there's a good chance that they'll stop too. We need to think about what we do *if* that ends up happening."

Eli hated the situation, feeling they were done for in pretty much any scenario if they were caught.

"No matter which way we cut it, we're outnumbered and outgunned by a long shot," Eli said. "If they stop, we'll at least have a better shot defending the barn than facing them out in the open. We're outmanned but we'd have cover, they'd have nothing."

"Or we could just give up the kid if they found us," Shane stated coldly, nodding towards Kit like he was a lame mule. "Hand him over and let them be on their way."

"What if you give me up and they *still* kill you?" Kit asked, clearly enjoying getting a jab in.

Eli ignored him and got off his horse.

"C'mon," Eli commanded softly. "We better get the horses in the barn with us to bunker down. And pray they don't find us."

ii. Kit

The combination of the oppressive sun, the tension of pursuit, and the thought of retying a noose around his neck made for a miserable trek so far, yet all of those were far more appealing to Kit than stepping into the barn. He had no desire to face his Blackcreek captors again, yet there was something *off* about this place, causing the primal senses in his brain to scream for him to stay the hell away at all costs. He felt that rush of sickness you only get from a bad hoof to the balls creeping into his throat. He didn't always trust his own intuition, but he *did* always trust the instinct of animals and could see the horses were clearly spooked by this place.

"Hey, hey. C'mon now," Eli reasoned with his horse like it understood fucking English.

The animal had fear in its black eyes, resisting entering the barn like a disobedient child. Kit wanted to smack the marshal and tell him *the horse knows something you don't, and whatever it is ain't good*, but there wasn't time to argue, nor other options for them to explore. Resigning to his fate, he swallowed the bad feeling in his throat and advanced towards the barn entrance as the marshal pulled his distraught horse along.

Approaching the doors, he could smell something rotten, like old meat spoiled by maggots. Eli pulled at one of the rotting doors, hitting everyone in the face with the sour smell of decay as it opened. They all frantically covered their faces, hopelessly trying to muffle the odor.

"Jesus Christ," Shane gagged. "What the fuck is that smell?"

Kit knew exactly what it was.

"That's death," he warned.

iii. Shane

An uneasy energy possessed the three men as they entered the nearly pitch-black barn. The memory of clean air was gone, overtaken by the pungent scent of sour milk and flesh that became more punishing by the second. The still, silent air from the outside world had been replaced by the humming of countless flies, buzzing at a level that was somehow subtle and deafening at the same time. Kit was right, this was death and they were stepping right into its belly.

Shane wanted to run. Leave this place, leave the bounty, leave it all. Everything about the place was wrong, the blanket of stink acting as a warning to keep out. His eyes adjusted to the dark, shifting from blackness to horrible clarity. He froze in terror when his adjusted vision allowed him to see *them*. He immediately wished he could unsee what would now be burned into his brain forever.

"Mother of God." Eli barely managed to mutter the words, his voice dry from repulsion.

Three corpses hung from the rafters above, strung up by their necks with old, damp rope. They had been savagely mutilated, disfigured to the point that made it impossible to make out any discernible difference between them. The bodies were stripped bare and skinned down to their exposed muscles, torn ribbons of flesh dangling from them like decorations. The floor below them was black with a puddle of congealed blood, long since drained from the bodies, which were now dry as salted jerky from the heat and exposure. The army of flies buzzing about happily made a feast of the former souls turned meat.

"Fuck me," Shane muttered, wrestling to keep the vomit down.

He thought he'd seen the worst humanity had to offer during his law days, but never had he seen something as deplorable as this. These mutilations weren't rushed. They were intricate, marked by craftsmanship. Whoever did this took their time. They had enjoyed themselves. The next wave of stench hit his nose. He bent over and retched, the hot stink of maggots on gelatinous rot assaulting his senses. Every bit of the rabbit from the night before violently left his body, hell swimming through his head and beating him between the ears.

"It was them..." Kit muttered from a place of isolated, distant horror living deep within him. His face had morphed into the type of shock that only comes from recognition. "Only *they'd* do something like this."

"Who?" Eli asked directly, sparing no time for nonsense.

Kit was hesitant to answer, knowing he couldn't unsay the words that left his lips after a hard gulp. "The Walker Brothers."

The cursed name was the last straw. Eli drew his pistol,

violently lunging at Kit like a fox on the coop. He grabbed him by the throat with precise force and violently pressed the barrel of his iron up Kit's nose.

"Is this a setup?" Eli snarled.

He pressed the barrel hard, the force making Kit's nose turn upright like a pig's snout. The pressure of the situation caused the kid to hesitate, amping up Eli's anger.

"I asked if this is a *fucking* setup!"

"No!" Kit screamed.

He was scared. Shane didn't blame him; they were *all* scared standing in this pit of death.

"Are they fucking hiding somewhere around here to break you free?" Eli raved, sounding paranoid now. "Did you set us up? How did you tell them we'd be here?"

"I didn't tell anyone shit!" Kit pushed back, sounding miraculously calm.

"I swear," Eli grunted, cocking the hammer and pressing the iron even harder, "I'll blow your fucking brains out if you're lying."

"If they are here, I'm as good as fucking dead!" Kit screamed back. There was terror in his eyes, none reserved for the gun in his face. "I'd rather you pull that fucking trigger over what they'd do to me."

Eli pushed the barrel harder. The kid must have realized he was one wrong word away from eating a bullet, lightening his stance slightly as he carefully picked his next words.

"You can't rip guys like that off and get away with it," Kit said. "I knew they'd kill me anyway when I saw all those bodies on the train, so I took the money. But that also means they'll never stop looking for me. You see them coming, do me a favor and put a bullet in me, because I'm *worse* than dead if they ever find me."

Eli lowered the pistol. It was clear that a true fear was eating away inside the kid greater than any threat Eli could throw his way. Between the rotting corpses hanging above them, their pursuers, and the looming threat of the Walker Brothers catching them, the need for any more spilled blood felt unnecessary.

"If you see them, save a bullet for yourself too," Kit offered, his voice serious, "because those guys don't take prisoners."

It was a grim statement that brought silence, amplifying the horrid hum of the flies littering the dead. They stood in the pit of death with the aura of doom permeating the air, yet the mention of the Walkers brought the topic of the robbery back into everyone's mind. After letting it soak for a minute, Eli acknowledged the elephant in the room, dropping the *real* question on everybody's mind.

"So, where *did* you hide the money?" Eli asked bluntly.

Shane obviously wanted to know the same thing but didn't have the stomach to bring it up. Buried gold made for a fun campfire story, but loses its luster quickly when you're standing under dangling flesh that was once human. It was the men looking for that gold that committed this atrocity, a fact Shane didn't want to lose sight of. He knew Eli's situation was bad, bad enough to tangle him into this whole mess, but hearing him actually ask about the gold while standing in this hellhole felt like all kinds of wrong.

"Sounds like you musta been a real upstanding lawman," Kit scoffed.

With that, the subject was dropped. It could be brought up again at an appropriate time and place. If they lived long enough to get there.

iv. Kit

Once the doors were shut, the barn became an isolated

island of blackness. The dark amplified Kit's senses, feeding more power to the vile smell of hot blood and rot, along with the angry buzz of the disease-carrying flies. He hadn't been afraid of the dark since he was a small child, but the turmoil he felt in his guts right now made him more afraid of it at this moment than he ever was as a kid.

It also made it damn near impossible to tell what time it was or how long they'd been there. An hour had easily passed, but after that the sense of time vanished. Had it been two hours? Three? The vacuum of their surroundings made time disappear. The loss of time also meant he had no idea how long they were going to have to wait. *As long as it takes*, he'd been told with no further discussion. His brain started to wander as he thought about waiting for the group to pass, a group that might not even be heading this way. And *if* the posse *did* come this way, they were outgunned several times over without a cunt-hair's shot of surviving a showdown. He wanted to scream *If I'm going to die, at least let me spend my last hours out in the life of the sun instead of in here with the death of the dark.*

He wished he could sleep. Not just because of the boredom, which was unbearable, but to mentally escape the prison he was in right now. The decay, the flies, the stench. Lucid and here was a far worse nightmare than any horror he could find in his dreams. This place felt like the end that awaited all of them if the Walker Brothers caught them.

Or *when* they caught them.

Maybe it *was* better that he couldn't sleep. God knows what kind of nightmares this place would breed in your head.

He didn't know how long he'd zoned out with these thoughts when the marshal snapped him out of the solitude of his mind, back to a place of sharp awareness.

"Shhh. Quiet!" Eli hushed, motioning for silence.

Everyone remained still. Even the flies seemed to pause,

respecting the peace in the air and making way for new sounds to haunt the senses. At first, Kit couldn't hear a thing outside of their breathing, but the marshal kept still as a tree to let his ears work without distraction. Finally, Kit heard it. The faintest *clop, clop, clop* off in the distance.

Horses, a group of them.

The dynamic in the barn changed then. Witnessed by the decaying bodies swaying above, the three men became allies instead of enemies, even if just for a moment. The desire to stay hidden outweighed the desire to be at odds with one another, banding them together within the confines of this hell pit. Without prompt, they swiftly made their way to the barn doors to peer through the small crack, seeking a glimpse of the outside world they all desperately couldn't wait to rejoin.

It was difficult at first to make out anything by peeking through the sliver of light. The sun seemed impossibly bright compared to the darkness they cowered in, taunting them that they might never be able to bask in its glow again. After his eyes adjusted, Kit made out a cloud of dust in the distance, rising from the trampling hooves of a dozen horses steadily heading in their direction.

Slowly, the marshal unholstered his pistol and quietly cocked the hammer. He nodded to Shane, who took the cue, carefully readying his rifle with shaking fingers. Kit had witnessed his share of frightened men in his time and couldn't help but admire how well his two captors hid their fear. He wished he had an iron of his own to join them, not that it would make much of a difference, but at least he would have died on his feet fighting if it came to that.

The riders drew nearer, Kit praying to God that they were the men from Blackcreek instead of the Walkers. He could find peace with the thought of a bullet to the brain or a simple hanging, fates he had always accepted as the way he'd eventually leave this world. What he couldn't stomach was what the Walkers would do. He'd be skinned alive by them or crucified out in the desert for the vultures to pick out his eyes. If it were the Walkers, there would be no mercy.

The sound of trampling hooves grew, the noise from the outside world sucking more of the air from within the barn. Things inside were now dead silent except for the flies, their awful sound humming loudly. The drone of their buzz pounded like thunder inside Kit's eardrums while they danced around the corpses above.

Don't worry, we'll be dancing around your flesh soon enough, he heard them say.

His eyes darted towards Eli, who refused to breathe, grasping his revolver tightly with the illusion that it would do him any good. Shane appeared to not be faring as well, his eyes clenched shut as his wrinkled hands shook around his rifle. Two armed lawmen under regular circumstances wouldn't stand much of a chance against these numbers, but two men crippled with terror after being locked up in this pit of hell, were beyond hope.

The riders had moved out of their line of sight, the view from the thin crack in the door now consumed with dust swept up from approaching hooves.

THUMP. THUMP. THUMP.

Kit swore he heard the marshal's heartbeat, thumping loud enough that it would give them away before it burst from his chest. The hum of the flies buzzed in sync with the growing, thunderous clopping of horse hooves. The *thumping*, the *clomping*, the *buzzing*, all synching together to form a symphony that chanted *Come on inside, they're in here. Skin them down to the muscle, we'd love more flesh to feast on.*

Just kill us and make it quick. Kit thought, wishing it would end swiftly.

But then, his ears were given reprieve as the notes began to dissipate. The thunder of hooves, which had become a charging rumble, had started to fade, like a storm that just reached its peak and was now starting to move away. The clear galloping began to decrease a bit at a time. The realization of the miracle hit all three men at once — their threat was riding past them.

It may have taken mere minutes, or it could have been an eternity, but the sound of the riders mercifully faded ever so slightly until eventually they were gone. Even the horrid sound of the flies faded with them. The pocket of hell they hid in mercifully formed back to reality. For a few minutes of almost psychotic peace, the three men waited in silence, until Eli finally built up the nerve to check through the crack in the door again.

"They're gone," he whispered, his voice cracking with thirst and relief.

"Thank fucking Christ," Shane sighed.

Kit swore it was the first time the old man took a breath since the riders arrived.

Guns were uncocked and shoulders let down. Everyone looked alive again, drinking in that sublime feeling you get from sniffing your own death before walking away from it without a scratch. Kit knew the feeling well and could see it on the lawmen by the way the color in their faces went from a deathly gray back to a healthy pink.

"You boys need to learn how to keep your nerves in check," Kit joked.

Neither of the men dignified him with a response, their faces transforming from relief to business as they began to calculate their next move. Kit felt like shit for making the comment, hating that he couldn't help himself from cracking wise. He knew it cost him, killing the illusion of them being equals and bringing back their status quo. The thrill of victory was gone, and they were back to the harsh truth of being stuck in a dilapidated barn filled with rotting corpses that stank of coagulated decay.

"We'll have to lay low here for a bit until they pass," Eli dictated, all business once again. "Let them get some distance from us."

The idea of staying here any longer was out of the question for Kit. This place was hell, and they'd already been here far too long for his sanity.

"Fuck that," Kit protested. "We can't stay here any longer."

"You don't have much of a choice," the marshal said, as both a threat and fact.

That feeling of being equals already felt like a long-lost memory.

"I could start hollerin'," Kit threatened. Of course, he didn't mean it, but being regulated back to bottom bitch soured his judgment. "I could make enough noise that we might catch their attention to come back."

"And I could cut your tongue out of your mouth," Eli answered without hesitation. "But I think we can both agree that neither one of us prefers that approach. So, let's just stay calm and wait things out here."

Kit nodded, reaching the closest they were going to get to civility right now. He wished he'd kept the chatter going longer, even if it was confrontational. Silence only made staying in the barn worse. Every quiet moment in this place ate a little piece of his nerves, gnawing at them like jackals on the ribs of a carcass.

"This is a bad place," Shane said, stating the obvious just to break the dreaded mute air. "I'm not ashamed to say it, this place scares me."

"I don't like it either," Eli admitted, "but the longer we wait, the more distance we put between us and them. That and..." he trailed off for a moment as he looked at the grim scene surrounding them, "it would give us some distance from the sick fucks that did this."

"I'd wait in this barn for a lifetime rather than see those sick bastards again," Kit shared without a hint of shame.

The thought of the Walkers made him sick, their surroundings suddenly feeling like a better alternative.

"Then it's settled," Eli agreed with forced confidence. "We lay low here for a while. After that, we ride for Arkell."

They nodded in unison, trying to keep their eyes on each other instead of the dangling fly-infested corpses above. The *buzz* dancing around the bodies began to hum again. The flies somehow knew they were going to be sticking around a little longer, happily playing their horrific chant louder for their guests.

CHAPTER NINE

THE CRIMSON STREETS OF ARKELL

i. Shane

*T*hings were different after the barn.

A fresh burst of life had been injected into the group, bringing the three men closer together, despite the very different interests they held. Before the horrors of the barn, every word and reaction between them was closely guarded and calculated. But after escaping that hellish place, it was easier to enjoy the journey and their surroundings. They could appreciate the outside world, share a couple stories and even laugh here and there. Shane learned that the kid had seen and done some interesting things in his life, some of them even hinting at a bit of a decent side under his skewed view of morality. He was able to see the kid as a person, not just a monster in a story. His personality shined in a way that made it pretty easy for Shane to grow to kind of like him. The new lease on life and view of their prisoner made the ride relatively pleasant, a blessing they all appreciated after what they'd been through.

But growing to enjoy the kid as a person created a new problem, one that bubbled to the surface as they approached the outskirts of Arkell. How do you claim to enjoy a man's company only to drop him off to be hung for your own monetary gain? The relationships had changed, but their end destination sure as shit hadn't. The air became thicker among them the closer they drew to Arkell, the sunny sentiment fading by the minute. Everybody had the same thing on their mind, a sense of finality beginning to weigh on their shoulders. Eli and Kit seemed to be hiding it pretty well, but Shane could read it behind their eyes. He felt a lump of guilt in his throat, a feeling that only reminded him of the noose that would soon be around the kid's neck.

When they eventually reached the edge of town, they stopped to soak in the night air of their final stop. The sky was clear, littered with endless stars above them, paired with the glow of the moon. The beauty of it felt mixed, contradicting the despair growing in their guts. Shane wished he had the courage to say something, *anything*, but couldn't get the words out. He felt even worse when it was Kit who broke the silence.

"You know, it's not too late," the kid said, as if it were all as easy as that. "There's nothing that says you boys can't cut me loose."

"I'm afraid this is the last stop for you, my friend," Eli told him solemnly.

"It doesn't have to be," Kit reasoned. "We could forget everything and all go our separate ways."

He managed to make the proposal sound elegant, like they were having a casual negotiation over goods instead of a man pleading for his life.

"Sorry kid," Shane responded, hardly believing the bitter words were his, "but we can't give up this reward."

The kid scoffed with amusement at the mention of money.

"You still want that piddly bounty? That's nothing," Kit dismissed, the dangling carrot coming out. "Cut me loose and we can split a *real* bounty. I'm the only person alive who knows where the Silverton gold is stashed."

The golden elephant reentered their world. Greed began to glow in the lawmen's eyes.

"Bullshit, you still have it." Eli dismissed, a twinge of curiosity in his voice betraying him.

"I swear on my Mama's life," Kit countered, his negotiating charm in full swing. "Whatever reward they're offering, it's not even close to what I stashed away."

"How about you tell us where it is and then we'll see?" Shane butted in, not believing how greedy the words in his brain sounded out loud.

"I tell you where it is and I hang anyway? Fuck that!" the kid laughed. "Let's turn around and I'll take you there."

"There is no hidden gold." Eli dismissed the idea with an obnoxious snort before locking disappointed eyes with Shane. "He's just saying whatever he can to weasel out of the noose."

The comment shut everyone up. Shane felt ashamed for letting his greed show, and stupid for falling for the story. He hated that this was going to be one of their last interactions with the kid, a grim reminder that they weren't friends. He'd heard dozens of outlaws promise rewards and hidden treasure in exchange for their freedom during his law days, and he never once fell for it. It was nothing but an old fairy tale, this time pret-tied up by the silver tongue of a likable murderer.

He snapped out of his own head when he noticed Eli's expression change, his crow's feet tightening as a disturbance hit his eyes.

"The hell?" Eli muttered, squinting off into the distance.

Shane couldn't make out what it was, but that didn't stop Eli from carefully drawing his pistol.

"Stay back and cover me," he instructed. "Somethin ain't right."

Without another word, Eli rode towards town. Shane still couldn't see what had caught his eye, but readied his rifle as instructed and awaited further orders.

Once Eli was out of earshot, the kid spoke up again.

"Your friend really wasn't interested in entertaining the idea of us getting rich together, was he?" Kit whispered, his tone secretive.

Shane thought the subject of the gold had been dropped, not feeling right about picking these talks back up with just the two of them.

"He's doing what's right," Shane defended. "He's upholding the law."

"Let's not insult each other and pretend that this is about upholding the law," Kit cawed. "It's about the *money*. It's *always* been about the money."

Shane was exhausted. He felt there was no sense in lying about their motives anymore at this point. If they were sending the kid off to hang, they didn't have to keep insulting him by bullshitting him as well.

"It's not personal, he just really needs this," Shane confided. "You know how the banks can be, they're looking to take the farm away from him and his boy. This bounty could push them off his back, so he ain't gonna go risking it all by chasing some *story* of buried gold."

"But you *know* I ain't lying," Kit pressed, his eyes bulging with excitement. "I have much more stashed away than some insulting bounty. Cut me loose and we can go get it. We'll split it together."

"Eli said no, so the answer is no," Shane stated as firmly as he could. The exchange felt slightly embarrassing, like he was scolding a kid who wanted permission to go out and play.

"Who said anything about Eli?" Kit asked, the words

sounding both sinister and logical. "That bounty split two ways is a hell of a lot more than splitting it by three."

The suggestion should have died immediately, but there was something in the night air that gave the idea just enough oxygen to allow it to linger. Eli would be too stubborn to go through with it, but Shane thought maybe there was a way to work out a deal without him and then pay him his cut later after the dust settled. A dozen scenarios of how to make it work raced through his head as he tried to balance what would be the most beneficial to everyone, while also justifying what was right.

Then the kid overplayed his hand.

"What if he suffered from some sort of *accident*?" Kit suggested, his voice even lower and oily. "It's mighty dangerous out here, so who knows?"

Shane's heart filled with disgust, shame hitting him for entertaining the idea long enough for it to get this far.

"You snake fuck," he spat. "I'm not like you. You're nothing but a gutless coward."

Kit's reaction didn't waver at the insult, but Shane hoped he felt it in his throat where he'd be strung up soon enough. He hated everything about the kid at that moment, especially the ugliness he had brought out of him. *Make sure that noose is nice and tight,* he thought.

Thankfully the dark matter was interrupted by a whistle from Eli. Shane turned away from the kid, shifting his focus to where his loyalty belonged.

"Whatcha find?" Shane hollered, relieved to change the topic.

Eli responded with a wave, beckoning them to come to him. From the look of it, Shane knew they should hurry.

ii. Eli

Eli had that sunken feeling in his stomach you get when that bad news you've been suspecting turns out to be true. His fading eyesight immediately recognized the shape for what it was, a figure lying face down in the dirt. It was the type of situation that was never good, more trouble on top of a journey full of it. Eli knew from experience that this person was either passed out drunk or they were dead, the drunk option being much less likely considering they were on the edge of town instead of outside the local tavern. Dead is what he expected riding up, and dead is what he found.

What he wasn't expecting was the horrid condition the body was in. The standard scenario, as standard as finding a dead stranger can be, would be that someone had a disagreement with this man before putting a bullet in him. One disagreement, one dead man, that would be that. But this didn't look like a disagreement, this looked sadistic. This crime was committed with savage glee. From what he could decipher, the body looked to be of a boy no more than seventeen or eighteen. The corpse of the young man had been severely mutilated, the injuries looking like they were inflicted well beyond the point of death. Deep gashes ran across his face and body, paired with streaks of blood strewn about that looked black under the moonlight. Whoever killed this boy didn't want the experience to end. Death was only the beginning; they wanted to keep going until he was more meat than man.

Eli whistled for Shane to join him and see his discovery, a rotten feeling in his guts, wondering how nobody in town saw this.

"Jesus Christ," Shane muttered as he approached, clearly not ready for such a grisly sight. "What happened?"

"It's not too late to turn around." The kid interrupted the scene, chiming in yet again at the most in-fucking-appropriate time possible.

"Shut your fucking mouth!" Eli demanded. He needed to think, and Kit's input was the last thing the situation needed right now.

"If it's the Walker Brothers," Kit started back up, "we ain't gettin out of here alive. They'll skin us like fucking animals."

"I said shut up!" Eli snapped.

He had to block the kid's bullshit out of his mind to stop him from making him eat a bullet. He turned his energy to Shane, stomaching as much stoicism as he could muster.

"Let's head in and let Sheriff Kelly know about this. Keep your eyes open. We don't know if whoever did this is still in town."

His old friend nodded dutifully and readied his rifle. Cautiously, they continued their trek into Arkell.

iii. Kit

Though he'd heard things here and there about the small — and before tonight seemingly unremarkable — town of Arkell, Kit had never actually been there before. He expected quaint, which was the furthest fucking feeling he felt upon finally reaching their destination. Nothing he could have been told, no matter how ghastly or outlandish, could have prepared him for the blood-soaked sights they arrived at. The welcome committee of the mutilated man on the outskirts wasn't a great start to the place's image, but it was appropriate in setting up what awaited them in the sleepy town.

Sleepy-town. A funny description that was thrown around often.

Sleepy-town, Dead town.

Shut up, I'm dead tired, his daddy used to yell.

This town is dead tired, Daddy.

Life had left Arkell completely, replaced with a monsoon of

blood. The town looked like a biblical rain had hit it, not a living soul in sight to tell what happened. A crimson mess had painted the streets, obscene amounts of blood soaking into the dirt roads. It felt like the place where a nightmare once slumbered before it continued on its way to haunt the next poor person that dreamed it up.

The men had seen their share of horrors on this journey, but this was different. Something vital was missing. The gallons of blood soaking into the earth didn't carry flesh counterparts, alone without the expected accompanying bodies. There wasn't a single corpse in sight to take ownership of the sea of red, making this hellish landscape all the more surreal and frightening. Somehow, the scene would have been more comforting if the missing, mutilated bodies were present.

"What happened here?" Eli asked, his voice bringing the reminder of life back to everyone. "It's a bloody ghost town."

"You got the *bloody* part right," Kit joked dryly.

Eli shot him a look telling him to shut up. He wasn't trying to be cute, he just needed levity to help swallow the awful lump forming in his throat from the grisly situation.

"Let's check the sheriff's office," Eli commanded, spotting their unlikely sanctuary ahead.

That camaraderie of all being in the shit together came back to Kit as they cautiously rode towards the sheriff's. It should have felt good; being together in the shit is better than being in it alone. But when the shit ran this deep, the idea of going to the gallows started to feel like maybe a better alternative than what they'd gotten themselves into.

iv. Shane

The waft of rotting stink pickled into the walls, paired with the horrid drone of flies buzzing about the sheriff's office, gave

Shane an unwelcome case of déjà vu. The three men covered their mouths as they entered, their eyes treated to the decoration of smeared blood spread across the floor and walls. Shane shivered at the thought of how he didn't retch from the putrid smell, recognizing that he was damn near accustomed to it, thanks to their episode in the barn.

Panic lived here before the massacre, the windows hastily boarded up with various planks and hunks of furniture. The tenants had tried to keep their intruders out, the mess inside displaying signs of a struggle that clearly showed these efforts were futile. The ripe stench and gore were combining in a way that made Shane dizzy, his mind hammered with the truth that things couldn't have ended well here for the sheriff.

Shane had met Sheriff Kelly, or Miles as he was known to friends, on a couple of occasions. He considered him a decent enough guy, if a little crass. Eli knew Miles better and considered him one of the few men left he'd still call a friend after the incident that ended his life with the law. It was because of that friendship that Shane made the extra effort to hold himself together, doing his part to prevent a spiral of emotional dominoes from toppling at the sight of the bloody office. As bad as the scene felt for him, he knew it must be so much worse for Eli.

Their horrific journey had conditioned Shane to stay sharp, his rifle ready for whoever or whatever might still be hiding in this house of decay. He clocked Eli to see if he could get a read on him, finding a small bit of relief that he was still in full business mode with his pistol drawn. *Maybe Miles got out just in time*, he foolishly thought to himself, the same stupid way kids do to block out the real horrors of the world. Those foolish thoughts died instantly when Shane turned a corner and saw the tattered remains of Miles Kelly hiding behind the desk.

If it weren't for the sheriff's uniform, Shane didn't know if he would have been able to recognize the mutilated corpse as

human. Sheriff Kelly's body was sprawled across the floor, his
death grip clutching the shotgun that couldn't save him. His face
and torso were ripped to shreds, peeled down to the muscle and
tendons by what appeared to be the claw marks of a vicious and
impossibly large animal. His tattered clothing was soaking wet
with blood, dripping down to a caked jelly on the floorboards
below him. Well-fed flies crawled through what remained of his
face, breeding inside his eye sockets as dozens more buzzed
around his corpse. It was the same viciousness they had seen in
the barn, except instead of strangers dangling from the rafters, it
was a familiar face gazing at them with what remained of his
one rotting eyeball.

"Eli..." Shane gasped weakly.

Gun cocked, Eli made his way over to Shane with the stance
of a hero ready to vanquish any evil he encountered. His heroic
stance died when he saw the corpse of his old friend. Never in
his life had Shane seen Eli's face turn to the shade of sheet-white
that it did in that moment. Not when he drunkenly shot that
woman, nor when they took his star away and transformed him
from a lawman into a mere disgraced and pathetic civilian. Not
even when he had told him that Ada had passed from the flu, a
moment so painful he had never brought it up again since. This
was a new look painted on his friend's face, a look Shane knew
he'd never be able to unsee for as long as he lived.

"Mary-and-fucking-Joseph," Eli muttered, closer to babbling
than words.

The vacant, glassy look in his eyes as he gazed at the mutilated remains of the sheriff sent a chill through Shane's bones.
He worried that an irreparable piece of his friend had been
broken at that moment.

Shane hadn't noticed the whiskey bottle sitting on the desk
upon first surveying the place, but it must have instantly hit Eli's
senses, even amongst all the gore and chaos. Ignoring the night-

mare around him, Eli briskly grabbed the bottle, pulled the cork and took a long, uninterrupted draw from it. Old habits made Shane think about stopping him, but he forced himself to allow his friend to take the necessary drink. The man might have his demons hiding in the bottle, but right now they were the comfort he needed. The swig from the bottle was drawn-out and greedy, like a man discovering water in the desert. He followed it up with another generous slug that dribbled down his chin. For a brief moment, the relief on his face suggested that the drink had fixed everything, like an elixir with the power to erase the death surrounding them. Like all highs, the pleasure quickly began to dissipate as the reality of their rotten situation came back. Any small bit of pleasure it gave him quickly dissolved.

Eli took one more swig before aggressively passing the bottle to Shane. Shane was reluctant to accept, worried that it was enabling his friend, but didn't see much choice. The manner it was thrust on him felt more like a demand than an offer. He took the bottle and gave a little swig in solidarity, the warm feeling in his throat giving him more comfort than he'd felt on this entire journey. He went to take another drink when Eli selfishly motioned for him to return it.

"We need our wits about us," Shane warned, noting the fog already glazing over Eli's eyes.

"We also need our nerves," Eli snarled as he lunged and aggressively snatched the bottle back.

The room was dead quiet outside of the buzzing flies, allowing the liquid hitting the neck of the bottle to give an audible *chug* with Eli's next swig. All eyes drifted towards the dead sheriff no matter how hard they tried to look elsewhere.

"Guess you might as well cut me loose," Kit interjected, somewhere between cutting tension and dead seriousness. "Now that the sheriff has, bluntly speaking, *retired*."

It was a spark that shouldn't have been introduced to Eli's

rapidly filling powder keg. The marshal snapped, drawing his pistol and lunging at Kit with that strength a man only finds from the darkest part of his soul. He violently tossed Kit towards the wall with what appeared to be minimal effort and jammed the gun barrel into the kid's mouth.

"Show some fucking respect," Eli howled as he shook the gun in place. "That was a man of the law who was put down like a dog and left to rot."

Kit tried to mumble something, his teeth against the metal barrel making a horrid *clicking* sound in a pitch that made Shane want to vomit. Eli made sure the mumbles didn't manifest into words by shoving the gun further into Kit's mouth.

"I should put you down right now," Eli threatened in a tone that sounded frighteningly logical. "See the sheriff's role of justice through to the end."

"Eli..." Shane interrupted, calmly, hoping he could pull his friend back into sanity.

Eli ignored him, answering with a cocked trigger.

"I told you," Eli continued, a bit of a slur creeping into his voice, "that Arkell was the end of the road for you."

"Eli!" Shane barked with more authority than he'd let out in years. "That's enough!"

He'd seen Eli commit a life's worth of mistakes, no need to add another one to the pile. The warning must have rattled through to him. His hands shook with contempt, but at least that vacant cloud had lifted from his eyes. Nobody said a thing, wordlessly avoiding eye contact with one another.

The silent, unbearable tension lifted when they all heard the sound of a pained moan. It sounded like an elderly woman, coming from the back of the office where the holding cells were. The three men turned their attention toward the horrid sound, that uneasy but welcoming feeling of a truce bubbling back. They paused as the moaning went silent, carefully listening until it started up again moments later. Shane couldn't tell if it was a cry for help or a warning, but the look on Eli's face confirmed that neither one of them wanted to risk finding out without being prepared for the worst. Shane drew his rifle, pointing towards the back. Eli nodded in agreement and readied his pistol.

It seemed that this wasn't the time for them to shoot their unarmed prisoner after all.

v. Eli

A new stench hit Eli's nose as they entered the holding cell area. It was different from the rotting flesh smell they'd all become accustomed to. It was something meaner, closer to the sour smell of infection. The odor reeked of disease and neglect, the sweet rot of decaying apples filling the air. Eli could taste the stink building in his throat, wishing that the tiny window near the ceiling in the corner of the room hadn't been boarded-up, to allow some of the tragic scent to escape.

Of the three cells, two were mercifully empty. The third was occupied by the prisoner whose vulgar appearance instantly explained the putrid, vinegar smell assaulting their senses. Left to die inside was an old woman, stripped nude and bound by her arms and legs with damp rope, a dirty rag shoved into her toothless mouth. She appeared to be at least eighty years old, though the neglect of every part of her body made her look even older. Her thin, wispy hair was a deathly gray; the unhealthy remains looked like it could be pulled from her scalp with an effortless tug. Her naked body was covered in boils and scabs that were visibly decaying, leaking pus and infected fluid. Every inch of her body looked like it *hurt* to the touch as she twisted her delicate skin, burning and scratching against the binding rope with each movement.

She didn't appear to care or notice when the three men entered the room, never raising her milky white eyes to meet them. Her horrid state looked like an existence of misery, yet none of this appeared to bother her as she rocked back and forth, moaning beneath the gag in a calm, almost rhythmic manner.

"Jesus Christ," Eli muttered with pity.

He wanted to vomit. Not just from the stench and the horrific condition of her body, but from the thought of pure neglect this woman had suffered. Who did this to her? How long had she been here? How was she the only person in town left alive? He ran to her cell door, not surprised to find it locked when he gave it a tug. As if they weren't there, she continued to rock back and forth, lost in her own world.

"Hey," Eli said softly, tapping on the cell door to try to get her attention. "I'm Marshal Eli Cooke, we're here to help."

She continued to ignore them, her expression blank as if her brain had decayed along with her body. Eli turned to Shane urgently.

"Keys!" he commanded. "Go check the sheriff, see if they're on him."

He could sense from the look on Shane's face that he didn't want to go back and deal with Miles' mutilated corpse, but the foul odor of the neglected old woman wasn't a much better alternative. Shane took a deep breath and headed back to the front, leaving Eli and Kit with the poor woman.

"You're going to be okay," Eli forced himself to tell her.

Deep down, he wasn't sure if he was talking to her or to himself. It felt like the type of thing you were supposed to say in bad situations, and this was as bad of one as he had ever been in. But the words did nothing for her, the rocking continuing as if they were never said.

"She's fucking crazy," Kit said.

Eli knew the statement was inappropriate, but a sick feeling in his bowels told him it wasn't untrue, either. He wanted to help her, but every moment they spent with her stirred up all sorts of awful feelings of dread.

"Got em!" Shane announced, returning with the keys and a blanket not a moment too soon. He handed them over to Eli, who didn't waste any time unlocking her cell door.

"You're just gonna let her out?" Kit asked, mortified by the prospect.

"What, are you afraid of an old woman?" Shane chirped with a bit of much needed levity.

"You don't know what she's done," Kit argued, showing no shame in expressing his fear. "Someone locked her up in here for a reason."

Eli didn't miss the irony of one prisoner bitching about another's freedom.

"Show some goddamn sympathy, we have no idea how long she's been in here," Eli said in a muted tone, trying not to upset the woman as he opened her cell. "Shane, find her some water."

Shane nodded dutifully and left the room once more.

Eli cautiously entered the cell. He slowly approached the neglected woman, carefully pulling out his knife and cutting the rotting ropes binding her blistered hands free. He delicately wrapped the blanket around her frail, naked body before gently removing the gag from her mouth. None of these acts registered behind her dead, milky eyes; she stared blankly ahead as if her rescuers had never come.

"Who did this to you?" Eli asked, a lump aching in his Adam's apple.

Registering him for the first time, she turned her shriveled neck to face him, giving him a blank, foggy stare.

"Diiiiaaa…llooooooossss," the woman croaked in a scratchy, unintelligible moan.

Her mumbled response sounded painful, like it scraped her throat to release it. The words didn't mean anything, at least not to Eli, but the look of conviction on her face said they meant the world to her. Replacing his fear with as much empathy as he could channel, he carefully took her old hands into his. They were delicate, like the texture of old paper, like they could crumble into dust if he pressed too hard.

"It's ok," he reassured her. He wanted her to know that this part of her nightmare was over. "You can tell us, what happened here?"

Something snapped inside the old woman, causing her to erupt with an explosive burst of energy. She lunged at Eli with surprising strength, her sour stench soaking into his nostrils as she descended on him. His first reaction was to try to calm her down, but he suddenly found himself putting real strength at forcing her back as she locked her milk-foggy stare on him.

"Diiaaa-booo-luuus," the decaying woman moaned with a hiss that sounded like she had swallowed half her tongue. "Diiaaaboooluuus."

Eli shook the woman off and ran out of the cell, scrambling to close the door behind him. He felt ashamed that he was actually afraid of her.

"I told you she's fucking crazier than a shit-house rat!" Kit screamed with a little too much *told-you-so* tone for Eli's liking.

Eli saw fear in Kit's eyes that said his flight mode was looking ready to kick in. Worried the kid might make a break for it, he grabbed Kit and threw him into the cell beside hers.

"Hey!" Kit screamed with confusion, the action unfolding before he could register what was happening. He clued in too late as Eli slammed the cell door shut and locked it. "What the hell are you doing?"

The putrid woman sank to the floor of her cell, calming

down like the end of a rainstorm. She lowered her head and continued her chant.

"Diiaaa-booo-luuus," she moaned in a low rhythm. "Diiaaa-booo-luuus."

She rocked back and forth, frothing at the mouth. The tone of her unintelligible chant was sinister, the feeling of an evil presence permeating throughout the holding cells. Shane barged back in, glass of water in hand. He handed it to Eli, who took it gratefully.

"Let me the fuck outta here," Kit demanded.

Eli had grown used to ignoring the kid by this point, easily doing so yet again as he carefully handed the water through the cell bars to the woman.

"Drink this," he said softly. "It'll help."

Her spark of energy came back, violently smacking the glass out of Eli's hand and sending it crashing into a shattered mess. She locked her cataract eyes with him once more, reaching down and picking up a piece of the broken glass with her fragile hands.

"Diiaaaboooluuus."

Her expression remained frozen as she squeezed the broken shard in her hand. The glass cut deep, adding a fresh injury to match the dozens that polluted her body. Eli wanted to wince and look away but was petrified still by her disturbing actions. He locked eyes with her, lost in the abyss of her milky yellow stare. He felt unsure if he'd ever be able to escape it until he was brought back to reality by a distant, familiar sound. He turned his sight to Shane, who looked as if he heard it too.

"Quiet," Shane hushed. "Just quiet down for a second."

He motioned with his hand for silence, somehow getting everyone to comply at once, like some sort of cheap magic trick. Even the old woman managed to stop her rocking and babbling at the command.

Through their silence, a muffled noise dampened by several walls and distance, started to take shape. It was a rhythm they'd been hearing their entire journey, one that had faded nicely into the background without them ever really focusing on it.

Clip. Clop.

Clip. Clop.

"You hear that?" Shane quietly asked.

Clip. Clop.

Clip. Clop.

It was the comforting, familiar sound of horse hooves. They all listened carefully, hopelessly trying to calculate how far away they were and how many. It sounded like a whole group, moving at a relaxed and loud enough pace to be considered an arrival.

"Shit," Eli muttered, recognizing they were in even deeper shit than they thought.

There was no back exit in the sheriff's, pinning them down with nowhere to go. Instinct told Eli to panic, but he thought of the whiskey in his belly and used it to calm the nerves and do the only dignified thing he could think of; He took a deep breath and bravely walked out to the front of the office.

"Wait! Where are you going?" Kit asked with real worry in his voice.

Shane knew where his place in this scenario was. Without hesitation, he left Kit and the old woman in their cells and sprinted to catch up with his friend, to face their destiny together.

Kit's face filled with terror as he saw he was being left alone with *her*.

"Wait, you can't leave me here with her!" he screamed. "Don't you fucking leave me!"

CHAPTER TEN

TO LIVE AND DIE IN DIXIE

i. Shane

*T*he rowdy posse weren't even trying to remain stealthy as they rode into Arkell, ringing clear as a bell by the time Shane had caught up to Eli. He perched beside him near the boarded-up windows at the front of the office, finding a decent sized crack between the boards to get a peek at their newly arrived guests.

There were at least a dozen men out there, all of them carrying iron of various sizes and caliber. It was the same pack from Blackcreek, easily identified by the boisterous braggart that led the group, along with the big bastard that had been acting as his lapdog. Shane recognized a couple of the other men from that night, but was more concerned with the guns and dynamite they were carrying, over how familiar their faces were.

"Shit," he whispered to nobody in particular.

He watched their pompous leader get off of his horse, posing in that theatrical way he did back in Blackcreek, as if he knew he was being watched.

"Marshal!" he called out in a loud, jovial tone. "Come on out, marshal. You and I have matters to discuss."

Neither Shane nor Eli responded to the challenge, knowing damn well that the two of them didn't stand a chance against the dozen out there. They held their breath, remaining dead silent as the hum of the flies pestering the corpse of the sheriff, amplified in their ear drums.

"I know you're here, marshal," the leader hollered through a devilish grin. "Even amongst all this death, I can *smell* the cowardice of you."

The word *smell* throbbed in the pit of Shane's guts as if the suggestion made it true.

"I smell your chicken shit ass, I smell your lapdog old man, and I sure as shit smell that cocksuckin' weasel of a prisoner you're hauling."

The crouching was starting to wear on Shane's old joints. He felt that weakness in his knees that you only get when you know you're truly fucked.

"Ready your rifle," Eli calmly commanded with stoic conviction. "I'm going to go out there and talk to them."

"But you..." Shane started before being quickly cut off.

"If it looks like they're ready to start shooting," Eli warned, "you start firing first."

"But there's too goddamn many of them," Shane said, trying to be the reasonable one.

Going out there would be a suicide mission, but Eli's eyes never lost that confident edge that said he knew exactly what he was doing.

"All you have to worry about is *him*," Eli said, motioning towards the group's de facto leader. "You cut off the head of the snake, the rest of the body will panic long enough for you to get the hell out of here."

Shane wanted to argue Eli's logic, but lost his words when the demands from outside started up again.

"This can go one of two ways, marshal," their leader boasted, the theatrics in full swing now. "One: we march our way into that office, where we *know* you're hiding, and we kill you all. You, the old man, and that piece of shit murderer you stole from us. Because that's what ya' did. You stole."

The words were self-righteous in their delivery, fueling up the murmurs of anger in the posse.

"Or two:" he continued, "you can come out here and we can have an exchange of words instead of lead."

Shane couldn't help but find himself being sucked into the crowd-pleasing demands. Eli wasn't fazed though, completely focused on psyching himself up to head out there into the nest.

"Now, I hope you'll make the right decision," the man warned. Shane could tell by his tone that this was where the threat part of the spiel would follow. "But my men are tired and more than a little pissed off. So instead of dragging this out, I'm gonna give you the count of ten to decide."

Eli took a deep breath as the counting began.

One. Two.

He made his way to the door.

Three. Four.

He walked out to greet their new arrivals.

ii. Dante

The long trek to Arkell had been nothing but one giant pain in Dante's ass. The entire journey was built on a foundation of angry spite, and was starting to feel more futile the closer they got to their destination. The heat was oppressive, his saddle was jabbing at his balls and asshole, and the company was filled with goddamned morons he barely trusted. Throw in the lack of proper sleep and a dose of resentment and you had yourself an ugly little recipe that had him questioning if the trip was actually worth it, or if his goddamn stubborn pride had gotten him into yet another jackpot.

That all changed as soon as they arrived in Arkell.

Seeing the young fella's mangled body spread carelessly on the outskirts of town reminded Dante why they had come here in the first place. An innocent boy murdered for no reason, his killer roaming free. Dante had an obligation to see justice, *real* justice, through.

The scene in Arkell only got worse the further they rode into town, blood painted everywhere without a body in sight. Dante didn't want to admit how fuckin' uneasy the whole situation made him. As a man who knew the importance of appearances, he'd have rather died than let any of the dipshits he was riding with know how scared this place made him and how goddamn much he wanted to get the hell out of there. But he also knew that they were twelve men strong and were well armed, far better equipped than the two disgraced lawmen and one pris- oner they were up against. Sure, something real bad must have happened before they got here, but he felt confident enough that the guns and dynamite they were packing was more than enough to give a confident *fuck you* to anyone that crossed them.

Putting emotion aside, he pushed the mutilations out of his head to focus on his target. Amongst the blood were fresh tracks, their imprint disrupting the streaks of red. They guided him to their destination, the trail leading to the sheriff's office, where their prey must be hiding like cowards. The thought that this could be a trap briefly crossed his mind, but knowing they were only against three men made him feel confident that the chips were in his favor.

He was ready, filled with the satisfied feeling you get from arriving at your destination after a long journey, combined with a strange adrenaline from the eerie feeling that this fuckin' place gave him. It all mixed into the perfect cocktail for the mood necessary for tonight, priming even the weakest of his men to be ready for a showdown if it came to that. Sure, he would let the marshal go if he cooperated, but the look of this place and the smell in the air made him think cooperation wasn't going to be on the table.

He put on that charm he had perfected over the years, to start calling out for the cowards, theatrically letting them know that they would be in some pretty serious shit if they didn't comply with his demands. The bloodstained streets told him that there was no reward to be had here, so he felt more than comfortable burning the sheriff's office down and roasting the inhabitants alive if the situation came to that. He didn't necessarily want things to escalate to that level, justifying that it was ultimately up to the men inside to decide their fate. They could stay inside and burn, or they could come out and talk the situation through like civilized folk.

He decided to present the ultimatum through a countdown, a tactic he was a sucker for thanks to how his daddy would implement it when he was just a boy. In his experience, speaking to any scared bastard like you're their daddy and ready to give them a whipping, almost always worked at getting you what you wanted. So, he started counting, the spanking of a torched fucking building at his disposal if they didn't cooperate.

"One. Two. Three."

What he wasn't anticipating was how high his count would get before they showed themselves and surrendered.

"Four. Five."

Most men made it out by the count of four, but when seven and eight rolled around, Dante was wondering if he might *actually* have to burn the place down. It was when he hit nine that the door to the sheriff's finally opened.

Out walked the marshal. Alone.

Dante was slightly disappointed to see that he wasn't hauling the murdering bastard out with him, but he had an appreciation for the negotiations that sometimes happened at this stage. Knowing he had the better hand, he had a little more patience to enjoy this part of the dance.

"Marshal," Dante greeted warmly, loud enough for everyone to hear clearly. "So glad to see that you have some sense to you. I was getting a little worried there for a second."

He flashed his devilish grin as he spoke, the smile coming genuinely instead of forcing himself to put it on. The marshal smiled back. It looked natural in a way Dante wasn't ready for. If the marshal *was* scared, he sure as shit wasn't showing it.

"Storming the door of a sheriff," the marshal said disapprovingly. "That's a little aggressive, wouldn't you say?"

"Aggressive?" Dante scoffed, finding the accusation more than a little hypocritical. "From the look of things around town, I'd say it was *you* that took the aggressive route. Murdered that kid in cold blood and left him there like a dog."

"Now, you know that wasn't us," the marshal calmly denied. "Personally, I thought it looked more like your style."

Dante didn't let the comment crack his exterior, even though he found it to be insulting. He may have dipped his toe into some unsavory waters over the years, but never as cold-blooded as butchering a boy like that. He was here on a noble mission to dish out justice when everyone else was either too damn scared or too damn greedy to do it themselves.

"Not my style at all, marshal," Dante answered. "We're not animals. Unlike that piece of shit you've been towing."

"What do you want?" the marshal cut back, getting right to the point.

Dante could appreciate the bluntness, politely taking the cue and returning the sentiment.

"You have something that belongs to me," he responded. It felt good laying out what each one wanted and cutting through the bullshit. "You surrender that piece of shit to us, and I'd be willing to let things lie. We'll let you go and be on our way. Simple as that."

As much as Dante just wanted to collect what was his, he admired how the marshal didn't let his face betray him as he mulled things over. He was impossible to read, staring back with the neutral expression of a great card player. For a brief moment, that admiration made Dante feel bad about the thought that he was probably going to kill this man tonight.

"Sorry, I'd love to help you," the marshal responded with that fake, law-filtered version of an apology that isn't really an apology at all. "But that man is now in the hands of Sheriff Kelly. Your problem is no longer with me, it's with him."

That was enough for Doc, finally cutting through the shit and letting his giant presence be known. He took an aggressive step forward, pushing his duster aside just enough for the marshal to see the solid bundle of dynamite strapped to his belt. It was slightly overdramatic, and it killed Dante's poetic momentum, but he had to admire the rabid dog spirit of it.

"How about I slit your throat from ear to ear?" Doc growled like a beast that had never once met elegance in his life. "What would the sheriff have to say about that?"

Dante calmly reached out and put a friendly hand on Doc's shoulder, signaling the big man to stand down. The giant felt tense, making Dante regret the decision before Doc reluctantly stepped back and relaxed slightly. Dante felt privileged to be the only person he knew who could actually reach out to Doc like that without having his arm ripped out of its socket, though he knew it wasn't something he should ever push. He had once seen Doc mash a man's nose into a sinewy pile of mush with a whiskey bottle over an ill-conceived joke, an image burned into Dante's mind that made him always be careful about how he approached Doc. Knowing that he could still keep the big dog on a leash was a matter of pride for him, but not something he ever wanted to abuse, having seen the consequences up close at the expense of another poor bastard's face.

With Doc stepping down, even if just for a moment, Dante allowed his signature grin to slide back on his face as he played his next card.

"Tell me, marshal, where *is* the sheriff?" he asked, calling the marshal on his bluff. Between the dead man on the outskirts of town and the crimson stains of the streets, he knew the sheriff was either long exiled or dead by now. "Perhaps he can come out here and straighten out this mess?"

"The sheriff isn't going to bow to the demands of a bunch of bandits," the stubborn marshal responded. "If he's forced to come out, it's only going to be trouble."

Dante couldn't help but chuckle. He knew it was a bunch of bullshit, but the son-of-a-bitch had such a serious look plastered on his face, it was as if he believed his own far-fetched lie.

"I have to hand it to you, marshal, you have balls. That was a hell of a fast one you pulled on us in Blackcreek," Dante said with admiration. "I got so caught up in the moment, I didn't stop to think *why the hell don't I recognize this marshal*?"

Doc spat in agreement. Dante could see his guard-dog's hand visibly itching to draw like it had a spider crawling on it. He knew he didn't have long before Doc would let loose, shooting the bastard down with or without his blessing.

"Stealing from us under the guise of the law? Ballsy. Impressive, but ballsy," Dante crooned. "Normally I'd have to applaud the stones to pull that off, but all of this traveling has worn my patience thin. So please, marshal, be a good boy and send that peckerwood out before my dogs tear you apart."

Dante thought the threat was crystal-fucking-clear, yet the stubborn bastard still didn't look fazed.

"You know you're drawing arms on a building of the law?" the marshal lectured, in a way Dante had no patience for. "Personal feelings towards me aside, you have to know that's a bad idea."

This self-righteous bullshit was oddly comical to Dante, even if his patience was long gone.

"That's where you got me confused," Dante said through gritted teeth, the grin evaporating from his face. "I don't think this is any longer a building of the law because I don't actually believe the sheriff is even in there."

He was through dancing around truths and negotiating with a man who didn't have any chips left to offer.

"Now, I'd never dream of shooting down a marshal. Not in a million years," Dante continued, letting that last point linger for a moment, "but I sure as shit wouldn't hesitate to gun down a lying, chicken-shit cocksucker such as yourself, if you don't bring out my prisoner right fucking now."

To punctuate, Dante cocked his pistol. That beautiful *clack* of the hammer pulling into place sang the opening note to a symphony of his men readying their irons in solidarity. The sound of a dozen ready arms made the entire trip worth it to Dante, clearly getting the message across. With no more bullshit left to sell, the lying marshal slowly raised his hands to surrender.

"Easy now," the marshal said, suddenly not sounding so sure of himself. "I'll go in and get him."

iii. Kit

While they were never going to be best friends due to the context of their journey, Kit still couldn't believe that Eli and

Shane actually locked him up and left him alone with *her*. It wasn't just the putrid stench of the old woman that was driving him to the edge of what little sanity he had left, it was the mumbling of her chants that signaled she was locked up for a reason. He knew she could snap at any moment and thanked God for the small miracle that at least he was locked into his own cell instead of sharing one with her.

He wanted to scream *let me out, I'm back here*, but he also wasn't a fucking idiot, and knew the price he'd pay if the posse outside caught him. A dozen-plus men against three weren't great odds any way you cut it, and once you knock that number down to two, with him being unarmed and locked up like a dog, those odds suddenly became much fucking worse. There wasn't much hope for them, but if there was a sliver of a chance to get out of here, he wasn't going to fuck it up by screaming and drawing attention to where he was. If that meant being caged back here with a naked old witch covered in rotting sores, he'd just have to suck it up and deal with that.

He knew those two bastards probably weren't going to be able to negotiate their way out of this mess, which would either end with them giving him up or being shot down before the posse would barge back here and put him down too. *Like shooting fish in a barrel*, his daddy used to say, though never in such a goddamned literal sense as this.

Staying locked up here wasn't a viable option for his survival. He needed an escape. The only way out he could spot was the small boarded-up window in the top corner of the room. It was a good eight feet up and damn narrow, even for his slim figure, but he thought desperation would allow him to squeeze through if he could manage to get himself up there. That is, if he could find a way out of this goddamn cage first.

"Diiiaaabbooollllusss," the old woman continued mumbling.

The reminder of her made his thought process foggy,

bringing her goddamned rotten presence right back to the front of his mind. The stench seemed to amplify, the stink of infection hitting his nostrils and shifting his focus away from an escape plan and over to trying to keep his last meal down. If only he could...

The thought was interrupted.

The distant sound of something new captured his attention, pulling his focus away from where he stood. Away from escape, away from the gang out front, even away from the goddamned witch of sores. It was the faint sound of an old confederate song being whistled off in the distance. A song Kit knew from his past. A song that turned his skin to gooseflesh. He froze in terror as memories flooded over him; he recognized where he knew it from.

iv. Eli

Knowing they were outgunned by a long shot, Eli had hoped his words might be able to buy them a little wiggle room. He had all the right ingredients to help him deliver the perfect bluff to the angry posse: the pain of seeing poor Miles mutilated body, the warmth in his belly from sloshing down half the bottle of whiskey, and the surreal sight and smell of the rotting old woman they encountered. The bluff came swift and confident but none of his lies were working, making it clear that if he didn't give Kit up, they'd gun him and Shane down before getting what they wanted anyway. Hell, they could still go forward with shooting him after he gave the kid up if they felt like it. He didn't have any chips left to negotiate with, and the posse's patience had long run out.

He raised his arms in submission, ready to surrender their prisoner, when the eerie whistling began. He recognized the song from a long-dead drunk from his past who used to tell of his confederate war days to anyone who would listen. "Dixie," he believed was the name of the song, a thoroughly upbeat ditty that sounded a lot more haunting as it echoed through the empty, blood-soaked streets of Arkell that night. What little he remembered of the lyrics wormed their way back into his brain, stealing valuable bits of his ever-fragmenting attention.

In Dixie Land I'll take my stand to live and die in Dixie. Away, away, away down South in Dixie.

He didn't know if it was safe to turn his back on the dozen arms drawn on him to see where the whistling was coming from, but he was so damn curious that he couldn't help himself. He slowly turned to steal a look at the whistling stranger, keeping his hands firmly raised and visible to display that he had no intention of trying anything.

He was surprised by the appearance of the meek intruder. Despite all the tension, the whistling was coming from a lone man dressed in a fine suit. The stranger was extremely well put together, looking even better compared to the horrid group of dirty misfits drawn on Eli. He was strolling towards them in an extremely casual manner, whistling his tune as if he were enjoying a morning walk, rather than that of someone marching into the middle of a standoff. He carried himself as if he had wealth, power, confidence, and the world in his hands. The whole situation felt *off*. His casual demeanor, the relaxed pace he took sauntering towards them, the unusually nice outfit. None of it sat right. But there was another thing that eclipsed everything else.

His eyes.

They were vacant, glassy, as if no light existed behind them. Just a blank stare pretending to carry a soul as he whistled his tune from a war since passed. Blank to how abnormal it was to be walking towards a dozen drawn guns, whistling like the sun shines on you and only you. Everything about his presence put the group on edge, and for Eli the anchor was those goddamn eyes.

v. Shane

Initially, Eli's plan to go out there alone felt crazy to Shane. It wasn't until he started using his words on the pissed-off group that Shane realized that what he was really doing was buying them peace. While instinct told him that camping inside the sheriff's office was the right thing for them to do, the only way that scenario would have ended would be with a massacre. The gang outside would have either barged in shooting or burned the place down with them inside. The only play they had was the gamble Eli took: going out to negotiate a deal between them with the hopes that they didn't blow his head off in the process.

Facing the crowd alone was a smart move, too. If they both went out, they'd be gunned down before a single word was muttered. One unarmed man created a safe atmosphere, one where nobody wants to start shooting unless they want to be deemed a coward, the worst crime in the eyes of a group like this.

Shane had done exactly as Eli commanded, drawing his rifle and keeping it aimed at the leader of the posse. He kept the words *the head of the snake* rolling in his ears, using them as a totem of sanity in case anything went wrong. Shane wasn't a bad shot, but he knew that if things went south, he could only pop off three, *maybe* four of these men, before he'd have to make a retreat to the back without an escape.

Thankfully, it was sounding like Eli had been getting somewhere in his talks, showing the benefit of words over bullets. From what Shane was able to decipher, it seemed like they'd have to exchange the kid's life for their own. It wasn't an ideal outcome, but considering they had brought Kit to Arkell to hang anyway, he figured he'd still be able to sleep at night when it was all over and done with.

Of course, that was before the creepy, whistling loner arrived and changed everything. Suddenly, the idea of a peaceful passage out of Arkell seemed less and less likely.

Everything about the arrival of the well-dressed stranger felt off, his unwelcome presence bringing an uneasy pinch in Shane's bladder. The man's dandy clothing, the contradictory glum-yet-cheerful confederate tune he was whistling, his swagger. Shane had always disapproved of the idea of gunning down an unarmed man, but something about the stranger made him start to rethink the direction his moral compass pointed on the issue.

However, as uneasy he felt about the approaching stranger, Shane stayed true to Eli's wishes and kept his rifle drawn on the leader of the pack. *The head of the snake.*

He started to doubt that the leader was the true threat of the scene, the evil aura of the stranger constantly pulling his focus. While the sight of his rifle kept its aim true, his eyes continued to waver, stealing as many uneasy glances as he could afford at the whistling wanderer.

vi. Dante

The stranger's stroll towards Dante and his men reached the *thats-fucking-close-enough* distance of about ten yards before he stopped, appropriately right as he reached the end of the tune he was whistling. He was but one lone man, yet he somehow had this baker's dozen of outlaws, fuckups, degenerates *and* a lawman in the palm of his hand. The stranger soaked in that energy, letting the silence build anticipation. If he had something to say, he damn well had everyone's attention. Theatrics: a quality Dante could appreciate.

Dante had no idea *who* the stranger was, but he could deduce from his own judgment *what* he was and wasn't.

The sheriff of this town? Not a chance.

Dangerous? Likely.

Stupid? Maybe.

Ballsy? Absolutely.

A threat? To be determined.

Did he want something? More than anything.

Dante knew *exactly* what he wanted. He wanted what they *all* wanted: the cowardly peckerwood hiding inside the sheriff's office who had been cheating the reaper for far too long.

There was no rousing speech from the stranger, nor any grand gesture to accompany his well-orchestrated entrance. Instead, he just stared down Dante and his men, who were all too dumbstruck to say anything as they silently stared back. Even the pathetic marshal kept his hands raised, standing there like a fool between the stranger and the rest of the group.

The silence held past the point of good theatrics that Dante could appreciate and into the realm of being plain uncomfortable. They all continued to stand there, waiting to see who would crack first by breaking the air with their voice.

It was, poetically, Mother Nature who broke the silence. First with a low roll of thunder, followed by a sudden and aggressive downpour of rain. The well-timed shower clouded over the town and began biblically washing the blood on its streets away. Dante couldn't help but laugh at the timing of the storm, taking it as his cue to cut through the impressive but tiring act the new player had been putting on, and getting to the fucking point.

"Son," Dante called out with authority, "I don't know if you're crazy or just plain stupid walking into a confrontation like this, but I'm gonna let you plead ignorance and give you one chance to step aside."

The stranger's face, which started as a blank, handsome

neutral, began to slowly contort into a wide, creepy smile. The words had broken through to him, striking a chord that twinkled in his vacant eyes.

"Stupid?" the stranger asked with little offence. "No, I'm definitely not stupid." He held his contorted grin, giving his ivory-white teeth a lick. "Crazy? Maybe. Maybe you're right about that."

Crazy. That was the goddamn understatement of the night. Up to this point in his life, Dante always believed that a man who referred to himself as crazy was actually quite sane, if cynical. Crazy never addressed itself as such, it just *was*. The grin and vacant eyes of the well-dressed stranger made Dante question that long-held belief.

He could see Doc getting impatient through the corner of his eye, itching to put this creepy cocksucker down. His darker thoughts hoped Doc *would* snap and shoot the prick, but his curiosity of what the stranger wanted had him hoping Doc would be able to show a little more patience.

"He said step aside," Doc ordered with surprising restraint. "He won't be asking again."

The stranger patiently surveyed the group with that shit-eating grin sprawled across his face. Dante didn't like it, feeling more like he was looking at a bunch of prized cattle instead of the threat he should be experiencing. A man who ain't scared when he damn well should be is a dangerous thing.

"I believe y'all have something that belongs to me," the stranger humbly said, finally getting to his fucking point. "You're harboring a weasely little cowpoke who reckons himself a bandit. I'd like him to come with me, please."

"Get in line," Dante snorted. He felt a slight bit of relief knowing that he was right about why the stranger was there, but still had no time to be taking any of his demands. "He's quite popular thanks to the reward on his head."

"Reward?" the stranger chuckled dismissively. "Lord no, I have no interest in such monetary trivialities." The grin contorted wider, his eyes refusing to blink as he spoke in his sickly pleasant tone. "No, see, I want my property back because he's been very naughty, and he should pay the price for it. I plan to spend a couple of days with him as I peel the skin off of his body, layer by layer, inch by inch."

Just another sick fuck in a world full of them.

Dante's patience was beyond gone. He wanted to hear the point, and now that he had, he'd heard more than enough. He drew his rifle on the lone freak, his posse following his lead and doing the same. The stranger, either too slow to react or smart enough to know better, didn't try to retaliate.

"Who the fuck are you?" Dante demanded, his rifle shaking.

"Oh lord, where are my manners?" the stranger responded politely, with a sheepish grin. "Here I am making demands without even introducing myself."

The stranger tipped his hat like a gentleman comfortably in his element.

"Gideon Walker. Pleased to make your acquaintance."

CHAPTER ELEVEN
THE BLOODY WALKER BROTHERS

i. Kit

*T*he horrid whistling had mercifully stopped, replaced not with gunfire but simple conversation. The voices were muffled, calm and indecipherable from the cell. The calmness turned Kit's skin to ice, knowing that it wouldn't last long. He didn't know exactly *what* would be coming, just that it would be coming soon and that they would all wish they were dead when it finally came.

"*Diiaaaboooluuus.*"

He'd only ever heard one other person whistle that old fucking war song before, pining for a horrific time that should be forgotten instead of celebrated. They whistled it with the same inappropriate cheer, a cloud of poison lingering in the air with it. He knew it was the harbinger of doom. It was *them*. He felt it in his bones.

"*Diiaaaboooluuus.*"

Why wouldn't she shut up? How was she not afraid?

He almost felt sorry for her when the whistling began, blissfully unaware that she was just as doomed as everyone else. The company of the infected woman was a dream compared to their new guests. A dream compared to the nightmare of the Walker Brothers.

He'd squeeze through these bars leaving his skin behind to get out of here if he had to. Anything to get away from *them*. His eyes kept drifting to the window in the top corner of the room. It was a way out, but useless to him trapped in this cell.

"*Diiaaaboooluuus.*"

It was still quiet outside. The screaming hadn't started yet.

ii. Eli

Eli felt his mouth go dry when he heard the stranger say his name.

"Walker..." one of the bandits mumbled dumbly, his brain trying to catch up to why he suddenly felt sick to his stomach.

"Of the Bloody Walker Brothers," Dante piped in, completing the dullard's thought. Bravado was still in his voice, but there was now a tinge of fear in it.

Never had Eli ever witnessed a dozen armed men look so uneasy at the sight of one lone individual. They had a right to be afraid, unknowing of what was surely coming. Eli recognized that he was standing smack in the middle of a hostile situation that was ready to explode, unarmed and helplessly waiting for the other shoe to drop.

"I always thought the name *the Death Walkers* had a better ring to it, but it just didn't stick," Gideon mused proudly. "Probably because anyone I ever proposed the new name to ended up dying shortly afterwards."

"I know who you are," Dante said, unimpressed. "I've heard the stories."

"You've heard the stories?" Gideon asked with a growing grin. "Tell me, what do these stories say?"

Eli could feel Dante's uneasiness, thrown off by how eager Gideon was to have his ego stroked with that creepy smile on his face. Dante couldn't help but take the bait.

"They say you're a sick fuck," Dante said bluntly. "That it ain't about the money, it's about the killin'."

Eli could see Dante using all of his willpower to hide his dread as he spat out the next hard truth.

"And that you never leave anyone alive."

Speaking these tales of the bogeyman out loud had Dante's men on edge, but the last note about no survivors was more than they wanted to hear. Without prompt, they all pointed their cocked guns at the lone Walker brother. They were tired of his threats, and more than a little worried that they might actually be true.

Eli carefully surveyed the hostile situation without making any sudden movements, his eyes hopelessly scanning the area for any potential escape. He knew damn well there ain't a lot of options for a man stuck right in the middle of what feels like a trap that's ready to go off at any moment.

iii. Shane

Nothing like a common enemy to bring rivals together, Shane thought, comforting himself in believing it was true, with all arms aimed at the newcomer. The setting was a powder keg, and it wouldn't take much to spark up a gunfight with all of the tension out there. He hoped the stranger had enough of a silver tongue to avoid any bloodshed, at least long enough for Eli to slip out of there alive.

Just use your words, he kept thinking as he looked down his rifle sight.

His focus shifted when something else caught his eye. He wasn't sure what gave off the reflection, the slight glimmer of a metallic sheen begging for his attention off in the distance. It was tucked snuggly in the alley across from them, between the buildings, easy enough to dismiss if the situation hadn't amplified every one of his senses, to make the slightest of movements stand out.

"The hell is that?" he whispered to himself, squinting to try to make out what it was.

iv. Bronco

That moment when they finally figured out what was about to happen to them was always the most satisfying feeling for Bronco. He had shot many men, women, and even children in the back before, but it wasn't nearly as rewarding as looking at them head-on and taking in that moment when they suddenly realized what was about to happen to them. It wasn't the fear that he enjoyed the most, but the *disbelief*. No matter how many people he killed, no matter how clear he made it to them that this was their unavoidable fate, none of them actually *believed* it was going to happen to them, right up until the end. The ignorant disbelief of death when it was staring right into their eyes was a human emotion like none other, and one Bronco never grew tired of inflicting.

The sheep were perfectly lined up in front of the sheriff's, just about to go through the same predictable experience of denying their reality. Bronco knew they wouldn't believe it would be their time either, even when it would begin and they'd watch each other being mowed down. *I'll get away,* they'd each think, just as they always did. They'd believe it, filled with an adrenaline that blinded them from accepting the truth. Their last thoughts were never about their mortality. They were about their survival.

He watched Gideon enjoying himself, spilling his exploits

and building up his legend as he toyed with the soon-to-be-dead men. Gideon may have been a fucking ham that loved the sound of his own voice a little too much, but Bronco accepted that it was just part of who his brother was. They'd fought together, robbed together, killed together and on several occasions, almost died together. Gideon always did his job, and he did it well. He earned the right to be a fucking showy asshole once in a while.

His wagon was filled to the brim with everything they could have possibly needed for tonight, and more. It might have been a little excessive, but a good survivor knows that it's always better to be over-prepared and have too much instead of not enough. Watching Gideon spin his yarn to over a dozen men reassured him that this was the right call. No matter how loaded their arsenal was, they were still heavily outnumbered. Amongst the supplies weighing down the loaded wagon was a healthy amount of dynamite, a few barrels of gunpowder and the true star of the show: his beauty that he had affectionately named *Peggy*.

Peggy was a beautiful instrument of death called a Gatling gun, an incredible weapon unlike any other he'd used before. He had never experienced anything as efficient and exhilarating as firing this man-made bringer of death. Spring-loaded with eight barrels, you hand cranked the fucker to pour a rain of gunfire on any poor bastard in your way. Be that a dozen poor bastards? Sure, *Peggy* here could handle that, no problem.

They had stolen *Peggy* from a militia group and damn near got themselves killed doing so, something Gideon never tired of reminding Bronco about. But now that he was standing here with her fully loaded with a belt of 7.8mm bullets looking down at his targets, only reaffirmed to him that the whole episode was worth it.

He patiently aimed her down at the unsuspecting men,

comforted by the fact that he was equipped with a whole wagon full of weapons that he was just itching to use.

Thankfully that itch was about to be scratched.

v. Silas

Silas still had his reservations about hanging the man that saved Maggie's life in Blackcreek, even after discovering that he was the monster responsible for the Silverton massacre. He never admitted it when his savior was taken away by the marshal, but he felt a sense of relief that the man's blood wouldn't be on his hands. So why the hell did he agree to ride with Dante all the way to Arkell to retrieve him?

He'd tried to justify it with a half dozen reasons, but the real answer was money. Of course, he was afraid to say no to Dante, as Dante wasn't the type of man you said *no* to, but Silas knew in his heart that the real reason he had agreed to go was the promise of that big fat reward. With a little money in his pocket, he could picture himself as a more attractive prospect to a gal like Maggie, proving to her that he wasn't just another degenerate that hung around Arlo's bar, but rather a true provider. He didn't feel great about hunting down the man who saved her life, but he was more than willing to make that deal with the devil if it meant he had her admiration and her hand.

Unfortunately, every part of the journey had made him regret his decision to go along. Most of the men he was traveling with were assholes, and if they weren't assholes, they were scary as hell, like that big bastard Doc who looked like he'd gouge your eyes out if you looked at him wrong. Plus, there had been the hot goddamn midday sun beating down on them, and very little downtime to rest the hell up.

The journey had been bad, but none of it nearly as a bad as reaching Arkell, which was a fucking nightmare from the moment they got there. From the dead boy on the outskirts to the blood-soaked streets, the whole place made his skin crawl. He was hoping they could pick up their prize and get the hell out of there, only to be met by the creepy, smiling asshole claiming to be one of the fucking Walker Brothers. At this point, he just wanted Dante to shoot this cocksucker dead, forget the bounty and head on home to Maggie. Unfortunately, their exchange gave Silas a bad feeling that it wasn't going to be that easy.

"They said all that about little old me?" the creepy stranger asked proudly after hearing Dante lay down his reputation. The cutesy tone of it made Silas feel sick in his guts.

"They did," Dante said, his gun pointed firmly at the bastard's head. "Hell of a reputation if I may say so myself."

Dante cocked the hammer on his pistol. *Please God let him do it,* Silas thought. *Shoot the bastard dead and be done with it.*

"You forgot one thing," the man corrected, that fucking smile still planted on his face.

"Yeah?" Dante chuckled in exhausted disbelief. "What's that?"

"My brother Bronco always travels with me."

Silas heard the whizzing of multiple projectiles fly by his head, smashing into the wall behind him before the accompanying, thunderous *BANGS* shattered his eardrums. He felt numb, everything slowly moving at a beautiful, almost frozen speed around him. His stomach felt warm, like it was full of a top-shelf whiskey reserved for men of a status he would never be a part of. It took him a moment to realize he'd been hit. He looked down to see the exit wounds of several bullets tearing through his belly – two, three, four and finally five.

His body tingled; he felt invincible. His knees wobbled before they gave out and brought him to the ground. He fell at a gentle pace, the mud below welcoming him like a pile of pillows. It should have been loud. There should have been the deafening sound of earth-shattering gunfire. He should have heard panic and screaming. But all he heard was ringing. Ringing and a bright light creeping into his vision, contradicting the dark and stormy night sky. He was cold, a comforting feeling as he thought of that mid-day sun.

It was nice. He dreamt of Maggie and closed his eyes to rest.

vi. Eli

There was a near-fatal delay in Eli's brain that didn't register what was happening at first, before survival instinct kicked in, forcing his body to move before his brain caught up. He quickly scurried for cover behind a stack of barrels as the rapid gunfire rained down, filling the night sky with a deafening roar of endless bullets tearing through the air into anything in their path.

A beautiful glow from the source lit up the alleyway, the crack of every bullet singing at an ear-piercing volume that drowned out the screaming. The chaos paired beauty and horror in an unlikely dance as every man tried to make sense of what was going on. Panic rose in their throats while they fought fear and tried to wrestle control of themselves to survive. It was a fucking bloodbath.

Eli had barely made it to his temporary sanctuary when he watched four members of the Blackcreek gang instantly ripped to shreds by the barrage of bullets. The speed and frequency of the shots tore their bodies into a mangled mess of meat and tattered clothing. What was left of their lifeless husks fell, splattering their inelegant mess across the dirt one after the other.

As each desperate man fled for cover, Eli watched Gideon Walker join in the participation of the massacre, a twisted smile stretching to his ears. One poor son-of-a-bitch tried to run, only to have Gideon aim his pistol and shoot him in the back of the head, sending brain matter splattering in every direction.

One of the drunks Eli vaguely recognized from Blackcreek, clearly out of his element, wisely cut his losses and tried to make a break from the group. He didn't stand a chance, a grim reminder that even the fastest man can't outrun a bullet. The gunfire from the alley turned, catching the lost soul and turning his fleeing body into torn meat. Dead and already forgotten among his peers, his blood became another stain in the soiled Arkell streets.

Taking advantage of the split second afforded to them from the gunfire's change of direction, the surviving members of the posse scrambled to find whatever pathetic bits of nearby cover they could as they fired blindly towards the alley. Through the chaos, a handful of men emerged from the bar across the street and joined in the gunfight, rushing into the madness and firing at Dante's men, who were cowering in cover from the incoming hail of death.

Bullets whizzed by Eli; he couldn't afford to steal a peek to see which direction they were coming from. He clenched his pistol, knowing a safe shot or escape wasn't likely. He thought of the bottle of whiskey in the sheriff's office. It felt like the only thing that had gotten him this far, a beacon to fight for. He needed it to survive. He'd kill every man here if it meant he could have one more swig from it.

vii. Kit

Kit thought he had gone deaf, his ears ringing under the barrage of chaos crashing through the glass and brick out front. He lay hopelessly on the floor of his cell, praying that none of the stray bullets would strike him. A cancerous thought crept into the back of his mind, telling him that this would be a better end than if the Walker Brothers made it back here.

The old woman continued her poisonous chanting, as fearless of the incoming hailstorm as she was of the infectious sores polluting her naked body. Kit wished one of the bullets would strike her skull, delivering him a slight bit of peace before his inevitable death. But the fatal bullet never came

The time to be stoic was gone. He forced himself to scream, praying his captors had the empathy to see he wasn't the real threat now.

"Get me out of here!" he hollered until his vocal cords were raw. "Get me the fuck out of here!"

viii. Eli

It was impossible to tell who was firing at whom from where Eli hid as hell continued to rain on Arkell. A few moments of reprieve saw a brave soul here and there try to make a move, only to have the gunfire start back up and send any survivors scurrying back to safety like mice. They were all pinned down and knew it would all come down to making a break for it when you saw some other poor bastard meeting his maker.

Eli scanned his surroundings, his eyes drifting to the sheriff's. His only chance at survival would be if he could make it there. He just prayed to God that Shane was still alive to join him.

ix. Shane

Shane hugged the ground, helplessly covering his head as chunks of wood and glass showered down on him.

"Help!" he heard the kid shouting from the back cell, under the riotous sound of combat. "Get me the fuck out of here!"

Returning any sort of cover fire as bullets tore through the office wasn't an option. He knew any wrong movement would end in his death, but with each precious second passing it was becoming clear that staying out front was no longer a safe option. He could die lying down here like a coward or he could die fighting.

He clutched his rifle tightly, hopelessly wondering if Eli was still out there. He forced himself to ignore the blood and glass that littered the entire floor and began to slide across it on his belly like a snake. Sharp bits of glass dug into his stomach as he pulled himself towards the back with his elbows, one slow inch at a time. The next forty seconds felt like hours. His eardrums were ready to burst, and each shard of glass made itself known with every part of his body it pierced. He dragged his body through hell, feeling every inch of the journey. He passed through the blood, the entrails, and finally made his way past the corpse of the mutilated sheriff, while thunderous shots passed above.

The sins of his past had brought him here, moment by moment, inch by inch, sin by sin. He had thought the barn of rotting corpses was his penance, his own personal hell, only to find himself here in a new circle. He feared what the next layer would be if he managed to make it out of here alive.

Kit's screams became clearer as Shane finally made his way through the back door into the holding cell area. The putrid, sour milk smell of the old woman's sores mixed with gunpowder and fear made him feel lightheaded.

"C'mon!" Kit pleaded upon seeing Shane. "You gotta get me outta here."

Shane hated how long he hesitated. While it wasn't exactly safe back here, the layer of bricks from the additional wall allowed some room to pivot and help the kid out. So why did he hesitate? The time of 'sides' went out the window the second a fucking Gatling gun came into the picture.

"If it's about money, fuck it – I'll give you the whole haul if we make it out of here alive," Kit begged.

Money was the last thing on Shane's mind, and he could see from the desperate look in the kid's eyes that it didn't matter to him either. He'd give away all the gold in the world if it would get him out of that cage.

"You're going to need as much help as you can get against those fucking maniacs. We're well beyond laws and bounties at this point," Kit pleaded, trying to stay as cool as he could in the situation. "Let me out to die fighting with some dignity, instead of stuck in here with *her*."

Shane was sold, feeling foolish that it had taken him this long to agree. He unlocked the cell door and drew his pistol, confidently handing it over to his former prisoner.

"Don't make me regret it," Shane said as Kit gracefully accepted the gun.

x. Bronco

Bronco's arm felt like jelly from the repetitive turning of the crank. He'd spent significant time training himself how to use *Peggy*, mastering both the control and crank, but he'd never continuously fired her for this long. Even with a brilliant machine that simplified the task, killing was hard work.

The final *clink* of the last shell, followed by the softer *clack-clack-clack-clack* of the empty chamber, didn't register in his ringing ears at first as he had fallen into a soothing rhythm from the repetitive crack of each bullet. It was only when the ringing died down that he realized that he was out of ammo.

"Shit," he muttered to himself, the euphoria quickly evaporating.

Without wasting any more precious seconds, he retrieved another belt of the high-caliber bullets and started reloading with militant precision. He knew that it put him in a vulnerable spot, but if he did things as rapidly and efficiently as he had trained himself to, he'd have enough time to tear down anyone stupid enough to take a rush at him.

It was mid-reload that he began to feel the presence of something nearby. Not a person, but something else in the air. Something foreign. Something unknown.

A deafening sound unlike any he had ever heard before hit his ears. It was a sound beyond the gunshots that had been echoing through the rainy night sky. Those sounded slight compared to this. This was something alive. Something primal.

CHAPTER TWELVE

A NEW GUEST IN TOWN

i. Kit

*N*ot that it made much of a difference with the miserable odds they faced, but Kit was grateful to have the pistol in his hand. The heavy weight of the iron was comforting, guiding his confidence like a compass to try to figure a way out of this mess. If he were to die tonight, the tool in his hand ensured he'd at least die fighting on his feet rather than crouching back here alongside the old, rotten witch.

The firing of the Gatling gun had momentarily stopped, allowing them a brief window to try to make an escape and find Eli. Leaving the sheriff's may have been a dangerous plan, but Kit felt confident that it beat the hell out of staying back here like frightened mice cornered by the family cat.

That confidence died when they heard the *sound*.

Kit had never heard anything like it before, the foreign *roar* echoing through the air like an approaching storm. It rang over the commotion in the streets, reverberating with a shivering crack like lighting making an example out of an ancient, powerful tree. His first reaction was something grounded, that it was the angry cry of some sort of animal. It was deep, making him wonder if it came from a bear, but what would a bear be doing this close to town? And if it *was* a bear, it seemed impossible that they would be able to hear it from inside, beneath the hail of gunfire.

"What the hell was that?" he asked, his tongue dry with fear.

The roar awoke something in the old woman, sparking a fresh breath of life in her. It was speaking to her, shaking her from the waking slumber she had been in. She promptly stood, responding like an excited dog taking orders, desperate to please. Her eyes were now alert, lucid underneath their milky fog.

"Dia-bo-lus," she spoke, clear as a bell.

Her eyes now had purpose in a way Kit didn't like.

"C'mon," Shane said, somehow forcing his brain to ignore her, "we gotta find Eli."

ii. Dante

"He's out of ammo!" Dante shouted like an enthusiastic general to whoever might still be alive. "Move! Move!"

The survivors didn't hesitate to take advantage of their small window. They all emerged from their hiding places like rabbits and began charging the alleyway, guns ready.

Dirty fucker thought he was pretty clever ambushing us with a chain gun, Dante thought. *Let's see how he deals with a rush.*

An ear-shattering *ROAR* echoed through the air, bringing their blitz to a halt. It was painfully loud, like a cannon shot right next to your ear. The awful, animalistic sound screamed in close proximity, causing every man to stop and freeze in their place.

"What the fuck was that?" Dante demanded, his voice showing more fear than he'd ever revealed before.

He was answered by another *ROAR* hitting the air. It sounded closer, smothering them from all sides. Dante couldn't decide if they should attack or run. Logic told him to keep moving while they had a chance, but as all eyes focused on their target, a giant shadow engulfed the entirety of the alley. The sight told his brain that he should be anywhere but here if his life meant anything to him.

iii. Shane

Shane ignored the hundreds of tiny shards his body absorbed as they crawled back through the path of blood and glass-littered hell to the front of the sheriff's office. While the oppressive firing of the Gatling gun had mercifully stopped, they didn't risk standing up from their painful trench in case it started back up again.

Their focus on survival didn't appear to be shared by the old woman, who fearlessly emerged from the back, disregarding any potential threats as she walked towards the front of the office. Shane thought he had done the right thing by freeing her, only to watch her foolishly march towards her own death.

"Diaaaboolus," she gurgled, lumbering towards the front door.

Let her get herself killed Shane thought. They had their own skin to worry about.

iv. Eli

"Jesus Christ," Eli gasped as he watched the shadow engulf the entirety of the alley.

He couldn't make out what he was looking at, his brain refusing to understand what could cast a shadow of that size. He felt all eyes gazing on the alley, fear and curiosity overtaking the group's opportunist mindset of charging it. Rushing while the Gatling gun had halted may have been their only chance at surviving, but now the thought of entering the mouth of darkness seemed incomprehensible.

A bloodcurdling scream erupted from the alley, cutting through the shared silence and echoing terror through the night sky. It was a grown man, reduced to a child, experiencing a level of agony none of them had known before in their lives. It was forged by pain and fear melting together, contagious to a degree that left Eli short of breath just hearing it.

Loud, destructive sounds of smashing wood accompanied the scream, paired with chaotic thrashing. For a brief moment, everyone stopped caring about killing each other while they tried to focus on the dark, frantic mess. They collectively attempted to make sense of what they were or were not seeing, silently watching in horrified awe.

With the trembling hands of boys pretending to be men, they readied their rifles and pistols for whatever was to come. Together, they all aimed in a collective, unspoken agreement that registered them as allies, united by a peace treaty inked in fear.

Everyone except for Gideon.

The cocky, well-dressed bringer of chaos had dropped his smarmy grin. He didn't care about *what* was in the alley. He was only afraid of what it was doing there.

"Bronco..." he muttered with an awful realization.

One last, horrific scream shot from the alley through the air like a high caliber bullet before the night rain drowned it out. The scream rang, gurgled, and then was cut short by the silence of death. Whoever made it would never scream again.

"Bronco!" Gideon hollered into the alley. He cocked his pistol, ready to face the devil alone if he had to.

His plea to his brother was answered, but not in the way he had hoped.

A large, free-flowing object was flung from the alley, capturing everyone's pure, unfiltered attention. It had been tossed with tremendous strength, bucking in the air at least thirty feet high. It flew in a messy arc towards the sheriff's, violently turning in the rain. It was difficult to identify what it was until it came crashing down to the earth.

Only when it splattered to the ground with a heavy, squishy *thud* was Eli able to make out that it was the mangled bottom half of a man's body. It had been ripped at the belly line, leaving red ropes of intestine tugged out of gnashed wounds. The torso skidded along the earth, painting another layer of gore onto streets that had already seen their fair share that night.

Seeing the legs of the dead man effortlessly tossed like a disposed chicken carcass had everyone's full attention. Most of the surviving men on the bloody streets had never seen a body mutilated to this degree. They remained still, waiting for whatever did this to come out of the alley and reveal itself. Every trigger finger itched like they were being held in a mosquito nest.

The silence broke when the sheriff's door burst open. Eli was amazed that the collective ball of nerves didn't snap and cause every gun to start shooting. Instead, they all watched as the naked old woman, covered in her putrid wounds, stumbled out into the street.

"Dia-bo-lus," she chanted madly. "Dia-bo-lus."

Fear curdled within the heart of every man there. They were all out of their element, knee-deep in shit and unsure of which direction to wade. The unsettling sight of the woman's naked, pus-covered body was too much for most of them to comprehend on top of everything they had already seen that night. They dumbly watched her wander right into the middle of the street and drop to her hands and knees. She lowered her head, chanting her God-forsaken prayer.

"Dia-bo-lus."

They watched her in a shared hypnotic daze. Her calm chants to whichever devil she spoke to felt almost comforting, knowing that she could find a grounded peace in the madness. The silence of the surreal scene was quickly interrupted by another one of the nightmarish *roars* in the alley, followed by a loud and rhythmic *THUD-THUD-THUD,* like massive footsteps shaking the earth.

The rain poured harder, a blinding blanket of water cloaking the town. Eli felt like it was a trick from God, laying down a layer to obscure the image of evil emerging. At first it worked, masking the shape of what was emerging from the alleyway. The layer of darkness and shadows through the rain made it difficult to make out any of its defining features, but it was also the sheer unnaturalness of the thing that made it impossible for the brain to register what it was seeing.

An implausible mix of imagination and nightmare that no one had ever witnessed with waking eyes stepped forth and let itself be seen. Everyone froze in terror, unsure of what to make of the *thing* that seemed too terrible to be real. When it finally stepped out of the darkness into clear view, every last man froze in stupefied awe. The monsters they feared in the dark from their childhood were real, and the worst of them was now standing before them.

Eli didn't know what the hell he was looking at. The only word he could think of was *creature*, but that seemed too simplistic to describe the horror before him.

Devil?

God?

His brain was pounding worse than all of the countless hangovers he ever experienced mashed together, wanting to explode out of his ears from the sheer disbelief of what it was trying to process.

This isn't real. It can't be real, he thought, *but if it isn't real, how is it standing here in front of us now?*

The only rational thing he could compare it to was some sort of bear, though the sheer size of the thing in question made that impossible. The creature stood effortlessly on its hind legs at a height three times taller than any bear he'd ever heard of, and at least twice as wide. Fuck no, this was no bear.

The front limbs of the thing looked more like arms than legs, blurring the image of animal and human together. Whatever the limbs were, they were equipped with sharp claws on the end of what appeared to be a cross between paws and hooves. Rotting antlers penetrated through fresh wounds on the top of the creature's massive head, poking through the skull like a crown of thorns.

Eli tried to make sense of the thing's face, his mind accepting it as the combination of something between a warthog and a wolf. He was mesmerized by its large, protruding snout and mouthful of glass-sharp teeth. Then there was the most captivating part of its grisly face: its eyes. The creature's eyes were depthless like a snake, their color a piercing, vile yellow that sank your heart to the pit of your bowels.

The skin of the thing stank, an unholy and illogical mix of organic flesh and plant. The *flesh* of its skin was visibly rotting; pus and viscous crimson poured from countless wounds, which had thick vines and roots like that of a tree woven throughout. The mixture of root and flesh intertwined painfully throughout the creature's body, perfectly coming together to create one awful, symbiotic entity.

Eli knew this was his only opportunity to make a run for the sheriff's while everyone else was captivated by the unnatural sight. But he didn't move. He just stared at the creature in all of its unholy and improbable glory.

v. Shane

When Shane finally built up the courage to peer through the boards, he instantly regretted the decision. His brain felt like it had cracked open like an egg, scrambled from the insanity he saw. None of what hit his eyes could be real, because there was no logical way he could describe it. But he wasn't the only one observing what he wished was a figment of his imagination. Every man outside shared his same, stupid look of awe as they stared at *it*.

His mind began to race for answers. How could everyone be sharing the same hallucination? Was he even really here or was this a dream? Maybe a bullet had struck his brain, and this was all part of the journey into hell, as he drifted to the other side. They say to pinch yourself to wake up if you think you may be dreaming, but he felt so numb watching the horrid vision that he couldn't bring himself to move.

He wanted to scream. Scream like a child, scream to wake up. But he couldn't.

He just watched.

vi. Dante

Time froze as every man on the bloody battlefield stared at the impossible *thing* that had emerged from the alleyway.

What the fuck is it? Dante wanted to know, his face agape like a goddamned imbecile.

The creature stepped away from its hiding spot and took a large stride towards the center of town. It let out another of its deafening roars, sending ripples through the puddles of rain and blood. Dante knew he should take charge, be a leader and step up to put this fucking thing down. Instead, he froze in place, his hand too stiff to draw.

It was Doc who snapped out of the united stare, summoning the courage that nobody else could muster. Not out of leadership, commitment, or egotistical bullshit; it was instinct. Doc was a man born and bred to kill, and this creature was made to put those skills to the ultimate test.

"What the fuck are you waiting for?" Doc screamed, fearlessly raising his rifle. "Kill the fucking thing!"

Without the better sense to hesitate, he began firing at the beast with his trusted repeater rifle.

BANG-CRANK-BANG-CRANK-BANG-CRANK

He didn't waste words, mechanically cranking to reload with each precise shot. Each bullet soaked into the thing like a sponge. It didn't matter how many shots he fired at it, the bullets had no effect on the creature except to make it visibly angry.

It shifted its yellow eyes to Doc. Pissed off and with a prey to focus on, it began to charge.

In all their years riding together, Dante had never once seen Doc afraid. He knew Doc had to be feeling something right now, but to his credit, he was doing a hell of a job at hiding it as he watched death charge at him. Recognizing that the rifle wasn't doing shit, Doc tossed it aside and reached for one of the sticks of dynamite on his belt that he'd insisted on hauling all the way from Blackcreek.

He was too late.

The creature leaped at Doc, effortlessly snatching its incredible jaws around his torso like a dog with a rabbit. Doc managed to give out the beginning of a scream before going silent as the thing bit down. His stomach burst open, disemboweling his hot guts into the dirt like discarded waste. The toughest man Dante ever met, dead with the squeak of a mouse.

"Fuck this!" Gideon spat, looking tired of waiting and ready for war.

He lurched forward and fired his pistol at the creature, his eyes filled with purpose instead of fear. The re-ignition of gunfire miraculously broke everyone out of their trance, aligning them to raise their arms and start firing at the thing together.

Bullets penetrated the beast from every direction, making it angrier with each shot it absorbed. It let out another ear-piercing howl, leaping at one poor soul and ripping him apart in mere seconds. Another poor son-of-a-bitch tried to run before he was quickly intercepted by the creature's long, sharp claws, which snatched him with cat-like precision. It pulled its latest victim towards its deadly maw with lethal efficiency.

Amongst the chaos of the gunfire, fleeing and hiding, the thing managed to sense everyone and their movements with deadly speed and accuracy. It spotted Charlie bravely making a run to the alleyway for the Gatling gun, leaping in front of him with impossible speed and freezing him in his soon-to-be-dead tracks. It took a quick swipe with its front claws at him, ripping his body cleanly in half like a sheet of paper. Intestines and blood splattered across the ground as the thing quickly set its sights on its next victim.

It was a fucking massacre.

vii. Eli

Eli longed for the hail of Gatling gunfire that had started the bloodshed. At least with gunfire, the victims had a shot in hell. As fast as a bullet is, it only travels in one direction. A living creature has senses — sight, smell, *taste* — and those senses can find you no matter which direction you run. Now those senses were finding *everyone* and making a meal of them.

Everyone but the old woman.

The blood-soaked streets saw every scrambling soul fleeing for their lives, yet there she was in the middle of it, calm, naked, praying, chanting, ignoring. She might as well have been praying in a church. She wasn't afraid, her fearlessness drawing Eli to an unsettling conclusion. She didn't mind the creature and the creature didn't mind her. Whatever the bond was between them, it was mutual and understood.

His thoughts on the old woman were shoved aside when the severed head of a young man splattered to the ground beside him. Its eyes were still open, looking right at him.

Hello Eli, the dead man's eyes said playfully, *are you ready to join me? Rolling around like this is so much better than crouching like a coward.*

They were making sense, and what they were really telling him was, that he had to get the fuck out of there.

Every eye and iron in town was on the creature, desperate to get in any shot they could. The gunfire was futile and any time someone made a run for it, the thing effortlessly caught up with them and mutilated them with humiliating efficiency. Eli convinced himself that their problem was focusing too much on the beast and not enough on where they were going.

Pretend it isn't there, he heard the eyes of the decapitated head tell him, *worry about where you're going instead.*

I'm going to the sheriff's, he responded in his own head.

Getting to the sheriff's was all that mattered right now. If Shane was still alive, he'd be in there. Eli shifted his focus away from the decapitated head and drowned out all other distractions.

The gunfire, the screaming, the crunching of bone and flesh between teeth. Put it out of your mind and worry about where you're going. You're going to the sheriff's, and there's nothing in your way to stop you.

He took a deep breath, waiting for another scream to signal that the creature was temporarily distracted.

The scream came and he made his run for it.

CHAPTER THIRTEEN
REUNITED

i. Shane

Thee was a unified, unspoken agreement in the air. While every single iron in Arkell had wanted to kill them mere minutes ago, Shane knew without exchanging a word that none of their differences mattered anymore. All that mattered was putting *it* down — whatever *it* was.

Shane and Kit frantically fired through the window boards, contributing what little they could to help bring the fucking thing down. Neither questioned their motives, nor spoke about it, silently fulfilling their duty in taking down the common threat while hoping it didn't shift its deadly focus their way.

With their attention absorbed in trying to kill the thing, they both leapt with surprise when the front door burst open. If Shane's gun hadn't been jammed through the slits in the boards, he was sure he would have turned and fired at their visitor out of instinct.

He was thankful he didn't.

"You're alive!" he exclaimed, ecstatic at the ghost he saw.

It was Eli, looking terrible with shock but thankfully unwounded as far as Shane could tell.

"Barely," he responded dryly. Shane was unsure if there was any humor intended or not.

"What the fuck is that thing?" Shane asked, knowing there wasn't an answer in this world that would satisfy him.

Eli shut the door behind him and ran towards the window to steal a peek from their vantage point.

"I don't know what the hell it is," he answered, "but we have to barricade this place up as best we can. Ain't nothing or no one out there that means us anything but harm. Is there any other way for it to get in here?"

"No," Shane reassured. "There's a tiny window in the back, but outside of that, the front door and windows are the only way in."

"Or out," the kid added grimly.

"Alright, at least we won't be ambushed," Eli said. "Let's barricade as much shit in front of the door as we can."

Shane didn't argue, grabbing one end of a nearby table while Eli took the other. It was heavy, which felt like a good sign. Eli took the lead, waddling backwards with the heavy piece towards the door while Shane followed.

"Grab that chair," Eli ordered the kid, "along with anything else you can find."

Eli positioned his end of the table by the door, dropping it in place and grabbing at his back. It was a slightly relaxed pose, his body appearing to breathe for the first time since they arrived in Arkell.

He paid for that moment of relaxation seconds later.

The door swung open with violent force, throwing Eli to the ground. The creature's horned head burst through, forcing its way through the doorway. It gnashed its horrific jaws at Eli, slashing a deep cut into his belly as Shane and Kit watched helplessly.

Eli desperately tried to stand, slipping in a fresh puddle of his own blood that he didn't even realize had formed with how quickly everything happened. The creature took advantage of the slip, snapping its jaws firmly around his torso.

"Eli!" Shane screamed.

He drew his rifle on the beast, aiming as it butchered his friend. He looked for a clear shot.

The creature bit down, Eli vomiting blood that paired with the red pool simultaneously pouring from his chest. There wasn't time to wait for a clean shot, Shane would have to just trust his aim.

BANG. BANG. BANG.

Shane and Kit fired repeatedly at the awful thing's head, hoping to hell they could draw its attention away from Eli. The shots appeared to pain the beast, but they weren't enough to get it to release its deadly grip.

It clenched its jaws harder, Eli's guts spilling out of his belly. He screamed for what remained of his life as loud as his punctured, gurgling lungs would allow.

Desperate, Shane defied good sense and reached out and grabbed his friend by the arm. Like a puppy playing a game, the creature tugged back effortlessly and ripped the arm clean off. Eli's screams were weakening, Shane unsure if they were even still happening or if he just wished they were as a sign of life. The severed limb dropped to the ground with a thud.

They kept firing at the thing, but it was futile. It reached an angry claw inside the door frame and pulled with all of its strength, gleefully gorging on its meal. It gave another tug, ripping the bottom half of Eli's torso away from the top, which sloppily fell to the ground. Shane looked in horror into his friend's vacant eyes. The dead stare told him it was over for Marshal Eli Cooke.

"Fuck!" Kit screamed, his voice a distant ring in Shane's ear as the thing struggled to pull itself further inside.

The two men unloaded their guns on the thing while it furiously squeezed itself further through the door frame, thrashing and snapping its lethal jaws every inch of the way. Shane watched dumbly, the thing now nearly halfway inside, before Kit violently pulled him out of the way of a near fatal snap.

"C'mon," Kit screamed. "He's gone, we have to move."

ii. Eli

This wasn't what Eli imagined it would be like; the great darkness, *the end*. You tried not to think about it too much in life, but it always found a way to creep into your thoughts when your head hit the pillow.

As a lawman, he'd encountered a lot of people in this position, and they'd almost always talk to him as their story concluded. They'd say the things you'd expect. They were scared. They were ready. Many babbled on about nothing, speaking nonsense like it was poetic. A lot of them said they felt cold, which was funny because Eli didn't just feel cold right now but also really *hot*. The blood in particular felt very warm as it pooled into his cupped hand along with a mushy, meaty substance that he realized must be his organs. He was sweating from the heat but also *freezing* at the same time. He'd never felt anything like it before, nor would he again.

None of it hurt. It was more of a tingle that ran through his entire body, allowing him to feel a numb buzz simultaneously in every part of himself. He felt an adrenaline high like that wonderful feeling you get from having a drink when you haven't had one in a really long time. Dizzy, good.

He wasn't scared, only confused. He heard people talk about seeing a light, but instead it was only getting darker. He was confused because he was waiting, but the thing he was waiting for wasn't coming.

He had always imagined that he'd see Ada again at this moment. That they'd be reunited and could run off together in the realm beyond. They'd be happy once again. He waited, seconds the speed of hours, the rest of the world and chaos gone from him. He had thought he'd see her again, even if it was just once more. But he didn't.

He only saw darkness.

iii. Kit

The horrific sound of the thing forcing its way into the sheriff's office pounded in Kit's ears as they retreated to the back holding cells. The smashing, creaking sound of the front door breaking off its hinges made it clear that they had mere seconds before it would make its way inside.

They were drenched in blood belonging to the dead marshal, which made it difficult for them to look at each other as they desperately searched for an escape route.

"Shit, there's no way out." Shane's voice was panicked, the color gone from his face.

There's no way out. Bullshit. Kit didn't accept the words. There was always a way out. How could he forget the escape that held his focus through every chant, gunshot, and scream tonight? He *knew* there was a way out, he had been fixated on it from the very moment they locked him up back here. He remembered the window that held his imagination for every single second he was trapped in the cell with *her*. It may have been boarded-up, out of reach and perhaps too small to fit through, but it was *there*.

"Up there," Kit instructed, pointing to the window in the corner.

It looked even smaller now that the idea of trying to fit through it was rapidly becoming a reality. The violent sound of crunching brick from the front entrance being tested swept any doubts they had away. Shane ran to the window and bent down on one knee, cupping his hands together to create a boost.

"C'mon," Shane ordered. "I'll lift you up."

Kit didn't question him, running over and taking a step into Shane's hand. He was impressed by the old timer's strength as he managed to lift him with seemingly little effort. God bless the supernatural adrenaline you got when death was nipping at your heels.

He reached eye level with the window, greeted by a rotten board of wood hammered into place by a pair of nails that were rusted to shit. He attempted to pull it, his fingers instantly beginning to blister from its refusal to budge.

"Open it!" Shane demanded.

Kit didn't appreciate the obvious orders. It wasn't like he was sitting up here with his dick in his hand.

"I'm tryin'," he screamed as he struggled to rip the goddamn thing off. "It's fucking stuck."

The thrashing was getting worse, more immediate. Kit put everything he had into pulling the board free, using that perfect combination of strength, adrenaline, and fear to force it to give. He couldn't help but grin when it finally came loose, giving him a good look at how narrow the window really was up close as he tossed the board aside.

Shane gave Kit an extra boost, sending him through the small opening face first. The fit was tight, but Kit had experienced his share of narrow escapes, giving him the training to know how to maneuver his way through. He wiggled rhythmically like a worm, breathing in the night air full of smoke and gunpowder until he fell through.

There was nothing on the other side to catch his fall, sending him on a clumsy tumble face down onto his belly. He was winded, his mouth filled with the taste of dirt and blood.

Never had a painful drop felt so good.

iv. Shane

Shane felt numb, still unsure if the hellish nightmare he just witnessed really happened. He had a memory of watching the creature mutilate Eli in front of him, but something that grotesque and horrible couldn't have been real. But if it wasn't real, why was he covered in Eli's blood? The question made his brain shut down, his body working automatically to do what had to be done. He was in survival mode.

He heard the heavy *thud* of Kit hitting the ground on the other side of the window. The kid made it, but Shane immediately felt regret that he may have made a fatal mistake. How the hell was *he* going to get out now? He was alone in here with no boost to the window and no way out. What was to stop the kid from cutting and running?

He stupidly waited for Kit to return, each second dragging for an eternity.

Nothing.

The thrashing grew angrier.

He felt like an idiot, pissed that he'd die hating himself for making the stupid goddamned mistake of trusting an outlaw. Why would the kid come back? After all, they *did* bring him here to hang.

Well played kid, enjoy the last laugh, he thought, *Eli and I will keep a spot in hell warm for you.*

A loud *crunch* followed by a *crash* made it clear that the creature had managed to get itself inside. He was out of time.

More infinitely long seconds passed. Still nothing from the kid.

He felt large footsteps wearing on the floorboards lumbering towards the back. This was it. It knew he was back here.

Still no kid.

Every last bit of common sense his mama taught him told him he should remain fucking silent right now, but he couldn't help it. He couldn't keep his screams in any longer, they had to escape before they burst through his chest.

"Hey!" he screamed to no one and everyone, "You can't just fucking leave me here!"

The thudding, heavy footsteps drew closer. Shane could feel them shaking the floor from where he stood. The end would be soon now. Hopefully it would be less gruesome than what happened to Eli. He took a breath and braced himself.

Through some miracle, the next face he saw wasn't the creature's.

Kit poked his head through the window above like a goddamned gopher, hastily reaching his arm down.

"Grab my arm!" Kit demanded. "Hurry!"

Shane couldn't believe the kid was actually there. Moving before his brain could catch up, he jumped and grabbed Kit's arm. The kid started pulling, his face beet-red. He could hear the breathing of the creature entering the room behind him.

"Come on..." Kit strained, trying to lift Shane through.

"PULL, GOD DAMN IT!" Shane screamed, his vocal chords threatening to snap like worn piano wire.

He could feel the hot breath of the thing on his tail. He was convinced if he turned to see it, his heart would stop immediately and drop him dead.

Kit tugged with the mad strength of a bull, pulling Shane up part way through the window. Shane felt the sensation of a large knife digging into the back of his ankle, followed by the hot wetness of blood. His body went numb to protect him from the pain, a warning that told him the gash must have been bad. Hell, he wasn't even sure if the leg was still there anymore.

Kit gave another pull that felt like it was coming from ten men, barely pulling Shane out of the window and free from the growling hell behind him. They tumbled out the other side onto a carefully parked wagon beneath the window, softening what would have been a painful fall. The kid must have placed it there to climb back up and get him.

The crazy son-of-a-bitch didn't leave me after all, Shane thought with gratitude.

He winced as he stepped off the wagon, feeling the injury on his leg for the first time. He snuck a peek at it, seeing a piece of bone protruding through the tattered gash. He forced himself to look away to avoid retching and carried on. Seeing how bad it was should have convinced him that he wasn't going to make it, but the adrenaline running through him from narrowly escaping the snarling thing from hell, gave him the push to move forward.

He limped onto the street behind Kit, fighting the urge to pass out from the agony of each awful step. His leg felt like it was being rolled in crushed glass as he hobbled along. He forced his mind off the pain and took in their situation, recognizing just how much carnage had occurred out here while they were hunkered inside the sheriff's.

Flesh and disassembled organs of mutilated corpses were strewn throughout the streets like tossed table scraps. The place was a ghost town again, not a living soul to be seen except for one. One survivor amongst the shells of men that were now just hunks of meat, ready to rot.

Her.

There she was, stubbornly planted in the middle of this hell. The putrid old woman, kneeling naked in the street, chanting her insanity, alive and undisturbed. Shane wanted to shoot her dead, remove one small part of the nightmare tormenting them. Instead, he just watched, thinking *you did this* as he fantasized about putting her down.

The violent, now familiar sound of thrashing from the sheriff's building stole his attention back. It was trying to escape to pursue its prey.

"Quick," Kit whispered, tugging at Shane's arm and pointing to the tavern across the street, "we'll hide in there."

It was as good a spot as any.

Shane pushed through the pain and followed Kit, stumbling and almost tripping over one of the many corpses littering the street. He looked down at the dead man who had something on him that caught Shane's eye: a bundle of dynamite.

Survival told him to run, but Shane knew it would be wise to have something that might actually do some damage to the thing if they found themselves cornered. He knelt to untie the bundle from the belt of the lost soul, dismissing the loud, screeching howl as the thing tried to force its way out onto the street.

"What the hell are you doing?" Kit scolded.

Shane ignored him, focusing on freeing the dynamite from the dead man.

"Stop fucking around!" Kit's panicked voice came out in a frightened hiss.

Shane pulled the dynamite free and powered through the knives in his leg, forcing himself forward to the tavern.

The beast howled. The old woman prayed.

CHAPTER FOURTEEN

A DRINK IS IN ORDER

i. Kit

*T*he tavern had been well barricaded, setting off panic when they arrived, but a precaution they were grateful for now that they were inside. Squeezing in had been difficult, taking their combined strength just to make a crack in the door wide enough for them to slip through, a fit that still felt tight even after the window incident at the sheriff's. Inside felt like a sanctuary though, absent from the death of the blood-soaked streets. This place was pure, untouched.

Once they secured the furniture back in front of the door, they decided to look around for anything else they could use to reinforce it. If the thing was going to try to come in here, it was going to have to work for its supper.

The next order of business was to brave a peek out the window, which had thankfully been boarded up even better than the sheriff's. Outside they saw the creature had managed to break free back out into the streets. It was sniffing around, hunting for survivors to feed its endless appetite.

Undisturbed by the creature, the old woman of rot, the

witch, whatever the hell she was, continued to chant and pray in the middle of the street.

Kit forced himself to stop looking, slinking away to take a quick breather from the madness. He could see in Shane's eyes that the old man was thinking about his friend, not an easy thing to ignore when you were drenched in his blood. Eli may not have been Kit's favorite person, but he seemed like a decent man outside of their differences, and didn't deserve his fate. The memory of the crunching flesh as Eli's screams gurgled to a pathetic nothingness was already haunting Kit, clearly having the same effect on Shane, who looked like he was trying to get out of his own head.

"Stay here and keep a lookout," Shane suddenly commanded with forced gusto. "I'm going to look around, see if I can find anything in here we can use against that thing."

Kit gave an exhausted nod, giving the okay for the old man to go on his own. Despite all the death and loss, he finally felt like the noose had loosened from his neck. If he was going to die tonight, it would be fighting along someone instead of alone on a gallows. For all the damage it had done, the creature had managed to throw the laws of both man and nature out the window. Kit knew he might have to carry injuries and mental scars from this whole nightmare for whatever remained of his life, but that impression of unity felt good.

After Shane disappeared to rummage around, Kit decided he should take advantage of where they were. What was the point of hunkering down in a tavern if you weren't going to have yourself a drink? The thought of the warm burn of whiskey in his throat and belly sounded heavenly, a small pleasure against all the pain to remind him that he was still alive.

He sauntered to the bar, feeling like he had finally gained a bit of control back in his life. It felt nice not having to run, taking his time to ponder the selection. He knew whiskey was what he wanted, but taking the relaxed moment to give himself the illusion of choice was a nice way to pull himself out of the reality of the surreal experience they had all just gone through.

He poured himself a generous glass, taking care not to overfill and spill any of the precious, amber liquid. He took a small sip, allowing himself to really *taste* the sting of the alcohol on his sunburnt lips. It tasted good on his tongue, oaky with a sharp smokey burn in his throat. He wanted to live in the glass, swim and ultimately drown in its peaty glory.

The next sip was interrupted by creaking floorboards to his left. He turned and drew his pistol, to find Dante standing there with his own pistol drawn right back.

"Hell of a mess you got us all in the middle of," Dante said, sporting his signature smirk.

ii. Dante

After witnessing the butchering of his men by the thing, Dante believed he was the only survivor left when he found refuge in the tavern. The first thing he wanted to do was have a drink, but resisted the temptation, knowing that hiding and having a clear head was the smarter choice. A few minutes later, when he heard the old man and the outlaw break in, he was pissed at himself that he didn't take advantage of the bar supplies when he had the chance. Now that he was here, pistol drawn on the kid, he didn't know if he'd ever have the opportunity to enjoy a whiskey again.

"Arkell is the last place I wanted to be," Kit responded, neither of them wavering their aim. "It was the rest of you assholes that were so hellbent on getting me here."

The kid wasn't wrong. Dante really *had* been hellbent on seeing him hang, but now it didn't seem like a priority. The idea of justice that seemed so important to him earlier was now washed away from his thoughts. He'd arrived in Arkell less than an hour ago, but it already felt like lifetimes had passed since their horrid dance with the devil.

"You did manage to get the attention of a lot of people," Dante smirked. "Can't blame them, it *was* a hell of a reward they were offering for your neck."

"I'm going to go out on a limb and say the reward is probably off the table at this point," Kit responded.

"True," Dante said, his smile unforced. The comment was funny, though not funny enough to absolve the killer of his sins. "Though I still owe you a personal hanging for what you did to Seth at that poker game."

"The way he was treating that gal in the bar," Kit answered blankly, "I didn't feel I had much of a choice."

It was true, Seth didn't hold his liquor well and Miss Maggie shouldn't have been treated that way, but it also wasn't up to this bastard to go and shoot him dead for it.

"Yeah, Seth always was an asshole," Dante agreed with a chuckle, "but he was *my* asshole."

Kit shared a little laugh at this. Even when at odds, Dante couldn't resist enjoying a chuckle when he knew he got a good one in. It made him feel smart, a feeling he longed for thanks to too much time spent hanging around the dullards of Blackcreek.

The chuckle died down, morphing to silence. The two men found themselves in a stalemate with their trigger fingers itching like crazy. Dante had no idea how this was going to play out and could sense the kid didn't either. So, he waited, patiently biting his tongue to let Kit be the one to break the silence.

"Seems we're in a bit of a pickle here," Kit finally said. "While it might be fun for the two of us to gun each other down and see who comes out alive, if we start shooting, we're likely going to attract the attention of that thing out there."

The kid had a point. Dying in a duel sounded outright

appealing compared to bleeding out while some fucking abomination ate you alive like a pathetic piece of livestock.

"We may draw its attention if we did that," Dante agreed, "or we may not."

"After what you've seen it do," Kit pondered, "do you *really* want to take that gamble?"

iii. Kit

"I'll take that bet." Their conversation was interrupted by the voice that haunted so many of Kit's nightmares.

He had been so caught up in bargaining with this asshole that he didn't hear the devil himself join them. He turned to see the speaker, praying the voice was only in his head. Before them stood Gideon Walker with two pistols drawn, one aimed at each of them. His venomous eyes pierced deep into Kit, competing with the thing outside for his fear.

"I've been looking for this gentleman for a long time," Gideon said, far too calmly for any man in their situation. "I've traveled too far and put up with too much to let anything, be it man or monster, get in my way."

Kit stole a quick glance at Dante to try to get a read on him, noting that even he appeared antsy about the new piece added to the board. He and Dante were far from fond of each other, but a quick look said that he'd take Kit over this animal any day.

"Your problem seems to be with the kid," Dante said. "How do I fit into this?"

"Collateral damage." Gideon shrugged.

While he and Dante still had their pistols drawn on one another, Kit could feel an energy between them, reassuring that they both knew where the true threat lay. Still, he safely kept his gun in place, knowing there wasn't room for any sudden decisions as everyone calculated their next move.

"There's two of us," Kit confidently warned Gideon. "Do you trust your aim with *both* hands before one of us can pull a shot on you?"

"Again, that's a bet I'm willing to take," Gideon said, not looking troubled by the threat. If he was anxious at all about the situation, he sure as hell wasn't letting it be known.

Beautiful silence hit the room once more. Kit felt like he could have reasonably talked things through with Dante, but that hope died the moment Gideon entered the equation. They had all survived an attack from this unthinkable thing that nobody would ever believe was real, only to lock themselves up and likely kill each other over petty bullshit instead. The reality of their situation was absurd, making Kit want to puke and laugh at the same time.

Fingers were itchier than a hair on your lip when the clear, distinct sound of a match being lit cracked through the room, breaking the silence and catching everyone's attention. All three men turned their heads in unison, seeing the source confidently standing in the doorway at the back of the musty tavern. The wrinkles on Shane's face glowed in the amber light of the match in his hand, the flicker of the flame dancing shadows across it like a piece of petrified wood. His other hand clenched a stick of dynamite, his bargaining chip over three assholes and their meager pistols.

"Here's another bet for you," Shane said, his voice coated with a cool demeanor Kit hadn't heard in all their travels. "You willing to bet you could survive a blast from this stick in a place as tight as this?"

A grin crept across Kit's face. The crazy old fucker was actually calling Gideon out head-on. Dante contributed a chuckle as well, welcoming the new development in their predicament.

"Who the fuck are you?" Gideon demanded, cracks of emotion finally starting to show.

"Well, this is interesting," Dante added. "I'm impressed, old man."

Kit could feel Dante's eyes searching around for the cavalry before the question followed.

"Where's your friend, the marshal?"

"He didn't make it," Shane stated bluntly, far more pain behind the words than he let on.

"Sorry to hear that, old man," Dante said with a true sliver of sincerity. "Even if I was gonna kill him, I can't help but admire the balls he had for pulling that bluff on us in Blackcreek."

There it was, the sign of mutual respect pitting three against one.

"You gonna' light that stick, old man?" Gideon snapped impatiently. "Or are we gonna just stand here and reminisce?"

Kit admired Shane's gamble, but hearing Gideon happily call him on it was a deadly reminder that this was a high-roller table that the old man might not have the skin for.

"He's got a point, old timer," Dante chimed in with a bit of pity. "From what I've seen, balls really ain't your strong suit. You *really* got the stones to blow yourself up along with us?"

The pendulum of Shane's position from Grim Reaper was quickly swinging back to pathetic old fool. Kit wished Shane could read his thoughts, mentally telling him that he had to make a move.

"You fire those guns," Shane started with an indifferent shrug, "it don't matter who is left standing. We're all dead once that thing hears us."

Finished with words, Shane calmly brought the match to the fuse. It lit up into a bright, aggressive spark, crackling in the silent air. The words were no longer a bluff, the bold move catching all of them by surprise.

"Now we can all die right here, right now," he said, calm as the fucking stars. "Or we can work together and kill this fucking thing."

The old man's eyes remained as still as a pond at night, never blinking, and sure as hell never betraying him by sneaking a peek at how much of the fuse was left.

"I promise," he added, "we can all go back to killing each other after we kill this fucking thing."

Kit realized he never knew how fast a fuse burned until this very moment. Every man in the room but Shane watched it rapidly burn away, doing their best not to flinch as the line to their deaths quickly depleted.

"My brother Bronco would never stand for this," Gideon snarled as if it was God's word.

"Good thing he ain't here anymore," Shane said coldly, eyes clear and still.

Kit wasn't sure of many things in this world, but he was sure from the look in Shane's eyes that this was no bluff.

Seconds passed, the fuse uncomfortably close to the stick, Shane refusing to waver. Finally, Gideon relented to the old man, lowering his guns in defeat. It was the first time Kit had witnessed the hideous Walker Brother afraid. A reassuring sign that he was indeed human.

Dante followed, lowering his iron in surrender, followed by Kit, who didn't hide the nod of approval he gave Shane. Holding up his end of the unspoken agreement, Shane pinched the wick, ending the immediate threat of their demise.

The mounting tension was suddenly gone, sweet lady death mercifully backing off once again. The satisfaction of brushing to the edge of finality felt as satisfying to Kit as ever.

A silent celebration was in order. Not a word was spoken as Kit took charge and marched to the bar. *Fuck it, we're partners now whether you agree or not,* his brain told him as he grabbed four dirty glasses, along with the whiskey bottle that he had a date with earlier. He poured the amber elixir, filling each glass generously.

In silence, the three other men apprehensively joined him at the bar and each quietly took a glass. In unison, the four of them drank together, forming an unspoken, uneasy alliance. The four glasses came slamming down on the bar simultaneously, prompting Kit to immediately pour another round.

"So," he started, taking the lead of the freshly formed posse, "let's figure out how we're going to kill this fucking thing."

CHAPTER FIFTEEN

FOUR HORSEMEN AGAINST THE APOCALYPSE

i. Shane

*W*hile Kit was sketching out some sort of plan at the bar in his own little world, the rest of them waited. Shane figured sneaking a peek at their harbinger of death felt like a good way to fill the time. It was also a way for him to get out of his own head, away from Eli's screams rattling around in there.

The view outside was hypnotic, sucking him in to the point that he was unsure how long he'd actually been peering through the narrow slit in the boards. The rotten witch didn't move from her spot, naked in the cool night air, praying in isolation. The creature was pacing in large circles like an uneasy dog, chewing on a corpse like a piece of gristle, while it covered a wide perimeter with its large strides. Once it finished chewing one dead man down to nothing, it would quickly sniff around and find another to gnaw on and repeat this ritual.

The pacing, the eating, and the hunting for new hunks of meat played out in a perfect, predictable rhythm, circling around the old woman like a dance partner. Watching the cycle,

Shane swore the creature was actually protecting her. He observed with morbid fascination, both sick to his stomach and intrigued by the nature of their relationship. He wasn't sure how many bodies he saw the thing devour during this process but was aware that the once ample supply of dead men was quickly dwindling.

Dante and Gideon were less interested in what was happening outside, happily planting themselves at a table with a bottle. If this was to be their last night, they opted to go through it pickled with whiskey. Their pairing wasn't comforting to Shane, too many volatile variables together. He couldn't read if they were just yammering on while sharing a drink, or if they were feeling each other out as they mentally prepared to kill one another. Recognizing that he was the least unhinged of the madmen, Shane would interject where he could to keep the topics of conversation neutral, focusing on their collective goal.

"What happens when it runs out of dead bodies to eat?" he asked, knowing he wasn't going to like the answer.

"Probably what any hungry animal would do," Gideon answered confidently. "Go hunt for fresh meat."

"It should eat that old fucking witch," Dante suggested gleefully. "Easy pickings."

Shane didn't disagree with the sentiment, biting his tongue to keep the focus on strategy over emotion.

"It's staying pretty close to her," Shane observed. "I don't know why, but she seems safe from it. Like she's being protected."

"I vote we blow her fucking head off," Dante proposed, with enough flair that Shane knew he wasn't joking. "We take her out, maybe it goes with her."

"Or," Shane countered, "it just *really* pisses it off."

The thing finished devouring another carcass, violently flinging the rib cage at the tavern door. The smash of bones against the building caused Shane to give a little jump, an embarrassing reaction he instantly regretted. His heart sped up, worried it was letting them know that it knew they were in here. He only let himself relax when the thing turned its attention back to a nearby corpse, continuing the eating and pacing regime.

"It'll be running out of food soon," Shane noted grimly.

Nobody else had anything to add to the thought, agreeing they didn't have a lot of time left. Their grim silence was interrupted by an excited *smack* on the bar top as Kit slapped it with youthful satisfaction.

"I think I've got something," he said optimistically. "Come take a look at this."

ii. Kit

Kit was more than ready for everyone to start making fun of the makeshift map he'd prepared, psyching himself up for the barrage of teasing and unoriginal jokes that were sure to come. It may have looked childish to an untrained eye, but Kit prepared maps like this for every robbery he'd ever done, several of them saving his life. Whether the task at hand was a simple robbery, or trying to kill an unstoppable creature, the visual layout always helped him plan better.

He'd found a pencil and some paper lying around, combined with the creative layout of some matches, glasses, bottles, and a deck of cards, which all came together to make a pretty impressive bird's eye view of the town. He'd carefully sketched out markers to identify places, landmarks, important objects and the beast itself, along with some arrows, circles and X's which were just begging to be explained. He didn't want to let on how proud he was of the map in the interest of keeping things serious, but he was pretty damn pleased with how it turned out.

They all huddled in to look at his masterpiece, grabbing a drink to feel slightly less silly for participating in the grown-up version of kids playing war. Pushing the hard sell of his life, Kit kept his voice clear and confident as he laid his plan out.

"We're here," he started, pointing to a spot on the south of the map crudely labeled *Tavern.*

No questions so far, telling him the geography was clear, which was a good start.

"And the Gatling gun is tucked in this alley back here," he continued, circling his finger around the glass in its place.

No questions, still good.

Moving on, he drew a big circle around the center of town.

"And *this* is the perimeter where that ugly fucking thing is circling. With the old lady..." he carefully pointed his finger to a shot glass inside the area, "...right here in the middle."

Everyone hung onto his every word. He didn't overthink it, continuing on to keep the momentum going. He drew a curved line from the tavern to the glass in the alley.

"Now if we were able to make it from here to the alley, and that's a *big* if, you'll see..." he re-traced his finger along the perimeter, stopping parallel to the glass, "...that part of the perimeter the thing circles is right in the line of sight of the gatling gun."

Dante and Shane nodded in agreement.

"We line it up in front of there," he continued, "and we have some serious firepower we can use to take it down."

Gideon looked less impressed.

"That's all well and good," Gideon interrupted, "but we all heard the Gatling gun stop before that thing attacked everyone. Bronco *never* would have stopped shooting unless he had to reload."

"And how long does reloading take?" Dante asked constructively, ready to find solutions instead of complaining about problems.

"It's not quick, but it's a lot less time if there's two of you," Gideon said, "and you both know what the hell you're doing."

Kit started back up, recognizing there wasn't room to have these two getting into a dick measuring contest. He pointed to a building on the map that read *Sheriff* with a big *X* underneath it.

"Now the sheriff's building is here..." he continued, tracing his finger down a straight line towards the alley, "...which we found out the hard way is right in the line of fire of the Gatling gun."

He traced his finger back up from the glass to the sheriff's office, tapping his finger on the X to stress his point.

"We've seen that thing get in and out of that building, but not without a hell of a struggle. We trap it inside there, we might just have a shot if we fire everything we've got from that Gatling gun on it while it's stuck"

Gideon forced a false grin at the plan, like a man faking emotions he didn't have, in a room he didn't want to be in.

"You're good at all this planning shit," he said through gritted teeth. "Is this what you did when you ripped me and my brother off? Draw yourself up a cute little map for your whole plan?"

"I *did* make one for the original plan," Kit said, refusing to accept the veiled threat. "But the rip-off part happened on the fly. Thankfully I didn't need a plan for that because I had quicker wits than everyone else."

The monster outside disappeared from the two men's thoughts as they eyed each other down. Suddenly the room felt like there might not be a need for a plan as a deadly confrontation threatened to play out right here and now.

The stare down was broken by another *THUD* of bones thrown at the front door by their threat outside. The creature let out one of its glass-in-the-ear roars, freezing all four men in place. It was clear that they were going to have to make their move soon.

"So how the hell are we going to get it back inside the sheriff's?" Shane asked.

Kit appreciated the old man's efforts to keep things neutral and on topic, turning his focus away from Gideon and back to the map.

"That's where the witch comes in," Kit said optimistically, pointing to her position on the map.

"I still vote we take her out," Dante interjected. "If this is a suicide mission, we might as well get the satisfaction of blowing her fucking head off."

"Whatever connection that thing has with her is the only leg we have to stand on right now," Kit continued, brushing off the crude comment. "From what we've seen, it appears to be protecting her. She stays close to it, and it stays close to her."

"So, what do we do then?" Shane asked, invested but to the point.

"We're going to move *her* to where we want *it*," Kit said, drawing a line from her position to the sheriff's. He stressed his point by then tracing his finger back and forth between the Gatling gun and where the beast would be trapped.

The group stared at Kit ominously, doubt and desperation behind their eyes. It was a flimsy plan at best, but Kit knew it would live and die on how confident he could sell his feelings on it working.

"I've seen a lot of posturing between all of you. Lots of talk about who has the balls to pull off what," he taunted. "Now it's time for y'all to actually prove if you've really got 'em."

iii. Dante

The tavern started to feel cluttered now that they'd quietly moved all of the furniture away from the front door. It was an overly cautious move to avoid anyone tripping or getting stuck on their way out, but they couldn't afford to have anyone slipping up, especially right out the door. The idea that they weren't protected by a barricade anymore should have scared the shit out of Dante, but his mind was too preoccupied thinking of the *real* horror that he was about to face next. Why worry about rain when you were about to run into a tornado?

He was kneeling beside Kit at the entrance, sneaking a peek through the crack in the door now and then. The slit was too narrow to make out much, but the glimpses he caught of the thing as it paced about were more than enough to remind him how little he wanted to be out there with it again.

"This is fucking suicide," he grumbled, no longer caring if anyone knew he was scared.

"Would you rather have my job instead?" Kit half-joked, half-offered.

Even *joking* about switching roles shut Dante the fuck up real quick. *Fuck. No. I. Do. Not.* he thought to himself as he pictured the terrifying task the kid was going to attempt.

Dante had enough of a sense of humor to appreciate the sick joke God was playing by pairing him up with Kit. Come here to hang the bastard, end up risking your life for him instead. He'd made questionable alliances in the past and was willing to patch things up when mutually beneficial, but never this quickly and definitely never under any circumstances like this. He went into the pairing without kicking and screaming because he knew that despite his feelings about Kit, he was hardly the short straw amongst the group when it came to picking partners. He may have come to Arkell to kill the kid, but he knew damn well that he was the best choice amongst a handful of bum cards.

The old man didn't seem too bad of a choice at first glance, maybe a little too noble for Dante's taste, but at least decent at his core. Problem was, that gashed up leg of his made him a liability. Sorry old timer, no room for any more handicaps when the odds are this bad.

Then there was the other one. The whistler. The dandy. The madman. Gideon Walker. They may have been forced to work together by circumstance, but that didn't mean Dante had to like it, and he damn well wasn't going to partner with him and be around him more than he had to. The guy was as sick and unpredictable as the fucking monster outside. *No thank you, I'll stick with the kid, thank you very much.*

Shane and Gideon were silently sitting at a table, mechanically stuffing rags into liquor bottles to make up a hefty share of explosives. They had a dozen or so ready, far too many to be around Gideon for Dante's peace of mind. He didn't feel any better knowing that Kit was currently working on strapping a bunch of dynamite to his belt, the formula practically begging for some idiot here to light a cigarette to get the party started.

"This is crazy," Gideon muttered as he stuffed the bottles, clearly not liking the structure of working as a team.

"What's the matter?" Shane ribbed. "I thought you Walkers *loved* crazy?"

Gideon shot the old man a dirty look.

"If that leg of yours holds you back," Gideon taunted, "you're on your own."

"Don't worry about me," Shane fired back. "Just make sure you keep your nerves about you."

While Dante enjoyed watching Shane hold his own against the sick fuck, he still had his reservations about that gash on the old man's leg. It had been patched up as best as they could with what little they had in the bar, raising its status from 'fucked' to 'temporarily usable'. It looked worlds better than the strings of tattered flesh it had been earlier, but Dante didn't envy the thought of the poor guy running on it. The old man was definitely a liability, paired with a second one, the wildcard Gideon. The more Dante thought about it, the more holes he saw, making him wonder what other lingering liabilities lay in their half-formed plan.

He snapped out of his headspace when Kit handed him the anxiety-inducing belt full of dynamite he'd been working on.

"Here," Kit said as casually as if he were handing him a drink. "Time to make our move."

Dante nodded stupidly and took the belt, burying his hesitation and fear of the shit they were about to get themselves into. He closed his eyes, breathing rhythmically to try to hype himself up as he put the belt on. When he opened them, he saw the kid looking at him like he'd gone off the deep end.

"Relax," Kit said with a mocking smile splashed across his face. "There's nothing to worry about."

"Kid, can you do me a favor?" Dante asked with false earnestness.

"Sure."

"If we make it out of this thing alive..." He smiled. "...make sure you let me be the one that shoots you."

They chuckled one last time before the sound died into the silence of dread. The time to put things off was over. It was time to move. Dante pulled a stick of dynamite from his belt, lit the wick and opened the door a crack. He gave Kit a nod that said everything — I *hate you. We got this. We're going to make it. I'll see you in hell* — and ran out into the wicked night streets.

iv. Kit

What the fuck was I thinking? How did I get myself into this fucking mess? The thought kept repeating over and over again in Kit's head as he watched Dante recklessly run out into the street, the wick from the dynamite glowing in his hand.

How did I get myself into this fucking mess?

As the wick wore down to uncomfortably close, Dante threw the stick as hard as he could into the middle of the street.

BOOM

The explosion rang through the night air like God's wrath. The thunderous, foreign sound caught the attention of the beast, a look of anger in its eyes as it searched for the source. Dante answered by lighting a second stick and bravely calling the thing head on.

"C'mon mother fucker!" he taunted.

The creature started moving towards him. Dante, bravely ignoring all instinct to turn and run, threw the stick of dynamite at his attacker.

BOOM

The second stick exploded inches from the monstrosity's face, causing it to howl in a combination of pain and hostility. Refusing to let his momentum die, Dante used the opportunity to light another stick.

"That's it," Dante taunted. "Come and fucking get me."

The beast shook off the blast like it was nothing more than a fly buzzing around its face. Dante patiently waited for the wick of the third stick to reach its sweet spot.

Kit felt numb watching the madness unfold from the tavern entrance, aware that he was going to be out there soon enough. He could sense Shane and Gideon were in the same headspace, mentally preparing themselves to be the next ones out.

"Now!" Gideon shouted, giving their cue.

Shane and Gideon rushed out the door on his call, taking a hard left towards the alley. Gideon tore out of the tavern like a jackrabbit, but Shane hobbled behind on his injured leg. Kit worried for the old man, knowing that if the thing shifted its attention his way and sensed weak prey, he'd be done for.

BOOM

Kit jumped at the sound of another stick of dynamite going off, nervously awaiting his turn to join everyone in the madness.

v. Shane

Every step Shane took felt like the skin on his leg had been peeled off and replaced with salt. But he had to keep up.

He watched Gideon dart past him, using him as a focal point to avoid looking at the thing. Dynamite explosions begged for his attention. Distractions he had to ignore, just like his leg. Right now, he had to stay in his own head, focus on reaching the alley, and keep up.

He knew he drew the shit end of the stick by being paired up with Gideon, recognizing that showing any sign of weakness could mean a bullet in his head. He couldn't imagine taking the thing head on with dynamite like Dante did, and he wasn't fast enough to do what Kit had to do, but being paired up with the sickest of the three put enough fear in him to miraculously make that leg work. Because if that leg *didn't* work, he knew Gideon wouldn't hesitate in putting him down like a dog if he saw him as a liability.

He had to keep up.

vi. Dante

"C'mon!" Dante taunted, throwing another stick at the thing.

He could feel the heat coming off of the last explosion near the beast's face, a warning that he was getting too close. The creature howled in pain, blindly taking a slash at him that brushed contact. He misread the distance, initially thinking it just caught his clothing, before feeling a warm dampness on his chest. He didn't have to look to know it was bad, but the fact that he was still standing gave him enough confidence in the moment to tell him it wasn't critical. He suppressed the pain by drinking in the thrill of the moment, opting to light another stick instead of worrying about the wound.

"I've got more where that came from fucker," he spat, gleefully prepping another stick.

He was actually enjoying himself.

vii. Kit

As the thing blindly howled from the latest explosion, Kit knew his moment was now or never. He saw that it was mad, but that anger was nothing compared to the shit storm that he knew was coming. He took a deep breath and jumped on the opportunity, making a run out of the tavern towards his target.

She was straight ahead of him, smack in the center of town, praying as if hell wasn't unfolding all around her. Kit could sense the anger of the thing nearby as it reoriented itself from the latest blast. He didn't dare look. He couldn't *afford* to look. He kept every drop of his focus on *her*.

He hunched as he approached the witch, turning his core inward as he slammed his right shoulder into her chest and picked her up, throwing her over his shoulder in one continuous motion. She wasn't heavy, but he overestimated how easily he thought he could continue to run at the same speed while carrying her additional weight.

Her chanting stopped, now replaced with the shrill screaming of a wounded child. She wriggled her sore-infested body wildly, desperate to break free from his grip like a fish pulled from the lake, gasping for air.

The thing let out a loud, angry roar that made Kit feel like his eardrums were going to burst. As anticipated, it knew the *moment* he grabbed her, filling him with immediate regret as he found himself being the sole focus of its rage.

He didn't dare look back, ignoring what was now surely chasing him. The screeches in his ear from the rotting woman trying to wriggle free rang in his head, making him feel dizzy as he kept his focus ahead. He pushed his legs as fast as they could go, praying they were faster than his pursuer.

The screeching became louder, echoing in the night sky. They weren't words, but Kit knew that she was directly communicating with the thing, pleading to it with her horrible shrieks. If her horrid noises *were* words, he was sure he knew what she would be saying.

She was screaming *Help*.

viii. Shane

The screeches, the roars, the explosions; they were all a thousand miles away in Shane's mind as he raced around the corner towards the stagecoach. He mentally blocked out his leg injury, miraculously keeping up with Gideon. He wasn't seeking any sort of recognition, especially from a coldblooded killer, but he couldn't help but feel a bit of pride for not collapsing from the overwhelming pain.

A deep streak of blood and entrails led to the stagecoach, a grim reminder of the fate of the last operator of the Gatling gun. The roof of the wagon had been torn off, effortlessly tossed aside like trash.

Shane jumped aboard with Gideon and started doing a mental inventory, noting the boxes of ammo, gunpowder, crates of dynamite, and rope crowding around the Gatling gun. It was enough to start a small war.

Shane wasted no time showing his worth, opening up one of the crates and getting to work. He expected Gideon to join in, but something on the coach had frozen him in place.

He turned to see Gideon staring at the top half of his brother's dead body, the remains covered in deep lacerations. The identity of the corpse was barely recognizable, except for the hazel eyes, which remained perfectly intact.

"Hey, we gotta move," Shane nudged, kind enough to show some empathy, but firm enough to get across that this wasn't the time to grieve.

They'd all lost people tonight, all of them better than this one.

Gideon didn't acknowledge Shane, continuing to stare back into his brothers dead, perfect eyes. Without any more time to play nice, Shane reached out and grabbed Gideon's stiff shoulder.

"WHAT?" Gideon roared, violently brushing his hand off.

Shane knew he better pick his next words carefully if he wanted to live long enough to even try to reload that Gatling gun.

"Let's keep it together," Shane reasoned, calmly holding out a belt of bullets as a peace offering, "and do this."

Gideon snatched the belt, his eyes unblinking and cold. Shane knew the look; he'd seen it from many good and bad men in his past. It was the look of pain, the look of hate. Most importantly, it was the look of wanting blood. Shane just hoped that it would be channeled in the right direction.

ix. Dante

The crazy son-of-a-bitch actually did it, Dante thought, watching Kit make the suicide run for the sheriff's with the old banshee screeching over his shoulders. Her shrieks were nearly as bad as the howls of the thing, reaffirming to Dante that maybe they actually *were* communicating with one another.

He threw another stick of dynamite to get the beast's attention, but as they'd predicted, it had its sights solely on Kit, and it was *pissed*. A part of him felt guilty that he was thankful that it wasn't coming after him anymore, finally allowing him to catch his breath. Not that he wanted to see the kid ripped to pieces, they were well past that point by now, but because he was finally feeling that gash on his chest, and knew he had more work to do.

He felt the wound when he'd breathe deep, like that feeling of bubbles in your lungs you get when you have a bad cough. He touched his chest and when he saw his hand was dripping dark red, he didn't dare investigate any further how bad the damage actually was. *Can't kill you if you don't know how bad it is,* he ignorantly thought.

His eyes shifted to the tavern, knowing what he had to do next. If everyone else somehow survived and managed to do what they were supposed to do, he didn't want to be the one who fucked it all up. He clenched at the gash on his chest, holding it as if to stop his lungs from spilling out, and made his run to get the next ingredient to their plan. It was time to bring fire in a bottle.

x. Kit

The thing was close enough that Kit could smell the stink of its hot breath on the back of his neck, turning his skin to gooseflesh. The flailing witch dug her nails into his back, flopping around and doing everything in her power to wriggle free and slow him down. The sheriff's office was a mere few feet in front of him, but it might as well have been a whole other town away. He closed his eyes, visualizing the inside as a sanctuary, blocking out the woman's screams and the angry howls behind him as he ran for his life.

Finally reaching his oasis, he leaned forward with his left shoulder, bursting the door open without stopping his momentum. He felt the wind of a near bite behind him, the gnashing jaws of the creature barely missing.

He gave the door a swift kick shut before it immediately swung back open with force. The thing smashed its primal face through the doorway, blindly biting in all directions as it violently bucked and thrashed to try to squeeze its way inside. Kit ignored it and pushed forward toward the holding cells, hoping to hell everyone else was in place.

xi. Shane

The loading of the Gatling gun was clumsier than Shane anticipated, truly proving itself to be the two-man job that Gideon promised it to be. Shane had never seen a weapon so complicated before, thinking how many times he could easily reload his repeater with his eyes shut, in a fraction of the time.

It wasn't just that it was overly complicated, it was also how *heavy* everything involved was. It might have been possible for one man to load this technical marvel himself, but he would have to be built like a goddamn bull to do it and it would take more time than they had. The opening of crates, the weight of the bullets, the disassembling, loading and assembling. He felt *old*, marveling at how technology moved one step forward and two steps back.

"C'mon, c'mon," he muttered nervously, working to load the machine with as much patience they could muster together.

The thrashing of the thing, now perfectly placed at the sheriffs, felt like a burning stick of dynamite ready to go off in their hands.

xii. Dante

The whiskey-soaked rags sticking out of the bottles burned

like acid as they brushed against the gash on Dante's chest. The original plan called for two trips, but he could feel his chest slowing him down, highlighting the ugly truth that another trip back to the tavern might not be in the cards.

He managed to carry about eight of the bottles in his burly arms, along with another in each hand for good measure. He considered trying to bring a few more but knew dropping them and covering himself in the flammable liquid would have been a hell of a lot worse than leaving a few behind.

This trip out of the tavern was just as nerve-wracking as the first, but at least with the relief of seeing the focus of the thing diverted as it thrashed at the door to the sheriff's. It wasn't looking for him at all, which only meant one thing.

God damn, the kid actually made it in there.

xiii. Kit

Kit carelessly threw the old woman in the first cell he came across. It was hard to feel sorry for her when her sore encrusted body hit the ground, scraping one of her scabs off into a yellowish streak across the concrete.

"DIA-BO-LUS! DIA-BO-LUS!" she screamed repeatedly.

Kit hadn't seen the woman so *alive* before now, her milk-fog eyes bulging as if they could come out of her skull as she aggressively writhed on the cold stone floor.

"DIA-BO-LUS!"

The sound of her voice made the thrashing of the thing angrier, like a mama bear trying to rescue her cub. Kit eyed the window, hoping it would be his savior once again.

He tried not to think too hard about how his only chance of survival relied on waiting on a group of men that had all wanted him dead earlier that night.

xiv. Shane

The whole contraption was as foreign to Shane as the language he once heard a group of rail workers speak. His mind was bending with frustration and curiosity as he and Gideon worked away at putting the pieces in place. It was a jumbled mess of chaos that he couldn't comprehend, until it all suddenly made instant sense when a final pull snapped into place, rewarding them with a satisfying and appropriate *CLICK.*

"Got it!" Gideon squealed with a shit-eating grin.

Gideon turned the crank with all of his strength, grunting like a tired bull while he built up momentum. After a few turns, the gun roared with a horrid, delightful repeating *BANG BANG BANG BANG.*

It sang like the world's angriest songbird, threatening to shatter their eardrums at this proximity as it unleashed its fury. A symphony of bullets galloped ahead, charging through the alleyway towards the sheriff's, where their target angrily thrashed to get inside. The barrage of lead began piercing the beast mercilessly.

Stuck between its prey and its safety, the thing was pummeled with confusion as it soaked in the blinding hail of bullets. Countless shots hit it repeatedly, causing it to flail around in a panicked cocktail of pain and anger.

The sounds of the gunfire and pained howling were too much to take. Shane wanted to cover his ears, afraid he'd never be able to hear again if he lived through the incident. Instead, he resisted. A smile spread across his face as he watched, joining Gideon, who was laughing like a delirious child with glee. Shane felt violent, death toll bells ringing in his head.

It was deafening and beautiful.

xv. Kit

A lifetime of shootouts and close calls had Kit's razor-sharp survival instincts perfectly tuned, sending him straight to the ground once the gunfire started. Wretched squeals filled the air, signaling that the thing was taking the brunt of the incoming fire as planned. Allowing curiosity to overtake good judgment, Kit snuck a peek to watch the creature thrashing and convulsing, while desperately trying to force itself through the entrance to get in. It was clearly in pain, every bullet from the assault fueling the fire of its anger. The gunshots weren't slowing it down though, only motivating it with cornered fear. It desperately scrambled until managing a final wiggle that allowed it to squeeze its massive body inside.

"Shit," Kit cursed, out of time and still stuck without his escape.

He had held up his end of karma by coming back for Shane, now it was time for God to return the favor. He ran to the window, waiting for his savior to pop through. Looking up at it, he felt like a fool for believing this was actually going to work.

The old woman wailed her horrid noises, letting the thing know where she was. The heavy sounds of thudding footsteps shook through the building as it drew closer.

"Fuck, fuck, fuck."

He scrambled in a nervous wreck, stupidly waiting for his miracle to come.

"Kid," he heard above him, "up here."

There was Dante, reaching down from the window like God's most fucked up angel.

Wails from the old woman bellowed behind Kit, accompanied by the loud, intrusive shatter of the thing entering the room. He desperately jumped, grabbing Dante's extended hand and praying to any God that would listen, that he wouldn't slip. Dante pulled like hell, using the effort reserved only for lifting your true brother out of the darkest depths of hell.

"Pull, goddamn it," Kit huffed, the hot snorting of the thing close behind.

"Fuck me," Dante spat through grit teeth. "I'm tryin'!"

"Pull!" Kit screamed, mentally ready to be ripped to shreds at any moment now.

Dante pulled like the devil, letting his weight fall from the other side of the window to help pull them through. Gravity did its magic and in one swift motion, Kit's torso slid free through the tiny escape.

He felt something sharp behind him on his way out. It dug deep into his leg, tearing a substantial chunk of flesh, like chicken meat from the bone. He screamed in agony as they fell cleanly, holding his arms out to soften the fall as they tumbled onto the wagon outside.

The snarls of the thing echoed right behind them, the creature angrily pushing its awful snout through the window and snapping. Their plan had worked, but they didn't have long to act before it would break free again.

Kit was impressed to see that Dante had loaded the wagon with what looked to be close to a dozen of the rag-soaked bottles. Thank Christ the crazy fucker actually held up his end of the plan. He jumped off the cart, favoring his injured leg as much as he could as they positioned themselves behind the wagon. He knew without looking that his leg was bad, but knew damn well it was the least of his worries now.

"Push!" Kit screamed, both men focusing on survival over their serious injuries.

They strained to push the wagon, the panicked sounds of the *thing* scurrying from the cells back to the front of the sheriff's office acting as an awful reminder of the stakes of this race.

Reaching the front of the sheriff's, they were greeted by the sight of the thing thrashing inside, preparing its escape. With the creature in sight, the Gatling gun started up again, pummeling the thing with a seemingly endless stream of bullets. The return of the gunfire scared and angered the hell beast, sending it into a hissing spree as it momentarily retreated back deeper inside.

Blood-tainted sweat beaded down Kit's brow as they took their opportunity, pushing the wagon towards the entrance as a makeshift barricade. Heads down, they suppressed their pain and pushed forward, until they were interrupted by a horrific sound — the sound of silence.

The gunfire had stopped.

xvi. Shane

Shane had grown so accustomed to the deafening gunfire that he didn't realize how loud it actually was until it stopped. Underneath the ringing in his ears came a repeated *click-click-click* from the continuous turns of the newly empty crank.

"Shit!" Gideon spat.

Showing his worth, Shane immediately readied the next belt of bullets. He quickly and efficiently joined Gideon in repeating the steps they'd learned, reloading together like a well-oiled train piston. Fast but precise, they worked at a brisk pace, while being careful not to move too quickly to avoid any costly mistakes. Stupid cost lives, and they'd lost enough of them for one bloody night.

xvii. Dante

The cease-fire brought the focus of the thing's hatred back towards Dante and Kit, pulling away from its retreat and back to its intent of getting the fuck out of the confines of the sheriff's. Their attempt to barricade the door was halted by the thing violently pushing its jaws through the entryway, snarling and slashing as it clumsily tried to escape.

Dante's chest felt like it was on fire, a grim reminder that they weren't going to last much longer trying to match the thing with brute force alone. He desperately grabbed one of the bottles from the wagon, sparking a match and praying to any god that would listen that his shirt hadn't soaked up enough of the whiskey to light him up as well.

"C'mon," he taunted, lighting up the booze-soaked rag.

He backed away from the cart, swinging the bottle like a torch. The beast howled in anger, its dark yellow eyes triggered by the sight of the flame taunting it.

Dante threw the bottle, flames exploding at the feet of the thing on impact. The fire began to spread, crawling up the thing's body like a scurrying spider. It began to flail around, reduced to a frightened animal. Kit took the reaction as his cue to join in, grabbing a few bottles and lighting them as the flames rapidly grew.

The thing cowered away from the wall of fire, conflicted as to whether it should fight or flee. It blindly slashed one of its claws through the door, snagging Kit and barely missing flesh. The impact caused him to drop one of the bottles, the cocktail shattering on the porch and spreading into a flaming pool around them.

The fires of hell burned inside and out of the building without discrimination, tempting the men to flee like cowards into the night. Yet they remained, dashing to the wagon for another fistful of bottles. They would face the thing head on or die trying.

xviii. Shane

The beautiful *click* rang once more, signaling that the

Gatling gun was ready to go. Shane grinned, feeling optimistic that they might actually come out of this night alive.

Gideon turned the crank, sending a rain of judgment at the beast as the thunder of bullets cracked through the night sky.

xix. Kit

Kit and Dante threw themselves to the ground when the gunfire picked up again. Glass showered from above, flames dancing around them like an accompanying rainbow from hell. The endless assault of bullets penetrated through the remaining boards, reducing the wood to tattered chunks as they stung the creature like a swarm of hornets. It flailed from the attack, stumbling backwards in a confused, fire-soaked rage.

Kit knew this was their last shot; the opportunity wouldn't come again. They each grabbed a bottle, clenching them with the respect of the holy cross as they ignored their increasingly serious wounds. They fumbled to light the alcohol-soaked rags and threw them through the windows, hitting the base of the creature's body. The bottles shattered on impact into fireballs, spreading flames to biblical proportions.

The inferno quickly spread throughout the building, the frightened creature and old woman trapped inside with no way out. Smoke filled Kit and Dante's lungs, their breathing bubbling and labored as they ran back to the wagon to grab more bottles to add to the hellscape.

Hot flames surrounded every inch around the creature, driving it to retreat to the front windows, only to be pummeled with more gunfire. Judgment cornered the thing at every turn, forcing it to cower deeper inside where the blaze intensified. Amongst the chaos, Kit caught a glimpse into one of the thing's horrid eyes. He swore that he could see the fear in them, briefly feeling sorry for the creature as he saw the scared animal inside its void pupils.

As the beast hopelessly flailed around, Kit and Dante pushed the wagon snugly in front of the doorway, blocking the creature's only way out. It began ramming its head at the cart out of fear, desperately trying to escape. Hopelessly stuck, it let out a howling, bloodcurdling scream that would haunt those that heard it for the rest of their lives.

The Gatling gun fire hit the remaining bottles on the wagon, shattering them into a fireball that spread across the flesh and root-infested head of the beast. A wall of fire quickly expanded, blocking the door as debris from the roof began to cave in.

Kit and Dante dragged themselves away from the burning building with bleeding fingernails, the flames searing their backs. They crawled like infants to freedom, their ears pierced by the dying screams of the thing, the woman, and the countless souls of the dead buried underneath the roaring fire.

The towering threat of the creature suddenly felt like it had evaporated, buried inside as it burned to its horrible death. The tomb it would die in was an inferno, burning away any evidence of its horrid existence. The nightmare had been replaced with the welcome, raging fires of hell that lit up the Arkell night.

The gunfire finally stopped, allowing the fire to do its job of cleansing the earth of the thing. Smoke filled the silent air, ashes dancing in the sky like playful fireflies. The flames from the sheriff's quickly began to spread to other buildings, inviting the rest of the structures to join in on the beautiful destruction. All of Arkell would burn tonight, too tainted from what had happened to be allowed to exist anymore.

As the heat grew to an unbearable temperature, Kit and Dante used what little energy they had left to drag themselves further away from the burning buildings. They felt every inch of the hot dirt scraping across their bloody injuries, refusing to let them forget the pain for even a moment. When they found themselves far enough from the heat, they forced themselves to sit up, to watch their shared nightmare burn away.

Kit took a deep breath of the smoky air, the blood in his nose giving the distinct smell of burning copper. He couldn't remember the last time he'd had a moment to relax, away from the running and fear that made up most of his life. He soaked in the orange glow, the climbing flames radiating in the air. Despite all the chaos and blood it took to get there, the scene felt oddly cleansing.

Grunting as he suppressed the pain from his chest, Dante stumbled and stood up. He offered a hand to Kit, a peace offering that he took without question. Rising to their feet, the two men stared at each other with the recognition of the unfinished business between them. The roar of the flaming buildings amplified the silence in the air, burning away what brought them together and bringing the reality of their rivalry back to the forefront. Kit wasn't sure what was going to happen, his body and soul feeling too weak to continue fighting.

Dante answered the lingering question of what would happen next with a simple gesture, placing his hand on Kit's shoulder with a warm smile. His teeth were a glowing white underneath his dirty, blood-caked face, feeling friendly and *real*. The feeling was contagious, Kit smiling back and planting the seed that maybe the mutual respect that had grown between them didn't have to burn away with the beast. Maybe there truly had been enough bloodshed, if just for tonight.

Nothing else had to be said on the matter, the two men opting to turn their attention towards the fire to silently watch Arkell burn together.

CHAPTER SIXTEEN
THE DEVIL YOU KNOW

i. Shane

*T*he heat from the buildings was hot enough that Shane could feel the warmth on his cool cheekbones all the way back in the alley. They had been watching the expanding flames in silent disbelief, the wind blowing loose embers their way as they stared in awe at the conclusion the strange and horrible night had reached. The events had all been too bizarre and horrifying to be real, an experience your brain would manipulate into believing was nothing more than a terrible nightmare as the years went by. They should have been dead several times over, a few more forgotten faces in the pile of corpses; yet here they stood, alive despite all odds. A stupid, childlike smile was cemented on Shane's face as he watched the buildings burn. Pride and disbelief filled him at the thought that an old guy like him managed to defy all odds and make it through this.

"We did it," he beamed, noting that even Gideon couldn't help but let out a smile. "I can't believe we fucking did it."

"I know," Gideon said, his voice infused with a hint of awe .

The notorious Walker brother placed a warm hand on Shane's right shoulder, a sign of respect. It was another strange and encouraging moment to cap off a night full of them.

"I know," he repeated, punctuating the words like a pinch, to say they weren't dreaming.

The moment was bittersweet. Shane wished Eli was standing there with him to share it. He sensed from the genuine reaction from Gideon, that he was channeling a connection with someone he'd lost as well. They'd both been through too much, their shared pain allowing a bridging of the gap between the two very different men, to share the moment.

The connection allowed Shane to justify Gideon pulling him closer, to give him a warm and sincere victory hug. If surviving against a thing like this didn't earn a hug, he wasn't sure what the hell in this world did.

Leaning into the hug, Shane felt a sharp, betraying pressure in his stomach as something pressed into his belly. He hadn't realized what was happening until it was already over, his body weight being used against him as he was pulled into the large blade in Gideon's fist. His face contorted with confused pain, looking down at the simple knife that would bring his death. There was a feeling of the warm, familiar liquid seeping through the fresh wound and soaking into his shirt. He helplessly reached down to try to pull the blade out, finding himself too weak to resist.

Gideon gripped tighter and gave the knife a twist, his face quivering with ecstasy while he leaned back and looked in Shane's eyes with an odd shade of sympathy. Shane felt an uncomfortable tightness in the area, dulling the wound and sending a tingling numbness through the nerves into his finger-tips. He tried to speak, but all that came out of his throat was a gurgling murmur.

"Shhhh," Gideon whispered softly. "Don't waste your breath."

His voice felt calming, like it promised to take away the pain in Shane's guts.

"You don't have many breaths left, and I want to savor all of them."

Gideon locked eyes with Shane. They were vacant and glassy like a bird's, making it clear that there was no soul behind them.

"There's only room for so many monsters in my world," he whispered.

Gideon let go of the knife, letting Shane collapse to the ground with it stuck in his belly. Gideon looked at his blood-soaked hand with satisfaction, giving it a primal, satisfied lick.

Shane tried to move, but every squirm felt like he was being shredded to pieces alive. He couldn't do anything, lying uselessly with the twisted blade in his abdomen as Gideon turned his attention to the Gatling gun.

ii. Kit

The shared silence amongst the men was welcome, but Kit knew it couldn't last forever. Unfinished business hung in the air between the two of them like bad breath, begging to be addressed so they could either kill each other or move on.

"So, now what?" Kit asked bluntly.

If they were going to kill each other, he'd rather get it over with while he still had the energy to stand.

"Now what," Dante repeated solemnly.

A stalemate. Kit pushed the matter a nudge further.

"Is this the part where things go back to the way they were?" he asked, straight to the point.

Dante let out a snort. It was a nice sound after all of the screaming that night.

"Kid, after the shit we saw, things can never go back to the way they were," Dante said, wisely but without sentiment. "Not with us, not with anything. What we saw and dealt with changes everything, forever."

It was true. What the hell did the next day look like after a night like tonight? There was nothing more to be said, so they left it at that and returned to the comforting silence of the fire crackling.

Then the silence ended.

Dante's torso transformed into a tattered mess of wet flesh in a matter of seconds as the dozens of piercings burst through him like hot butter. Kit's face was already wet with Dante's hot blood before his ears registered the familiar, thunderous *BANG-BANG-BANG* of the Gatling gun, that was once again sending hell his way.

He dove to the ground, seeking shelter behind a pile of crates as the countless barrage of bullets tore Dante apart, shredding the once charismatic leader of Blackcreek into nothing more than ravaged meat.

The refuge of the crates was short-lived, bullets pummeling through them and shattering them bit by bit. Two bullets whizzed through Kit's arm before passing clean out the other side. His screams were muted into nothingness by the gunfire.

With no other man or beast left, he found himself the only focus of the gunfire. He drew his pistol, aware he had mere seconds before the sanctuary of the crates would be completely gone.

iii. Shane

Gideon cranked the Gatling gun with demented determination, reveling in finally being the sole force of destruction in Arkell. His focus was clear, firing on his helpless target while cackling with glee as a self-appointed representative for the reaper.

Shane knew he was dying; he knew the moment he felt the blade sink into his gut. The question he didn't know the answer to was how long he had left, whether it was meager seconds or precious minutes. Calling on a higher power, or perhaps the devil himself, he used every ounce left in his soul not to scream as he used his numb hands to pull the knife out of his belly.

Hot blood and hunks of organ came spilling out of the wound, the ruby soaked knife clenched in his shaking fist. Spots began to appear in his fading vision, things becoming dark and blurry. He channeled what little focus he had left towards Gideon, who was gleefully operating the Gatling gun to hunt down his target like a hungry wolf.

Slithering on his own entrails like a dying snake, Shane mustered the strength to pull himself the mile-long inches towards Gideon. He felt no other sense in his body outside of pain, sharply stinging every nerve like venom as he clenched the blade between his blood-soaked fingers.

He readied the knife, preparing to strike like a scorpion on a much larger predator that was bound to kill it the moment it was alerted. He mustered a sloppy swing of the blade with what little energy he had left, plunging the knife deep into Gideon's left heel. Gideon howled like a snared rabbit, the gunfire ceasing as he fell to his knees in primal levels of pain. Tears filled his soulless eyes as he looked down at Shane, the old man staring right back with pure courage on his face.

I'm still here mother fucker, he wanted to scream, speaking only with his eyes now that speech was no longer a luxury he had in what little remained of his life.

It had been his one shot and it worked to stop the gunfire, if only temporarily. If it gave the kid a fighting chance to get out of

there, it was worth it. He now braced for the curses, the screaming, the threats and finally the bullet that would bring his end.

They didn't come.

Instead, Gideon turned his attention to the mutilated corpse
of his brother.

"Should I teach him a lesson, Bronco?" Gideon asked the
dead man.

Shane could tell Gideon believed he could hear the corpse
speaking back to him.

"I'll show him who he's fucking with," Gideon muttered hatefully. "We'd like that, wouldn't we?"

Gideon leaned down with buckling knees, grinding his teeth
hard enough that Shane thought they would shatter. He slowly
pulled the knife out of his heel, his ear-piercing scream unfiltered and full of raw pain that he would surely redistribute. He
grabbed Shane by the throat, bringing the dripping, crimson
soaked blade forward.

Shane tried to scream when he felt the tip of the knife slowly
pierce into his neck, but no noise came outside of a small gurgle
from the blood and bile stuck in the back of his throat. He was
paralyzed, unable to do anything but experience the pain of the
knife prick as it slowly plunged deeper.

Then the pain softened. Shane felt drunk and warm. He
realized he was just having a bad dream as things went dark.

iv. Gideon

"Bleed, piggy."

Gideon buried the knife deeper into the pathetic old man's
neck, disgusted by how the flaps of wrinkles reminded him of
the wattle of a turkey.

"That'll teach him, won't it Bronco?"

He carefully sliced, carving into the throat like a piece of fileted meat. What started as a scream out of the old man fizzled quickly, morphing into gurgles when the life behind his eyes faded.

But it wasn't enough, not after what had happened to Bronco.

Gideon kept digging, rhythmically moving the blade back and forth into the throat in a sawing motion. The tendons and spine were tough, but he relished working through them with glee.

When he finished sawing through the last of the meat, he gave an aggressive pull and a twist to finish the job. He gripped the old man by his wispy, white hair and tugged to snap the last bit of the spinal cord, before pulling the head completely free from its body. He lifted his bloody prize and turned it to face him, looking directly into its soulless, pathetic eyes.

"Look at you now," Gideon grinned. "Look at you now."

He spat in the severed face of the old man and unceremoniously tossed it aside, enjoying the sound of the clumsy *thud* it gave when it hit the dirt.

He had given the old man more thought and attention than most of his victims, wasting valuable time when there was still more work to do. More blood to spill. It wasn't over yet. His real trophy was still out there.

Fighting through the pain from his butchered ankle, he hobbled back to the Gatling gun and took aim. He let his eyes adjust, carefully looking for any movement from his frightened target. He scanned the area, but the rotten weasel was nowhere to be found. He'd wasted too much time on the old man, allowing this slippery son-of-a-bitch to break free. Gideon felt stupid about the sloppy mistake, the bastard likely already trying to get the jump on him.

He dismounted the Gatling gun, carefully favoring his good foot as he stepped down from the stagecoach. Any pressure put on his left ankle would bring him crumbling down like a wounded deer, forcing him to hobble on one foot like a fool.

He drew his pistol, anticipating the inevitable. Sensing he wasn't alone, he turned and caught the sight he feared. The thieving bastard was already here.

v. Kit

Kit knew in his heart that Shane was dead the moment the Gatling gun fire started up again. They had their differences, but he knew Shane wouldn't allow the murder of unarmed men to happen like that. The old man wasn't a sadist. He was fair. He was kind. Now he was dead.

He wasn't sure what miracle had caused the gunfire to stop, but he sure as hell wasn't going to let the opportunity go to waste. He ran like hell to get out of the line of fire, slinking into the alleyway to get the jump on the sick fuck while he had the chance.

When he reached the alley, he saw Gideon hunched over in the wagon, distracted by something in a hypnotic daze. Kit took advantage of his good fortune, drawing his pistol and sneaking to the side of the cart before Gideon even realized his target was missing.

Once Gideon finally figured out Kit was gone, it was too late. He hopped off the wagon, helplessly turning to find himself face to face with Kit, pistol drawn on him, ready to put him down like the dog he was.

Gideon raised his iron, too slow and sloppy to react in time. Kit fired a clean shot at the Walker brother's hand, blowing three fingers clean off. Gideon's pistol hit the ground with a heavy thud, along with the severed, mutilated digits. He screamed in agony, the nubs on his hand shooting a deep, flowing red geyser. The shock led him to carelessly step down on his weak foot, the pressure on the injury instantly sending him crumbling down on his knees.

Gideon eyed his fallen pistol, soaked in the red dirt surrounding the fingers that had been on his hand moments ago. Kit knew the bastard wanted nothing more than to reach for that gun, a gambit he was more than willing to let him try to take. It was hard to justify shooting an unarmed man, but he'd have no problem shooting him dead the moment he tried.

Gideon must have known he didn't stand a chance, opting not to take the risk of reaching for the pistol. With nothing available in his arsenal, he let out a devilish smile in his defense.

"So, what are you gonna do now?" Gideon asked in a reasonable tone. "Shoot me down in cold blood?"

Kit had killed better people for less. He wasn't accepting the manipulation, having no qualms about shooting this unarmed piece of shit if it came to that.

"You shot those people on the Silverton train in cold blood," Kit said, justifying what he was going to do out loud. "They were unarmed, every very last one of them."

Kit's eyes shifted to a round, bloody object lying on the ground nearby. Dread filled his heart when he realized what he was actually looking at. It was Shane's severed head, sloppily removed from his body and tossed aside like filth. Kit's mouth went dry, imagining the poor old man's final moments. Another tragedy caused by the man on the other end of his barrel. A bullet suddenly felt too good for him, the screams from Silverton suddenly flooding back into Kit's ears.

"The people you murdered here, you ambushed them like a coward," Kit accused as calmly as he could. "You murdered my friends and then tried to shoot me down the same gutless way."

He cocked the hammer to punctuate his point.

Gideon spat a rotten wad of blood and phlegm, his awful Cheshire grin never fading.

"Well then bandit, go ahead. Do what I'd do," Gideon encouraged. "Earn that reputation I helped you build, and finish the job. After all, who do you think they're going to blame for what happened here?"

Blame.

Kit had taken his share of it, enough for a lifetime. He was sick of carrying everyone else's blame.

"That thing," he answered with confidence, nodding at the burning buildings, "that fucking *monster* in there is to blame."

"Monster?" Gideon questioned dismissively. "All I see is a bunch of burning buildings. The only thing that remains for you to throw blame at is a pile of ashes. Nothing but a story."

A pile of ashes. It sounded so reductive. It was so much *more* than that. It had taken so much. It had killed Eli, and who knows how many others. But now? Now it was just a pile of ashes.

"Monsters are just stories we tell ourselves to justify the bad in the world," Gideon said, smiling like a snake. "When one monster disappears, a bigger one always comes along and takes its place. First there was me, now there's you."

That feeling of *blame* came back in the air. Kit felt his hand start to shake as doubt of the validity of the story he'd tell of what happened here crept into his mind.

But he had taken enough blame.

He mentally forced his hand to steady, knowing how closely he was being scrutinized. He kept his eyes locked with Gideon, coldly staring him down. Both men refused to blink, neither committing to the first move that would end this once and for all.

The silence was broken by the familiar sound that bound them once before.

The *ROAR* from the thought-to-be-dead thing rang from the burning wall of fire, accompanied by the aggressive sounds of thrashing and waving flames. Both men turned their hatred away from one another, watching the nightmare that they thought was over, reemerge to haunt them.

Completely engulfed in flames, the creature bashed its head at the entrance of the sheriff's. Kit could see the structure of the building had weakened from the inferno, hunks of burning wood and stone flying with each ram the angry thing delivered to the frame of the doorway. It was struggling and visibly weak, but the anger and fear it displayed as it tried to escape, showed its survival instincts weren't letting it go down without a fight.

Kit felt paralyzed with disbelief at the sight. How was this fucking thing still alive? What else could they possibly do to stop it? He was tired of fighting, crippled with injuries that left him unsure how he could possibly go toe-to-toe with the devil again.

The same paralysis didn't hit Gideon, who used the situation to his advantage. He quickly made a go to grab his fallen pistol, forced to use his left hand, which presently still had all five digits remaining. Kit's instinct kicked back in, firing on Gideon, who was too slow for the gamble he played.

BANG. BANG.

Kit fired two shots in rapid succession at Gideon's wrist, severing his hand clean off with the perfectly placed shots. Gideon squealed in shock, trying to tend to the bloody stump with the two pathetic fingers he had left on his remaining hand. Trigger-less, with no way to ever operate a pistol again, Kit ignored Gideon in favor of the more imminent threat.

He climbed aboard the stagecoach, manning the intimidating Gatling gun with a hope in hell that he'd instinctively know what he was doing. He'd never fired one of these before but picked up enough of the logistics during their planning in the tavern to feel confident enough to bet his life on it. He turned the gun's crank, greeted by a dull *click-click-click* signaling it was out of ammo.

"Fuck!" he screamed, frustrated by his dumb fucking luck.

He looked to the nearby ammo crate for answers, blood pooling around it from Shane's nearby, headless corpse. He glanced back at the sheriff's office, the thing breaking free from the fiery coffin far too quickly. God wasn't on his side on this one. Reloading the Gatling gun wasn't going to happen, there just wasn't enough time.

His eyes darted around the stagecoach for a solution, finding a potential answer with the gunpowder barrels, dynamite, and rope he spotted. It was enough to blow the thing straight to hell, but his brain knew one more element was missing from the equation: bait.

Needing something to lure the beast, his eyes shifted to Gideon for fresh meat. He grabbed the rope, hopped off the coach and grabbed Gideon by the collar, like a bad dog by the scruff.

"What the fuck are you going to do with that?" Gideon screamed, true fear behind his words, without the cocky coolness he always seemed to have an overabundance of.

Kit ignored his pleas, throwing Gideon's worthless body back up on the stagecoach. He hopped up, grabbed Gideon by the hair, and violently started tying him to the heavy Gatling gun. He pulled tightly, the rough, dirty, frayed bits of rope squeezing and rubbing against Gideon's wounds. Gideon tried to fight back, the pathetic effort futile thanks to him being down eight of his ten fingers.

"You mother fucker!" Gideon howled, hitting the pitch of a frightened eleven-year-old boy. "You chickenshit coward cocksucker!"

Kit ignored the insults, calmly grabbing the blood-caked knife off the ground and approaching his tied-up prisoner.

Gideon was unsure which of his predators to focus on, as a loud crash echoed through the sky. The creature roared with victory as it finally broke free, flames covering its entire body.

"Just kill me!" Gideon demanded as Kit drew the blade near. "Stop being a cunt and fucking kill me now."

With cold precision, Kit knelt down and dug the knife into the gash in Gideon's ankle. He surgically sliced off a thick piece with care, ensuring Gideon wouldn't be going anywhere.

"Stop!" Gideon begged, the agony in his voice desperate. "Please stop!"

His eyes bulged, tears running down them as he turned to see the flame drenched demon angrily approaching.

Knowing Gideon's fate was sealed, Kit ignored him and grabbed a stick of dynamite from the stagecoach. He dashed off, finding a pile of nearby rubble to hide behind as best as he could, while Gideon howled.

"You fucking coward!" Gideon screamed. "Come back here you chickenshit!"

The smell of burnt, rotting flesh polluted the air as the thing sluggishly limped towards the alley. It was visibly weak, but anger fueled its terrible body to keep fighting. It spotted Gideon, the smell of fresh blood from his injuries reducing him to nothing more than a cheap meal in its eyes. It barreled towards the coach like a cannonball, unstoppable with its thirst for blood.

"Stay away from me!" Gideon screamed, reduced to a cowardly ant as he stared into the yellow eyes of hell. "Stay the fuck away from me!"

The thing pounced on the stagecoach like a mountain lion, nipping at Gideon with its long, jagged teeth and effortlessly pulling his body free from the Gatling gun. He tried waving his useless stumps, kicking and crying defenselessly. His vocal cords snapped when he gave a bloody scream that would be his last, as the creature gorged on him alive.

Kit silently watched the thing feast, guilt climbing into his throat at how much he enjoyed watching his enemy suffer. It was captivating and surreal, seeing a man you wished to hell being dragged there in front of your eyes by the devil itself. He wanted to keep watching but knew his advantage wouldn't last much longer.

Keeping his breath still, he lit the stick of dynamite in his hand and patiently waited as the wick burned down to an uncomfortably close nub. He closed his eyes, took a deep, smoky breath and threw the stick at the stagecoach with everything he had. The moment it left his grip, he ran as quick as his body would allow, knowing death would be right on his heels.

The dynamite stick landed perfectly in the coach with a satisfying *thud*, drawing the creature's attention to it. It growled with awareness, ready to leap and strike at its attacker.

But it was too late.

The lone stick exploded, triggering a chain reaction from the gunpowder and dynamite on board. The cargo fed the explosion, building into one hellblazing fireball. Chunks of stagecoach and charred flesh of the creature flew violently in every direction.

Kit dove for safety from the expanding flame, his hair singing, along with a stinging sensation on the flesh on the back of his neck. He hit the ground with tremendous force, catching a mouthful of dirt on impact, knocking out two of his teeth for good measure.

The explosions didn't stop, the flames finding new sources to feed, to keep expanding. Kit crawled away as fast as he could in the wake of the chaos, finally collapsing when he felt far enough to rest safely. He lay still, the unbearable flames cooking away at his skin. He was charred, bruised, and critically bleeding. But he was alive.

His mouth tasted of dirty coins that had been handled too many times, his head pounding against the hard earth. Yet, it was away from all the death, a stillness after endless running. It felt comfortable, like your own bed after being away from home for far too long. He wanted to stay there forever, wondering if the surreal images floating in his mind from what he'd just experienced, had actually happened.

It could have been seconds or days when Kit finally felt rejuvenated enough to force himself to fight through the pain and stand up. He soaked in his surroundings, a symphony of deep red, charred bodies and dancing flames of fire and destruction. Countless bits of ash from the corpse of the creature danced in the air, raining down as the wind took them through town. Through the makeshift gray snow, the first bits of amber sunrise began to peak through the horizon, creating a surreal scene of beauty.

Everything that was once Arkell was now gone, fading away like a memory as a new dawn was born. Kit couldn't help but marvel at the miracle, watching what once existed of a town disappear right before his eyes. Nobody else would see it, nobody would believe it. But there he was, watching it.

There he was, alive.

EPILOGUE

THE COYOTE TRAP

i. Kit

The sound of crunching snow beneath each step his horse took, still had the power to make Kit feel like a kid again. It was like a magic trick that allowed him to travel back through time, even if just for a moment. It didn't happen all the time, usually a couple times a season, when he found himself in a peaceful mindset and alone. Without fail, season after season, he was able to channel it at some point no matter how dark the year might have been. And this had been a dark year.

During his days as an outlaw, his greatest fear had always been that the Walker Brothers would one day catch up to him before the law did. Now that they were long dead and gone, he should have felt a little more at ease in life. But he was never able to completely let his guard down, not after what he had seen. Nobody else knew it, but the world was different now.

He'd become afraid. Afraid of things he didn't think existed before, things that seemed to only exist in the darkest corner of a child's imagination. He'd become afraid of loss, growing close to people only to see the worst outcome happen. He'd become afraid of the unknown. He was afraid of what people would think and say if he ever tried to explain the things he'd seen.

He'd spent a lot of time since the *incident* in isolation, mostly afraid of what people would ask if they knew he had been in Arkell that fateful night. They'd have questions, and he didn't have the answers they would need. After it happened, he thought he'd tell the truth, but the further from the incident he got, the crazier he realized the truth sounded. So, he decided it was better to run, stay alone, and keep the darkness of the truth to himself.

But there were debts to be paid.

After what they saw together, friend or enemy, he felt he owed these men more than to just let them be forgotten. None of what happened should ever be forgotten. But to preserve memories of someone, you need someone who actually cared about them to carry them on.

Shane had nobody. Kit tried to look for his family, or at least someone who cared for him, but all roads led to the story of a lonely old man who mostly kept to himself and clung to an old friendship. A friendship that Kit, unfortunately couldn't make good on after what happened in Arkell.

Eli was different. Eli disappearing from the world didn't go unnoticed. He had someone important in his life, someone who mourned, someone who cared. Kit had spent most of his life living for himself, but knew his soul wouldn't be at rest unless he tried to make things right with that person.

Kit never considered himself a religious man, but after the incident in Arkell, he lost the urge to blindly take whatever he wanted in life, and was now trying to do more of what was *right*. The problem was that as a man who had never really done the right thing before in his life, he wasn't sure where to begin.

The bags of gold clanging around the side of his horse felt

like a good start, at least that's what he told himself. Money had a funny way of making a lot of problems go away, a language everyone spoke. Everything he'd ever done in his pathetic life had been for money. He had killed and almost died for far less than what he was hauling now.

He'd never had an exchange like this, giving instead of taking, at least without having an ultimatum. He wanted to think he was just giving it to be kind, nothing attached to the gift. But he knew that wasn't true, he knew that he was really hoping to buy a piece of his soul back, now that he had met the devil face to face. There wasn't a price he wouldn't pay to avoid seeing that thing again, the thing that had replaced the Walker Brothers in haunting his dreams every night when he shut his eyes.

It had taken him time to reach the old farmhouse, both in locating it and navigating his way there. Staying isolated and anonymous wasn't overly difficult when your only intent was finding a meal for your belly and a place to rest, but it became much riskier the moment you had to ask someone for information. People were always hesitant to let you know where to find someone without asking questions. Pay or no pay, it always ran the risk of word getting around that someone was asking for you after the fact. It made finding the place difficult, time consuming, and frustrating. Now that he was finally here, he realized that he never should have been in a rush to get here in the first place. Yes, it was good to pay amends, but that also came at the very steep cost of facing your demons.

Getting off the horse, Kit felt all of his old injuries emerge at once throughout his body. They didn't necessarily *hurt* anymore; *ache* was a much more accurate term. They were always there, always *aching* to make sure they were never forgotten. They had started to feel like an extension of him, something that would burden him forever instead of passing. Each one of the many injuries felt like they had aged him a few years, bundling together to fade away the youthful good looks he carried just a few short months ago. Now he was just another gruff, broken loner that melted into the scenery of the pathetic taverns he gravitated to.

He lugged the bags free from the saddle, feeling bad for his horse now that he was the one carrying the burden and feeling how heavy they were. He remembered when carrying weight like this wouldn't have made him flinch, but the injuries from Arkell made everything a little more difficult. Everything was a little heavier now.

He approached the front door of the farmhouse; a cold sweat started to break out on his brow. He began to panic, wondering if this whole idea was a big mistake. The effort to find this place, to find out who Eli *really* was, it all felt stupid now that he was here. There would be questions, questions he knew he didn't have answers to, at least not acceptable ones.

He wanted to turn and leave, but that haunting feeling that brought him there to do what was *right,* wouldn't let him. He couldn't just *go*; enough injustice had already been dealt out in this kid's life. He at least deserved to know *something*, along with a little gold to ease the pain of life without his daddy. Kit would have to stay, pay his penance, and face his sins.

He knocked on the door, loudly but with less urgency than the bastards at the bank tended to use. *A man is to be heard, he's not a mouse,* his father used to lecture, something Kit grew to both hate and take to heart. He wanted to approach with authority, standing up as a man being held accountable for what he had been a part of. Sometimes you had to do things you weren't comfortable with in life, take your lashings standing up.

His heartbeat started to pick up as he waited for someone to answer, his palms now clammy with sweat. Nothing. He gave it a solid minute before trying again, not wanting to be a bother, but also making sure that he was heard. The place was secluded enough that he felt it would be safe to just leave the bags there on the porch to be discovered later without being stolen, but the boy deserved some sort of closure to go with the gift. Kit had to at least *try* to talk to the kid, look him in the eyes as he paid him the blood money. He wasn't sure what he'd say, but that didn't mean he didn't have to say it.

Nothing still. The bags grew heavier by the second, his injuries feeling like they were ready to burst freshly open from the strain. After another minute, he decided he'd at least put the bags down to give his body a rest. If the boy weren't around, Kit figured he could wait. His solitary life of late had lifted the burden of hurry, allowing him to not worry about rushing out of there.

Standing alone on the porch as time passed, the sharp pain of the winter air started to amplify the agony throughout his body, tempting him to give into old instincts, to break inside for warmth. He brushed them aside, figuring he could always build a fire if the cold became unbearable.

More time passed. Still nothing. The kid was either out, or off somewhere around the property. Kit decided moving would be a better way to get the blood pumping than standing still, and figured he'd have a look around the grounds. Confident the bags would be fine at the front door, he trudged out into the snow to have a look around.

There was little noteworthy around the immediate perimeter of the house. It looked lonely, and if it weren't for the few signs of life like the pile of freshly chopped wood, he would have guessed that the place might have been abandoned at this point. He had heard the mumblings between Shane and Eli about *trouble from the banks,* which led to the gamble that cost them their lives. He worried he might have been too late, arriving at just another place repossessed by the money men.

The sad sight of the pile of wood pointed to a lonely life, but life nonetheless, which gave him hope that his purpose wasn't lost.

He eventually came upon what looked like tracks, leading to the nearby woods. They had been snowed over, but were still visible and clearly human. Confident that his sidearm would comfort him in case he met an animal that confused him for supper, he followed them deep into the inviting maze of white and green ahead.

Navigating the peaceful, seemingly endless rows of trees, he spotted something bright and beautiful splattered along a patch of crisp, white snow. Approaching closer, he found the deep red on white was exactly what he suspected — blood.

It was a significant pool, a spotted trail leading away from it suggesting an escape. The poor thing had been here not long ago, hopelessly trying to get away. This wasn't a bite that did this. The animal was unaware that it didn't stand a chance against the greatest predator: man. Kit banked it must have been the kid, giving him hope to continue following the crimson trail.

It was beautifully tranquil in the woods, a sad contrast to the trail of suffering he was following. Everything had beauty before man touched it, the salt and oil from his pores degrading all things with its touch. Kit had ruined countless things of beauty in the trail of his life, a regret he was hoping he wouldn't be repeating now as he followed the blood.

The blood became heavier at a point, as if the wound had become worse the further the thing moved. He was close, he could smell the desperation. He continued along, finally coming across the victim of the mess.

A dead coyote lay unceremoniously in the snow, a large pool of red gathered where it was missing a paw. The savage removal of the appendage, paired with the blood on the poor thing's teeth, told Kit that it had gnawed its foot off in an attempt to escape a trap. It paid for it by dying here, alone and scared.

He stared at the poor creature solemnly, too many of the demons of his past mistakes crawling into his mind over the next few minutes. He had to shake them off, partly out of guilt but mostly because he knew he could have stayed with them all day. It was time to go.

He started to leave when he realized that he wasn't quite sure which direction he had come from. He'd become so transfixed on the coyote that he managed to disorient himself. He felt like a damn fool, his mind racing to the old stories he'd heard of someone wandering in the woods to take a shit only to never return after getting lost. He wisely decided he'd use the blood tracks as a guide, only to find the damned thing must have been wandering in a few different directions in a confused panic, spreading bits of the blood splatter in every direction he looked.

He couldn't get a proper read on the sun through the trees, but with a rough estimate, along with a steady stream of blood to follow, he picked a direction and started swiftly following it with purpose. His feet were getting cold, the idea of breaking into the farmhouse for warmth suddenly not feeling beneath him anymore.

He tried not to panic as he picked up the pace, dreaming of warmth and a hot drink to keep himself grounded. He moved briskly, trying to push away the fear that he could be heading in the wrong direction. He thought of the summer, of warmer times. He thought of the sun guiding him. He thought of everything except being cold and lost.

He took heavy strides until he was stopped in his tracks, the loud metallic *THUNK* hitting his ears before the excruciating pain shot through his entire body like an orgasm. His movement halted. He instinctively tugged his leg to move forward only to find it stuck. That's when the pain increased exponentially. The sensation of multiple teeth stabbing through his ankle and into the bone, amplified every one of his senses to a level he didn't know existed. He screamed in agony, looking down at the sight of his leg caught in a rusty bear trap.

I'm gonna fucking die! his brain screamed in full panic mode, *Alone in the woods! I'm going to lose this fucking leg! I'm going to die lost and alone in these fucking woods!*

He had to get a grip, pull back the panic as his body went into shock. He'd been through worse than this and come through countless times before. This was just another story he could add to the many when his grandkids asked him why he walked with a funny limp.

Ha ha, Grandpa caught it in a bear trap when he tried to pay off his guilt to the boy of the father he saw eaten by a monster in front of him. Ha ha, isn't Grandpa funny?

He took a deep breath, wincing in pain as he tried to compose himself. Assessing what he was working with, he forced himself to look back down at his ankle. It was bad, the flesh mangled to ground chuck, buried under tattered clothing and snow. He thought of the coyote's leg, the morbid image of it gnawing off its foot to cling onto freedom. It took every bit of willpower to not throw up, the sight of the metallic teeth tearing through his bone too sickening to comprehend.

He focused on the snow, thanking the cold for partially numbing his leg. It was a soothing thought, helping him find the willpower to bend down to try to open the trap. He was shaking from the adrenaline, pain and cold making any attempt to pry it open quite difficult. It wouldn't budge.

He told himself it was fine. Breathe, try again.

As he made another attempt, he couldn't help but feel that sensation of being watched. After enough robberies and narrow escapes, you grew a knack for knowing when nearby eyes were planted on you. He looked up, careful not to make any sudden movements, and saw his companion.

Several yards away stood a boy of twelve or thirteen with a

rifle drawn and aimed at him. Kit ignored the unbearable pain, slowly raising his hands to play nice.

The boy looked familiar, like a dream of an old friend. He reminded Kit of Eli.

ii. Weston

Weston had been tracking the stranger from the moment he arrived. At first, he thought that he was just another one of the men from the bank, before recognizing him as something else, something different. He was a little less polished than the bank men and looked lost, unlike the vultures who always knew exactly where to go to harass you. Plus, the bank men never ventured into the woods, and they definitely wouldn't leave any of their belongings on your front step. As soon as the man left the porch and made his way into the woods, Weston realized who it was. He realized that it must be *him*.

"Easy," the man said, his tone condescending, like Weston was an ill-tempered horse. "Easy now."

Weston didn't reply, trying to calculate what the man wanted. There were no real answers to what happened to his father, but after asking around, he heard stories about an outlaw Shane was chasing right before he came to Pa that day. *You're in charge.* his father said, promising he'd be back in a few days after hearing whatever news Shane came bearing. It was the last time Weston ever saw him.

"You're Eli's boy, aren't you?" the man asked, his tone too familiar.

The man was squinting, like he could see the resemblance if he looked hard enough. Weston tried to keep emotion away from his trigger finger, but hearing the man bring up his father made it difficult.

"You look just like him."

You look just like him. The reminder of his father's face, never to be seen again, stung like a wasp. Weston let the moment stand, refusing to speak and forcing the stranger to calmly keep talking while his ankle bled out like a pig in the trap.

"I'm sorry to hear what happened to your father."

He didn't like the passive implication. He wanted to scream, but the thought of his father helped him keep his composure.

"You're sorry to hear?" Weston questioned, trying to suppress the lump forming in his throat. "You wanna know what I hear? I hear Shane tracked down some bandit and my father went with him to hunt him down for a reward. Neither of them came home after that."

He saw a shift in the stranger's face, regret in the form of recognition. Weston gripped his rifle tightly, relieved he was at least now aiming at something closer to the truth.

"We had our differences," the stranger responded with sincerity in his voice, "but he was a good man."

"So was Shane," Weston added, refusing to let him be forgotten as well. "They were both good men who never came home."

The air was clear now as they stood there in a cold, silent standoff. The man looked remorseful, true regret behind his aging eyes. But he was also a killer, a killer that was likely the last man to see his father alive. Weston had never shot a man before, sincerely worried at that moment that it might be something he was going to have to do. Something he might *want* to do.

iii. Kit

The aggressive cold surrounding his wound was the only thing keeping the screams suppressed inside Kit's throat. The numbness it created was making him uneasy, wondering how much of it was caused by the cold and how much was dead nerves. He felt his brow sweating, a bad sign of fever creeping in. Every small movement felt like his ankle was grinding against broken glass, amplifying the urgency to work through the unfinished business he had with the boy.

"Say kid, what do you say you help me out of this thing, and we can go inside where it's warm to talk?" Kit suggested, addressing the kid head on.

He'd known from years of being talked down to that kids this age were closer to manhood than most people gave them credit for, and that they appreciated being talked to on the same level. They didn't feel like kids and they sure as hell hated being talked to like they were.

"That's what men do," he added. "They talk."

The kid didn't respond, his focus never leaving his rifle sight. His face looked like there were a million things he wanted to know, all of them quietly buried deep behind his chestnut eyes. Kit patiently waited, knowing the temptation to start asking questions was too great. The kid might shoot him, but not without looking for some answers first. It took a cold, drawn out minute, but the kid eventually caved and blurted out the big question.

"What happened?" he asked, his voice hitting that cracked note of a kid putting on a tough face. "What happened after my father left here for the last time?"

The kid had every right to know, but there was no logical way to answer his question. Kit had thought about that night every single day since it happened, but when he tried to put the events into words to himself, none of it ever made any sense. Things like *that* don't exist in the real world, even if he saw it with his own eyes.

Maybe it would be easier to accept what happened if he wasn't the only one who survived that night, making it real with somebody else outside of his own crazy head. There were over a dozen men in Arkell that night, but every single one of them, aside from Kit, were now dead. The shared experience died with them, making the only memories of that night live in his thoughts and his alone.

"Kid," Kit finally answered with an exhausted smirk, "you'd believe any other lie I could come up with before you'd believe the truth."

The kid's eyes weren't accepting his answer.

"I've had enough time to imagine a thousand different scenarios," he said hatefully. "Try me."

Kit had seen that same look he was getting now a thousand times before, recognizing he was going to have to pick his next words very carefully. Instinct usually makes a man try to bull-shit their way out of situations like this, but Kit found what *actually* worked best was the truth. The problem comes when your truth is unbelievable. He didn't rush to answer, realizing that too much of the truth was going to sound like the world's biggest lie.

"Your father and Shane found me hiding out in Blackcreek," Kit began. "When they arrived, they stopped a posse from hanging me. They convinced them they were still lawmen, kidnapping me with the intent to collect a bounty in Arkell for my arrest."

His leg was hurting, he kept his mind on the story to keep from passing out.

"When we arrived in Arkell," he continued, "we were ambushed."

"By *your* men?" the boy asked coldly.

He was shaking but hanging on of every word of the tale.

"No," Kit said, sympathetically shaking his head. "By men that wanted me dead. Men that wanted anyone who got in their way dead."

"And yet here you are, alive," Weston said doubtfully. "I take it you ran?"

Kit took offense to the accusation, suppressing the urge to snap back. He swallowed his pride and put reason forward.

"No, we fought," he answered proudly. "Your father, Shane and I. We were outnumbered and outgunned. These men wanted to kill us, so we fought back, together. They fought well. They were good men."

"But they didn't make it." Tears welled in the boy's eyes.

"No," Kit said with regret. "Nobody else did. Just me. Barely."

Silence crept in again, the icy wind picking up. The kid was angry, but looked like he was accepting this truth. Kit swore the kid wasn't blinking, keeping his eyes locked on him behind the rifle.

The pain in his ankle was starting to take its toll, flaring up phantom injuries from Arkell all over again. The trap felt like the jaws of the thing, trying to pull him into the dirt below. It scared him, scared him *bad*. That feeling of it coming back, bringing him to hell with everyone else that was there that night. Dragging him to see Eli and Shane. Dragging him to rest forever with the Walker Brothers. He couldn't stand the thought, forcing a friendlier tone to try to wash the taste of the nightmare away.

"I brought you something," Kit said, desperation creeping into his voice. "That's why I'm here."

The kid didn't dignify him with a response.

"Gold," he added, his voice now overly cheery. "A whole pile of it. I left it up on your porch."

"Why?" Weston asked, cold and not accepting the bullshit.

The feeling started gnawing at Kit again, the scent of his blood calling the beast from his nightmares.

"I know that your pa was having some money trouble with the bank," Kit started. "And that..."

"It's to clean your soul," Weston cut him off. "It's blood money. And it wasn't your blood that spilled to earn it."

Again, Kit found himself having to pick his next words carefully, knowing that the wrong ones would be his last.

"It doesn't matter where it came from," Kit finally said, matter of fact. "It's no good to anyone else now."

"My daddy's soul ain't for sale," Weston said with finality.

The topic of conversation was done, there was no room to negotiate.

Neither spoke, staring each other down in a long, horrible silence. The throbbing in Kit's leg started again, making him feel weak in the cold, winter air. Neither wanted to say anything, but his worsening condition forced Kit to crack first.

"So, what now?" he asked bluntly.

He saw the kid's eyes wavering for the first time, stealing glances of the dead coyote off in the distance. The kid readied his rifle. He was going to have to make a decision about what to do soon.

WICKED HOUSE PUBLISHING

Come find us!

Amazon: Wicked House Publishing
Mailing List: Sign Up Here!
Facebook Group: The Wicked House Cult of Slightly Insane
Readers

Printed in Great Britain
by Amazon

45861193R00158